PRAISE FOR ANNE TYLER

"One of the most beguiling and mesmerizing writers in America."

—Cleveland *Plain Dealer*

"A novelist who knows what a proper story is . . . a very funny writer . . . not only a good and artful writer, but a wise one as well."

—*Newsweek*

"Tyler's characters have character: quirks, odd angles of vision, colorful mean streaks, and harmonic longings."

—*Time*

"Her people are triumphantly alive."

—*The New York Times*

Also by Anne Tyler

THE
TIN CAN
TREE

Anne Tyler

BALLANTINE BOOKS • NEW YORK

A Ballantine Book
Published by The Random House Publishing Group
Copyright © 1965 by Anne Modarressi
Copyright renewed 1993 by Anne Tyler Modarressi
Reader's Guide copyright © 2005 by Anne Tyler and The Random House Publishing Group, a division of Random House, Inc.

www.ballantinebooks.com/BRC

Library of Congress Catalog Card Number: 96-96672

ISBN 0-449-91189-6

This edition published by arrangement with Alfred A. Knopf, Inc.

Manufactured in the United States of America

9 8 7

First Ballantine Books Mass Market Edition: October 1992
First Ballantine Books Trade Edition: August 1996

≬≬≬

1

After the funeral James came straight home, to look after his brother. He left Mr. and Mrs. Pike standing on that windy hillside while their little boy wandered in circles nearby, and the only one who saw James go was Joan. She looked over at him, but she didn't say anything. When he was a few steps away he heard her say, "We have to go home now, Aunt Lou. We have to go down." But Mrs. Pike was silent, and all James heard for an answer was the roaring of the wind.

Going down the hill he took big steps—he was a tall man, and the steepness of the hill made him walk faster than he wanted to. It was too hot to walk fast. The sun was white and glaring and soaked deep in through the mat of his black hair, and his face felt slick when he wiped it with the back of his hand. Partway down the hill he stopped and took off his suit jacket. While he was rolling up his shirt sleeves he looked back at the grave to see if the others were coming, but their backs were still turned toward him. From here it seemed as if that wind hardly touched them; they stood like stones, wearing black, with their heads down and their figures making straight black marks against the sky. The only thing moving was little Simon Pike, as he picked his way down through the dry brambles toward James.

Simon looked strange, dressed up. He had always worn Levi's and crumpled leather boots, but today someone had made him put his suit on. That would be Joan. Mrs. Pike had looked at nothing but the ground for two days now, and couldn't notice what Simon wore. Joan would have polished those white dress-shoes that Simon was getting all grass-stained, and taken out the last inch of cuff on his sleeves so that they could cover his wrists. There was a thin faint line above each of his cuffs where the old hem had been; James could see it clearly when Simon came up even with him. He stood staring at the cuffs for a long time, and then he shifted his eyes to Simon's face and saw Simon frowning up at him, his eyebrows squinched into one straight line across his forehead and his mouth held tight against the wind.

"I'm coming too," he told James. His voice had a low, froggy sound; he was barely ten, but in a year or two his voice would begin to change.

James nodded and finished rolling up his shirt sleeves. There was a band of dampness beneath his collar. He loosened his tie and unbuttoned the top button of his shirt, and then he began walking again with Simon beside him. Now he went more slowly, bracing himself against the steepness of the hill. Each time he took one step Simon took two, but when he looked over at Simon to see if he was growing tired, Simon ignored him and walked faster. He wasn't sweating at all. He looked cold. James wiped his face on his shirt sleeve and followed him down between the rocks.

"Getting near lunchtime," he said finally.

Simon didn't answer.

"Want to eat with Ansel and me?"

"Well."

"Don't worry about your mother. I'll tell her where you are."

Simon said something to his shoes, but James couldn't hear.

"What's that?" he asked.

"I wouldn't bother."

"We'll tell your cousin Joan then," said James. "Soon as she gets back."

The wind was so hot it burned his face; it made lulling sounds around his ears so that he couldn't hear his own footsteps. He pushed his hair off his forehead but it fell into his eyes again, hanging in a tangled web just at the top of his range of vision. Beside him, Simon was letting his hair do what it wanted. He had greased it down with something (it needed cutting, but Joan had been too busy with her aunt to see about that) and now it ruffled up in thick strings and stood out wildly in every direction. When James turned to look at him he nearly smiled. With his face sideways to the wind the roaring sound was quieter, so he kept looking in Simon's direction until Simon grew uneasy.

"What you staring at?" he asked.

"Nothing," said James. "Some wind we got." He looked straight ahead again, and the roaring sound came back to hammer at his ears.

The ground they were treading was wild and weedy, with rocks sticking up here and there so white they might have been painted. There was no path to follow. Below them was the whole town of Larksville—the main street hidden by trees, but the outlying houses and the tobacco fields laid bare to the sun. At the foot of the hill was the white gravel road where Simon and James both lived. They lived in a three-family house that looked like only a long tin roof from here. No houses stood near it. James's brother Ansel said whoever built their house must have been counting on Larksville's becoming a city someday, but Larksville was getting smaller every year. When anyone went away to college it was taken for granted they'd never be back again, not for any longer than it took to eat a Christmas dinner in the house they'd started out in. Yet the long crowded house sat there, half a mile from town as a bird flies and a mile by car, and its three chimneys were jumbled tightly together with the smoke intermingling in wintertime.

The sight of that green part of town was cool and inviting; it made James think of cold beers in the tavern opposite the post office. He looked down at Simon, but Simon was hunched into the jacket of his suit and he still seemed cold.

"Do you like sardines?" James asked him.

"Not much."

"Or cold cuts?"

"No."

They stepped through a tangle of briars, with the thorns making little ripping sounds against their clothes. "I could eat a pizza," Simon said.

"You better talk to Ansel, then. He makes pizzas."

Simon tripped and caught himself. He looked down at the small rock that had tripped him and then began kicking it ahead of him down the hill, swerving out of his course to recover it every time the rock rolled sideways. Gray streaks began to show on his shoes, but James didn't try to stop him.

When they reached the gravel road they turned right and began heading in the direction of the house. Simon's rock rolled into a ditch; he left it lying there. It looked as if they might get all the way home this way—

not talking much, and not saying anything when they *did* talk, just as if this were an ordinary walk on an ordinary day. That suited James. He had been thinking too much, these last two days—turning things over and over, figuring out how if just some single incident had happened, or hadn't happened, things might have been different. Now he ached all over, and thinking made him sick. He was just beginning to feel easier, ambling along in silence beside Simon, when Simon turned and began walking backwards ahead of James, fixing his frowning brown eyes on a point far down the road. He opened his mouth and closed it, and then he opened it again and said, "James."

"What."

"How far down in the ground before it starts getting cold?"

"Pretty soon," said James.

"*How* soon."

"Pretty soon."

"I'm just thinking," Simon said.

To keep him from thinking any more, James said, "But then it gets hot again, down towards the center of the earth. That's beyond digging distance."

"Six feet under is stone, stone cold," said Simon.

"Well, yes."

"Good old Janie Rose, boy."

"Now, wait," James said. "Now, Janie Rose don't feel if it's cold or it's not, Simon. Get that all straight in your mind."

"I know that."

"Get it straight *now*, before you go bothering your mother about it."

"I know all about that," said Simon. He spun around and began walking forward again, still ahead of James.

Strands of his hair rose up and floated behind him, like the tail plumes of some strange bird. "You don't get what I mean," he called back.

"Maybe not."

"Now, you know Janie Rose."

"Yes," said James, and without his wanting it the picture of Janie Rose came to him, sharp and clear— Janie Rose looking exactly the way he thought her name sounded, six years old and blond and fat, with round pink cheeks and round thick glasses. He hadn't been planning to think about it. He said, "*Yes*, I know," and then waited for whatever would follow, keeping part of his mind far away.

"She just hated cold," said Simon. "Playing 'Rather' in the evenings after supper—which would you rather be, blind or deaf; which would you rather die of, heat or cold—she chose heat any day. She had a twenty-pound comforter on her bed, middle of summer."

"I already said to you—" James began.

"Well, I *know*," said Simon, and he started walking faster then and whistling. He whistled off-key, and the tune was carried away by the wind.

When they reached their house, which stood slightly swaybacked by the road with its one painted side facing forward, James stopped to look in his mailbox. There was only a fertilizer ad, which he stuck in his hip pocket to throw away later. "See what your mail is, why don't you," he told Simon.

Simon was walking in small neat circles around the three mailboxes. He stuck out a hand toward the box with "R. J. Pike" painted on it and flipped the door open, and then made another circle and came to a stop in front of the box to peer inside. "Fertilizer ad," he said. He pulled it out and dropped it on the roadside.

"Letter for Mama." He pulled that out too, and dropped it on top of the first. "She'll never read it."

James picked the letter up and followed Simon along the dirt path to the house. Halfway through the yard the path split into three smaller ones, each leading to a separate door on the long front porch. Simon took the one on the far left, heading toward James's door, and James took the far right to deliver the Pikes' letter. The Pikes' part of the porch had a washing machine and an outgrown potty-chair and a collection of plants littering it; he had to watch his step. When he bent to slide the letter under the door he heard a scratching sound and a little yelp, and he stood up and called to Simon, "Your dog wants out, all right?"

"All right."

He opened the door and a very old, fat Chihuahua slid through, dancing nervously on stiff legs as if her feet hurt her. "Okay, Nellie," he said, and bent to pat her once and then stepped over her and continued down the porch. On his way he passed the Potter sisters' window and waved to Miss Faye, smiling and shaking his head to show her he couldn't come in. She was sitting behind closed glass, full face to the window and as close to it as she could get, and when James shook his head the corners of her mouth turned down and she slumped back in her chair. Neither she nor Miss Lucy could climb that hill to the funeral, and they were counting on James to tell them about it.

Simon was standing at James's door, his hands in his pockets. "Why didn't you go on in?" James asked him, and Simon just shook his head.

"I reckoned I'd wait," he said.

"Ansel'd let you in."

"Well, anyway," said Simon, and stood back to let James open the door for him.

The inside of the house was cool and dim. It had unvarnished wooden floorboards, with no rugs, and when Simon walked in he clicked his heels sharply against the wood the way he did when he was wearing his boots. Walking that way, swinging his thin legs in heavy, too-big strides, made him look younger, like a small child entering a dark room. And he didn't look to his left, although he knew James's brother would be on the couch where he always was.

"Ansel?" James said.

"Here I am."

James closed the screen door behind him and looked toward the couch. Ansel was sitting there, with his back very straight and his feet on the floor. Usually he spent the day on his back (he had anemia, the kind that never got much better or much worse so long as he was careful), but today he had made a special effort to be up. He was wearing his Sunday black suit, and he had slicked his pale hair so tightly down with water that it was the same shape as the narrow bones of his head. Probably he had thought that was the least he could do for Janie Rose. When James came in Ansel didn't look in his direction; he was watching Simon. He waited until Simon finally turned around and faced him, and then he stood up and stooped toward him in what looked like a bow. "I hope this day wasn't too hard on you," he said formally, and then sat down and waited while Simon stood frowning at him.

"We got back before the others," James said. "I promised Simon lunch."

"Oh. Well, I doubt that he—Here, you want to sit down?"

He patted the couch where he sat, which meant that he was extending special privileges. Ordinarily he didn't like people sitting there. After a minute Simon shrugged and clicked his heels over to the couch, and Ansel moved aside to give him room.

"I haven't really talked to you since the, uh—It's been quite a few days. But I wanted to say—"

"I been busy," said Simon.

"Well, sure you have," Ansel said. "I know that." He was sitting forward now, placing the tips of his fingers together, gazing absently at the floor with those clear blue eyes of his. It made James nervous (Ansel had been known to get too serious at times like this) but before he could change the atmosphere any, Ansel had begun speaking again. "Uh, I wanted to tell you," he said, "I been meaning to say to you—sheesh! James, will you close the door?"

James gave the inner door a push and it clicked shut.

"Too much wind," Ansel said. "Well. I been meaning to, um, give you my condolences, Simon. And tell you how sorry I am not to go to the funeral. James said I shouldn't, but you don't know how I—"

"You didn't miss much," said Simon.

"What? Well, I just wish I could've come and paid my respects, so to speak. That's what I told James. But James said—"

Simon sat tight, his hands pressed between his knees and his eyes straight ahead. When James started into the kitchen Simon half stood, with that squinchy little frown on his face again, so James stopped and leaned back against the wall. He wasn't sure why; always before this it was Ansel that Simon followed, leaving James to Janie Rose. But now Simon sank back in his seat again, looking easier, and began kicking one foot lazily in the direction of the coffee table. Ansel rambled on, his speech growing more certain.

"I had never been so shocked by *any* news," he said. "I was saying that to James. I said, 'Why, she and Simon were over here not but a while ago,' I said. 'Why, think how Simon must *feel*.' "

"I feel all right," Simon said.

"I mean—"

"I feel all right."

Ansel rubbed the bridge of his nose and looked over at James, and James straightened up from his position against the wall. "Mainly he feels hungry," he told Ansel. "I promised him lunch."

"Why, sure," said Ansel. "If he wants it. But I doubt he does. You hungry, Simon?"

"I'm starved," Simon said.

"You going to eat?"

"I *reckon* I am."

"I see," said Ansel.

Simon stood up and came over to James. When he got to James's side he just stood there and waited, with his eyes straight ahead and his back to Ansel. "We going to get that pizza?" he asked.

"Anything you want."

"Pizza?" Ansel said, and Simon turned then and looked up at James.

"That's what I promised him," James said.

"Why, Simon—"

"Hush," said James. "Now, Simon, we got three kinds of pizza mix out there. Sausage, and cheese, and something else. I forget. You go choose and then we'll cook it up. All right?"

"All right," Simon said. He turned and looked back at Ansel, and then he went on into the kitchen. When he was gone, James came over and sat down beside Ansel.

"Listen," he said.

Away from outsiders now, Ansel slumped back in his seat and let his shoulders sag. There were tired dark marks underneath his eyes; he hadn't slept well. "You're on my couch," he said automatically. "Do I have to tell you, James? Sitting like that makes the springs go wrong."

"Simon's folks are still on the hill," said James. "We've got to keep him here; I promised Joan he wouldn't sit in that house alone."

"Ah, sitting alone," Ansel said. He sighed. "That's no good."

"No. Will you help keep him busy?"

"The couch, James."

James stood up, and Ansel swung his feet around and slid down until he was lying prone. "I don't see how he can eat," he said.

"He's hungry."

"I *wonder* about this world."

"People handle things their own ways," James said. "Don't go talking to him about dying, Ansel."

"Well."

"Will you?"

"Well."

There was a crash of cans out in the kitchen. A cupboard door slammed, and Simon called, "Hey, James. I've decided."

"Which one?"

"The sausage. There was only just the two of them."

He came into the living room, carrying the box of pizza mix, and Ansel raised his head to look over at him and then grunted and lay back and stared at the ceiling. For a minute Simon hesitated. Then he walked over to him and said, *"You're* the pizza-maker."

"Who said?" Ansel asked.

"Well, back there on the hill James said—"

"All right." Ansel sat up slowly, running his fingers through his hair. "It's always something," he said.

"Well, maybe—"

"No, no. I don't mind."

And then Ansel smiled, using his widest smile that dipped in the middle and turned up at the corners like a child's drawing of a happy man. When he did that his long thin face turned suddenly wide at the cheekbones, and his chin became shiny. "We'll make my speciality," he said. "It's called an icebox pizza. On refrigerator-defrosting days that's the way we clean the icebox; we load it all on a pizza crust and serve it up for lunch. You want to see how I make it?"

He was standing now, smoothing down his Sunday jacket and straightening his slumped shoulders. When he reached for the pizza mix Simon walked forward and gave it to him, not hanging back now but looking more at ease. Ansel said, "This is something every man should know. Even if he's married. He can cook it when his wife is sick and serve her lunch in bed. Do you want an apron?"

"No," said Simon.

"Don't blame you. Don't blame you at all. Well—" and he was heading for the kitchen now, reading the directions as he walked. His walk was slow, but not enough to cause James any worry. James could judge the way Ansel felt just by glancing at him, most of the time. He had to; Ansel would never tell himself. When he felt his best he was likely to call for meals on a tray, and when he was really sick he might decide to wallpaper the bedroom. He was a backward kind of person. James had a habit of looking at him as someone a whole generation removed from him, although in reality he was twenty-six, only two years younger than James himself. He was thinking that way now, watching with narrow, almost paternal eyes as Ansel made his way into the kitchen.

"Naturally there are really no *rules*," Ansel was saying, "since you never know what might be in the icebox." And Simon's voice came floating back: "Fruit, even? Lettuce?" "*Well*, now . . ." Ansel said.

James smiled and went over to the easy chair to sit down, stretching his legs out in front of him. It felt good to be home again. The house was a dingy place, with yellow peeling walls and sunken furniture. And it was so rickety that whenever James had some photography job that required a long time-exposure he had to run around warning everyone. "Just *sit* a minute," he would say, and he would pull up chairs for everybody in this house and then go dashing off to take his picture before people started shaking the floors again. But at least it was a comfortable house, not far from town, and Ansel had that big front window in the living room where he could watch the road. He would sit on the couch with his elbows on the sill, and everything he saw passing—just an old truck, or a boy riding a mule— meant something to him. He had been watching that long, and he knew people that well.

Thinking of Ansel and his window made James look toward it, to see what was going on, but all he saw from where he sat was the greenish-yellow haze of summer air, framed by mesh curtains. He rose and went over to look out, with his hands upon the sill, and peered down the gravel road toward the hill he had just come from. No one was in sight. Maybe it would be hours before they returned; Joan might still be standing there, trying to make her aunt and uncle stop staring at that grass. But even so, James went on watching for several minutes. He could still feel the wind, gentler down here but strong enough to push the curtains in.

For a long time now, wind would make him think of today. He had climbed that hill behind all the others, and seen how the wind whipped the women's black skirts and ruffled little crooked parts down the backs of their hairdos. And when the first cluster of relatives had taken their leave at the end, stopping first to touch Mrs. Pike's folded arms or murmur something to Mr. Pike, the words they said were blown away and neither of the parents answered. Though they might not have answered anyway, even without the wind. The day that Janie Rose died, when James had spent thirty-six hours in the hospital waiting room and finally heard the news with only that tenth of his mind that was still awake, he had gone to Mrs. Pike and said, "Mrs. Pike, if there's anything I or Ansel can do for you, no matter what it is, we will want to do it." And Mrs. Pike had looked past him at the information desk and said, "Just falling off a *tractor* don't make a person die," and then had turned and left. So James had let them be, and went home and told Ansel to keep to himself a while and not go bothering the Pikes. "Not even to give our sympathy?" asked Ansel, and James said no, not even that. He hadn't liked the thought of Ansel's going to the funeral, either. Ansel said he had half a mind to go anyway—he could always rest on the way, he said—but James could picture that: Ansel toiling up the hill, clasping his chest from the effort and gasping out lines of funeral poetry, calling out for the whole procession to stop the minute he needed a rest. So James had gone alone, and quietly, and had promised to report to Ansel the minute it was over. The only one there that he had spoken to was Joan; the only two sounds he carried away with him were Joan's low voice and the roaring of the wind. He thought he would never like the sound of wind again.

Out in the kitchen now, Janie Rose's brother was talking on and on in his froggy little voice. "I never saw *peanut* butter on a pizza," he was saying. "You sure you know what you're doing, Ansel?"

"Just wait'll you taste it," Ansel said.

James left the window and went out to the kitchen. "How's it going?" he asked.

"It's coming along," Ansel said. He was swathed in a big checked dishtowel, wrapped right over his suit jacket and safety-pinned at the back, and on the counter stood the almost finished pizza that Simon was decorating. The kitchen was rippling with heat. James took his shirt off and laid it on the counter, so that he was in just his undershirt, and he opened the back door.

"Aren't you hot?" he asked Simon.

But Simon said, "No," and went on laying wiener slices down. On the floor at his feet were little sprinklings of flour and Parmesan, and the front of his suit was practically another pizza in itself, but the important thing was keeping him busy. It was too bad the pizza-making couldn't go on for another hour or so, just for that reason; they would have to find something else for him to do.

Ansel said, "Now the olives, Simon."

"I don't think I like olives."

"Sure you do. Olives are good for the brain. Will you look at your shirt?"

Simon looked down at his shirt and then shrugged.
"It'll wash," he said.

"Your mama'll have a fit."

"Ah, she won't care."

"I bet she will."

"She won't care."

"*Any* mother would care about *that*," said Ansel.
"Makes quite a picture."

"Pictures," James said suddenly. He straightened up.
"Hey, Simon. You seen my last photographs?"

"No," said Simon. "You get another customer?"

"Not in the last few days, no. But I took a bunch on
my own a while ago. When you're done I'll show you."

"Okay," said Simon.

"Olives," Ansel reminded him.

James went over to the back window and looked out.
There was the Pikes' Nellie, burrowing her way through
a tangle of wild daisies and bachelor's buttons. He had
been planning to pick Joan a bunch of those daisies,
before all this happened. They were her favorite flowers. Now he couldn't; the house would be stuffed with
hothouse funeral flowers. And anyway, he couldn't just
walk in there with a bunch of daisies in his hand and
risk disturbing the Pikes. The daisies would have grown
old there, waving in the sunshine on their long green
stems, before he could go back to doing things like that
again.

The pizza was in the oven. Ansel slammed the door
on it and wiped his hands and said, "*There*, now."

"How much longer?" Simon asked.

"Oh, I don't know. Fifteen-twenty minutes. We'll go
out where it's cool and wait on it. You coming, James?"

James followed them out to the living room. It
seemed very dark and cool here now. Ansel settled

down on his couch with a long contented groan, and Simon went over to Ansel's window and stood watching the road.

"Anybody seen those people?" he asked James.

"What people?"

"My mama and them. Anybody seen them?"

"No, not yet."

"Well, anyway," said Simon, "I reckon I'll just run on over and have a look, see if maybe they haven't—"

"I think we'd have seen them if they'd come," said James. "Or heard them, one."

"*Still* and all, I guess I'll just—"

"You two," Ansel said. "Do you have to stand over me like that?" He was lying full length now, with his head propped against one of the sofa arms. "Kind of overwhelming," he said, and James moved Simon gently away by one shoulder.

"I almost forgot," he said. "You want to see my pictures?"

"Oh, well I—"

"They're good ones."

"Well."

James went down the little hallway to his darkroom. There was a damp and musky smell there, and only the dimmest light. He headed for the filing cabinet in the corner, where he kept his pictures, and opened the bottom drawer. The latest ones were at the front, laid away carefully (taking pictures for fun wasn't something he could afford very often), and when he pulled them out he handled them gently, examining the first two alone for a minute before he returned to the living room.

"Here you go," he said to Simon. "Your hands clean?"

"Yes."

His hands were covered with tomato sauce, but he held the pictures by the rims so James didn't say anything. The first picture didn't impress Simon. He studied it only a minute and then sniffed. "One of those," he said. James grinned and handed him the next one. Neither Simon nor Janie Rose had ever liked anything but straight, posed portraits—preferably of someone they could recognize, which always made them giggle. But when James wasn't taking wedding pictures, or photographs for the Larksville newspaper, he turned away from portraits altogether. He had the idea of photographing everyone he knew in the way his mind pictured them when they weren't around. And the way people stuck in his memory was odd—they were doing something without looking at him, usually, wheeling a wheelbarrow up a hill or hunting under the dining-room table for a spool of thread. Old girlfriends of his used to object to being photographed in their most faded blue jeans, the way he remembered them from some picnic. But almost always he won out in the end; the pictures of people in his mind and in his filing cabinet were nearly identical. Joan he imagined in a dust storm, the way he had first seen her (she had come down the road with two suitcases and a drawstring handbag, spitting dust out of her mouth and turning her face sideways to the wind as she walked). For a long time now he had waited for another dust storm, and last week one had come. That was in those first two pictures, the ones that Simon had barely glanced at. Even when James said, "That's your cousin Joan, if you don't know," thinking to make Simon look twice, Simon only raised his eyebrows. It was the third picture he liked. In that one Ansel was lying on his couch, looking up at the sky through the window and absently playing with the cord of the shade. "Ansel!" Simon said, and Ansel turned his head and looked at him.

"What now?" he asked.

"I just seen your picture here."

"*Oh*, yes," Ansel said.

"Of you on your couch and all."

"Oh, yes. Here, let me look." He raised himself up on one elbow, reaching out toward the picture, and Simon brought it over to him. "That's me, all right," said Ansel. He studied it for a while, smiling. "It's not bad," he said.

"I think it's a right good picture."

"Yep. Not bad at all." He handed the picture back and lay down again, staring up at the ceiling and still smiling. "They're wonderful things, pictures," he said.

"Well, some of them."

"Very *remaining* things, you know?"

"I don't like them other kind, though," Simon said. "Dust clouds and all. I can't see what *they're* for."

"They're for me," said James. "Here, I got another one of Ansel."

"James," Ansel said, "do your legs ever get to feeling kind of numb? Kind of achey-numb?"

"Prop them up."

"Propping *up* won't do it."

"It's what you get for not having your shots," James said.

"Oh, well. Right behind the knee, it is." He propped his legs against the back of the couch and slid farther down, so that his feet were the highest part of him. "This couch is too short," he said. "Here, Simon. Hand me the next one."

The next picture had Ansel sitting up, looking self-conscious. When Ansel saw it he smiled his dippy little

smile again and brought the picture closer to examine
it. "This is one I posed myself," he said. "Had James
take it like I wanted. James, I believe it's my *shoes*
aggravating that feeling."

James set the rest of the pictures beside Simon and
reached over to untie Ansel's shoes. "If you'd get the
right *size*," he said.

"No, it's to do with my illness. I can tell."

"It's on Wednesdays you get your shots," said James.
"This is Saturday. That's five times you missed."

"Lot you care. Listen—" He twisted around, so that
he was facing Simon. "What was I talking about? The
picture. That's right. I was about to say, in my estima-
tion this picture is the best of the lot. The one of me
sitting up." He tilted the picture toward the light. "He-
roic, like," he said. "Profile to the window and all."

"The other one's better," said Simon.

"What other one?"

"The first one. You lying down."

"That's because you're used to me lying down," Ansel said. He sighed and tossed the picture onto the coffee table. "Everyone's used to it. When I stand up they
hardly recognize me. Faces change, standing up. Become more bottom-heavy. Pass me the next one."

"I think the pizza must be done," said James. "Hey,
Ansel?"

"Well, take it out. This one of Mr. Abbott—I'd be
insulted if I was him. Troweling up the garden plot with
his back to the camera and his rear end sticking out."

James got up and went to the kitchen. The pizza-
smell filled the whole room, and when he opened the
oven he thought it looked done. From a hook on the
wall he took a pot-holder and then hauled the pizza out
and set it on the counter, burning one finger on the way.

"Ansel!" he called. He came to the living room doorway. Ansel was just bending over a picture, rocking slightly back and forth and frowning at it, and Simon was sorting through the rest of them. "Ansel," James repeated.

"This one here," said Ansel, "ought not to've been included."

"Which one?" Simon asked.

"I'm ashamed of James. You ought not to see it."

"Well, I just *saw* it," said Simon. "What's the matter with it?"

"Nothing's the matter. I'll just set it aside."

He pulled himself up and laid the picture face down on the back of the couch, looking over his shoulder to make sure Simon hadn't seen. "Shamed of James," he said.

"Well, for heaven's sake," James said from the doorway. "What's all that about, Ansel?"

"It ought never to've been included, that picture."

James crossed the living room and picked up the picture. It was a perfectly ordinary one—he'd done it as a favor for Miss Faye, who wanted her screened back porch photographed now that her nephew had spent half the summer building it. She had led James way behind the house, deep into the wild grass that grew there among scattered piles of rusted stoves and old car parts, and she directed him to photograph the whole long house so that her people in Georgia could get an idea how the porch was proportioned. "I think this is too *far*, ma'am," James told her, but she insisted and this was what had come of it—a wild, weedy-looking picture, with the house rising above a wave of grass like a huge seagoing barge. Miss Faye's porch was only a little bump sticking out along with a lot of other bumps—

Janie Rose Pike's tacked-on back bedroom, the woodshed under James and Ansel's bathroom window, and the rusted old fuel barrel on its stilt legs beside the middle chimney. He hadn't shown the picture to Miss Faye yet, for fear of disappointing her. But it wasn't all *that* bad; he couldn't see what was upsetting Ansel.

"I don't get it," he said.

"Well, never you mind. Just give it back."

"What you trying to pull, Ansel?"

"Will you give it back?"

James handed it across, but before Ansel's fingers had quite touched it Simon reached out and took it away. He swung away from the couch, avoiding Ansel's long arm, and wandered out into the middle of the room with his eyes fixed frowningly on the picture. Ansel groaned.

"You see what you done," he told James.

"Ansel, I don't know why—"

"Then *listen*," Ansel said. He leaned forward, talking in a whisper now. "James, someone *departed* is in that picture—"

"Where?" Simon asked.

"Oh, Lord."

"Well, I don't see."

"Me neither," said James. "What're you up to, Ansel?"

Ansel stood up, supporting himself with both hands on the arm of the couch. When he walked over to Simon he walked like a man wading, sliding his stocking feet across the floor. He poked his finger at one corner of the picture, said "There," and then waded back again. "I'm going to lie down," he said to no one in particular.

"Ah, yes," said James. "I see."

"I don't," Simon said.

"Right here she is."

He pointed. His forefinger was just touching the Model A Ford that stood behind the house, resting on cinder-blocks that were hidden by the tall waving grass. All that could really be seen of the Ford was its glassless windows and its sunken roof—it had been submerged in that sea of grass a long time—and in the front window on the driver's side, no bigger than a little white button, was Janie Rose's moon-round face. She was too far away to have any expression, or even to have her spectacles show, but they could see the high tilt of her head as she eyed James and the two white dots of her hands on the steering wheel. She was pretending to be some haughty lady driving past. Yet when James drew back from the picture he lost her again immediately; she could have been one of the little patches of Queen Anne's lace that dotted the field. "I don't see how you found her," he told Ansel.

"No trouble."

Simon stared at the picture a while and then tilted it, moving Janie Rose out of his focus. "She just blurs right in again," he said. "She comes and goes. Like those pictures in little kids' magazines, where you try and find the pig in the tree."

"The *what?*" Ansel said. He raised his head and looked at Simon, open-mouthed.

"But it's here, sure enough," said James. "Isn't that something? I never saw her. Not even when I was enlarging it, and I looked it over right closely then."

"It's funny," Simon said.

"You hungry, Simon?"

"I guess." But he went on staring at the picture. He seemed not so much to be looking at Janie Rose as turning the whole thing over in his mind now, holding

the picture absently in front of him. With his free hand
he was pulling at a cowlick over his forehead.

"When our mother died," Ansel said suddenly, "I
was beside myself."

Simon looked over at him.

"I couldn't think about her. I couldn't think her
name. Yet people are different these days. I see that."

"Oh, well," Simon said. He returned to his picture.
"James, is there such a thing as X-ray cameras? Could
you take a picture of our house, like, and have the people show up from inside?"

"I don't know," said James. "I doubt it."

A fly buzzed in, humming its way in zigzags through
the room, and Ansel followed it with his eyes. When
the fly had disappeared into the kitchen he lay back
again, gazing upwards. "I'm doing all my dying in one
room now," he told the ceiling.

"Oh, stop that," James said.

"It's true. I'm getting contained in smaller and
smaller spaces. First it was the whole of North Carolina; then this town; then this room. Soon no place. We
all got to go."

"Look," James said. "I know of one stone-cold
pizza in the kitchen. What do I do with it? Throw it
out?"

"Well," said Ansel. He sat up and peered over at
Simon. "Why do you keep looking at that picture?"

Simon put the picture down. He looked from Ansel
to James, and then he stood up and stuck his hands in
his pockets. "When I come to think of it," he said, "I
don't want no pizza."

"Well you don't have to eat it," said James.

"I think I'll just pass it up."

"All right."

"It's hard to say what's happening to people," Ansel said. "They don't seem to realize, no more. Don't think of *themselves* being dead someday; don't mourn no more. It's hard to say what they *do* do, when you stop and consider."

"Don't die of anemia no more, either," said James.

"What do you know about it?"

Simon was tilting gently back and forth, from his toes to his heels and his heels to his toes, with his shoulders hunched high and his eyes on a spot outside Ansel's window. He didn't seem to be listening.

"Nobody's perfect," Ansel said. "Janie wasn't exactly a pink-pinafore type, I admit it. Rattling through her prayers in purple pajamas: Deliver us from measles. But she's under the earth like you'll be someday, have you thought of that? *You* in that clay, and your survivors calling you a pig in a tree?"

"Ansel, there's not a thing in this world you do right," James said.

But Ansel waved him aside and sat forward, on the edge of his couch. "What will you do about *me*?" he asked. "How *about* that, now? When I am—"

Simon was crying. He was still rocking back and forth, still keeping his hands jammed tightly in his pockets, but there were wet paths running through the flour on his cheeks and his eyes were frowning and angry. "Well—" he said, and his voice came out croaky. He took a breath and cleared his throat. "Well, I reckon I'll be getting on home," he said.

"Oh, now," said Ansel.

But James said, "All right. It's all right."

He crossed over to open the door and Simon went out, stumbling a little. James followed him. He stood on the porch and watched Simon all the way down to

his end of the house, hoping Simon might look back
once, but he never did. He walked stiffly and blindly,
with his sharp little shoulder-bones sticking out through
the back of his jacket. When he reached his own door
he hesitated, with his hand on the knob and his back
still toward James. Then he said, "Well," again, and
pulled the door open and went on in. The screen door
slammed shut and rattled once and was still. James
could hear Simon's footsteps clomping on across the
hollow floor of the parlor.

The aluminum porch chair was still beneath the window, where Ansel had been sitting in it to watch the
funeral go by. After a minute James went over and sat
down on it. He let his arms rest along the arms of the
chair and the metal burned him, making two lines of
sunbaked heat down the inside of his forearms. Behind
him was the soft sound of the mesh curtains moving,
and the sleeves of Ansel's rough black suit sliding across
the splintery windowsill. "Hot out," Ansel said.

James squinted toward the road.

"I wish it was the season for tangerines."

There were no people passing now, only the yellow
fields across the way rippling in the wind and one gray
hound plodding slowly through the yard. In the house
behind James were the soft, humming sounds of other
people, murmuring indistinct words to one another and
moving gently around. James closed his eyes.

"Hey, James."

He didn't answer.

"James."

"What."

"James, I told you he wouldn't eat."

The wind began again, and James rose from his chair

to go inside. He didn't want to sit here any more. Here it was too still; here there was only that wind, rushing over and around the house in its solitary position among the weeds.

2

J oan Pike was twenty-six years old, and had lived in
bedrooms all her life. She lived the way a guest
would—keeping her property strictly within the walls of
her room, hanging her towel and washcloth on a bar
behind her door. No one asked her to. Her aunt had
even said to her, once, that she wished Joan would act
more at home here. "You could at *least* hang your coat
in the downstairs closet," she said. "Could you do that
much?" And Joan had nodded, and from then on hung
her coat with the others. But her towel stayed in her
own room, because nobody had mentioned that to her.
And she read and sewed sitting on her bed, unless she
was expressly invited downstairs.

If they had asked her, point-blank, the way they must
have wanted to—if they had asked, "Why do you have
to be invited?" she wouldn't have known the answer.
It was what she was used to; that was all. When she
was born, her parents were already middle-aged. They
weren't sure what they were supposed to do with her;
they treated her politely, like a visitor who had dropped
in unexpectedly. If she sat with them after supper they
tried to make some sort of conversation, or gazed at
her uneasily over the tops of their magazines until she
retreated to her room. So now, a hundred miles from

28

home and on her own, it felt only natural to be living
in another bedroom, although she hadn't planned it that
way. She had come here planning just to stay with the
Pikes a week or two, until she found a place of her
own, and then the children made her change her mind.
When Janie Rose's hamster ran away, and Janie Rose
stayed an hour in the bathroom shouting that it wasn't
important, brushing her teeth over and over with scald-
ing hot water that she didn't even notice and crying into
the sink, Joan was the only one who could make her
come away. After that the Pikes asked if she would like
to live with them, and she said yes without appearing
to think twice. This bedroom wasn't like the first one,
after all. Here there was always something going on,
and a full family around the supper table. When she
went walking with Simon and Janie Rose, she pretended to herself that they were hers. She played sense-
less games with them, toasting marshmallows over
candles and poking spiders in their webs to try and
make them spin their names. For four years she had
lived that way. Nine months of each year she worked
as a secretary for the school principal, giving some of
her salary to the Pikes and sending some home to her
parents, and in the summers she worked part-time in
the tobacco fields. In the evenings she sat with James,
every evening talking of the same things and never
moving forwards or backwards with him, and she spent
a little time with the Pikes. But she still lived in her
bedroom; she still waited for an invitation, and when
any of the Pikes wanted to see her they had to go knock
on her door.

Today no one knocked. Her aunt and uncle had gone
straight to their room after the funeral and were there
now—the sound of Mr. Pike's murmuring voice could

just be heard—and Simon was alone in his room and seemed to be planning to stay there. That left Joan with a piece of time she knew would be her own, with no one interrupting, and at first she thought it was what she needed. She could sit down and get things sorted in her mind, and maybe catch some sleep later on. There was still that heavy feeling behind her eyes from the long aching wait in the hospital. But when she tried sorting her thoughts she found it was more than she could do just now, and then when she tried sleeping her eyes wouldn't shut. She lay on top of her bedspread, with her shoes off but her dress still on in case her aunt should call her, and her eyes kept wandering around the bland, motel-like cleanness of her room. It seemed every muscle she owned was tensed up and waiting to be called on. If she were alone in the house she would have gone down and scrubbed the kitchen floor, maybe, or at least had a long hot bath. But who knew whether her aunt would approve of that on a day like today?

When she finally thought of what she could do, she sat up quickly and frowned at herself for not thinking of it sooner. It was the one thing her aunt had asked of her all day: she had been sitting at the breakfast table, digging wells in her oatmeal and staring out into the back yard, and suddenly she had caught sight of Janie Rose's draggled blue crinoline flapping on the clothesline. "Take everything away, Joan," she said.

"What?"

"Take Janie's things away. Put them somewhere."

"All right," said Joan, but she was hunting raisins for Simon's oatmeal and hadn't really been thinking about it. Now she wasn't sure how much time she would have; Simon might come in at any moment. She wanted to do the job alone, keeping it from the rest of the family, because different things could bother different people. With her it had been Janie Rose's pocket collection—modeling clay and an Italian stamp and a handful of peas hidden away during supper, sitting on the edge of the tub where they had been dumped before a bath five nights ago. She didn't think any more could bother her now.

She opened her door and looked out into the hallway. No one was there. Behind the Pikes' door the mumbling voice still rambled on, faltering in places and then starting up again, louder than before. When Joan came out into the hall in her stocking feet, a floorboard creaked beneath her and the murmuring stopped altogether, but then her uncle picked up the thread and continued. Joan reached the steps and descended them on tiptoe, and when she got to the bottom she closed the door behind her and let out her breath.

Janie Rose's room opened off the kitchen hall. It had had to be built on for her especially, because the Pikes had never planned for more than one child and the room that was now Joan's had been taken up by a paying lodger at the time. Janie didn't like her room. She liked Simon's, with the porthole window in the closet and the cowboy wallpaper. When Simon wasn't around she did all her playing there, so that her own room looked almost unlived in. On her hastily made-up bed sat an eyeless teddy bear, tossed against the pillow the way Janie Rose must have seen it in her mother's copies of *House and Garden*. And her toys were neatly lined on the bookshelves, but wisps of clothes stuck out of dresser drawers and her closet was one heap of things she had kicked her way out of at night and thrown on the floor.

It was the closet Joan began with. She pulled back

the flaps of a cardboard box from the hall and then began to fold the dresses up and lay them away. There weren't many. Janie Rose hated dresses, although her mother had dreams of outfitting her in organdy and dotted swiss. The dresses Janie chose for herself were red plaid, with the sashes starting to come off at the seams because she had a tendency to tie them too tightly. Then there were stacks of overalls, most of them home-sewn and inherited from Simon, and at the very bottom were the few things her mother had bought when Janie Rose wasn't along—pink and white things, with "Little Miss Chubby" labels sewn into the necklines. While she was folding those Joan had a sudden clear picture of Janie Rose on Sunday mornings, struggling into them. She dressed backwards. She refused to pull dresses over her head, for fear of becoming invisible. Instead she pulled them up over her feet, tugging and grunting and complaining all the way, and sometimes ripping the seams of dresses that weren't meant to be put on that way. She had a trick that she did with her petticoat, so that it wouldn't slide up with her dress—she bent over and tucked it between her knees, and while she was doing all this struggling with the dress she would be standing there knock-kneed and pigeon-toed, locking the petticoat in place and usually crying. She cried a lot, but quietly.

When Joan had finished with the closet, the cardboard box was only two-thirds full. The closet was bare, and the floor had just a few hangers and bubble gum wrappers scattered over it. It looked worse that way. She reached over and slammed the closet door shut, and then she dragged the box over to the dresser and began on that.

Upstairs, a door slammed. She straightened up and

listened, hoping it was only the wind, but there were Simon's footsteps down the stairs. For a minute she was afraid he was coming to find her, but then she heard the soft puffing sound that the leather chair made when someone sat in it, and she relaxed. He must not want to be with people right now. She pushed her hair off her face and opened the next dresser drawer.

Janie Rose had more sachet bags than Joan thought existed. They cluttered every drawer, one smell mixed with another—lemon verbena and lavender and rose petals. And tossed in here and there were her mother's old perfume bottles with the tops off, adding their own heavy scent, so that Joan became confused and couldn't tell one smell from another any more. She wondered why Janie Rose, wearing all this fragrant underwear, had still smelled only of Ivory soap and Crayolas. Especially when she wore so *much* underwear. On Janie Rose's bad days, when she thought things were going against her or she was frightened, she would pile on layer upon layer of undershirts and panties. Her jeans could hardly be squeezed on top of it all, and if she wore overalls the straps would be strained to the breaking point over drawersful of undershirts. Sometimes her mother made her take them off again and sometimes she didn't (''She's just hopeless,'' she would say, and give up), but usually, if the day turned better, Janie peeled off a few layers of her own accord. On the evenings of her bad days, when Simon came in for supper, he had a habit of reaching across the table and pinching her overall strap to see how many other straps lay beneath it. It was his way of asking how she was doing. If Janie was feeling all right by then she would just giggle at him, and he would laugh. But other days she jumped when he touched her and hunched up her shoulders, and then Simon would say nothing and fix all his attention on supper.

Out in the parlor now Joan heard the squeaking of leather as Simon rose, and the sound of his shoes across the scatter rug. She stopped in the act of closing the box and waited, silently; his footsteps came closer, and then he appeared in the doorway. "Hey, Joan," he said. There was something white on his face.

"Hey."

He looked at the cardboard boxes without changing expression, and then he went over to the bed and sat down, picking up the teddy bear in one hand. "Hey, Ernest," he said. He laid Ernest face down across his lap, circling the bear's neck with one hand, and leaned forward to watch Joan.

"I'm packing things away," she told him.

"Well, I see you are."

She folded the flaps of the box down, one corner over another so as to lock them, and then stood up and pushed the box toward the closet. "Some of your things're on the shelves there," she told Simon while she was opening the closet door. The box grated across the hangers on the floor. "You better take out what's yours, before I pack it away."

"None of it is," said Simon, without looking at the shelves.

"Some is. That xylophone."

"I don't play that any more. Don't you know I've stopped playing with that kind of thing?"

"All right," Joan said.

"I gave it for keeps."

"All right."

"Unliving things last much longer than living."

"That's true," Joan said. She chose an armload of

things from the shelves—dolls, still shining and unused, a pack of candy Chesterfields, and an unbreakable yellow plastic record ordered off a cereal box. She dumped them helter-skelter into a second box and returned for another armload. "James give you a good lunch?" she asked.

"No."

"What was wrong with it?"

"Nothing," said Simon. "There just wasn't any. Because I didn't eat it."

"Oh."

"If I *had* of eaten it, it would have been a pizza."

"I see."

She dumped another armload in the box. It was half full now, and junky-looking, with the arms of dolls and the wheels of cars tangled together.

"I better make you a sandwich," she said finally.

"Naw."

"You want an apple?"

"Naw."

He crossed over to where she was standing and laid the bear gently on top of the other things. "James has got this photograph," he said, and went back to sit on the bed. "That Ansel, boy."

"What about him?"

"I just hate him. I hate him."

When it looked as if he weren't going to say any more, Joan began removing the last few things from the shelf. Every now and then she looked Simon's way, but he sat very quiet with his back against the wall and his face expressionless. Finally she said, "Well, Ansel has his days. You know that." But Simon remained silent.

The room was bare now; all that remained were the things on the clothesline. She pushed the second box into the closet and then said, "I'm going out back a minute. After that I'll fix you a sandwich." Simon stood up to follow her. "I'm only going for a minute," she said, but Simon came with her anyway, and they went down the hall and through the kitchen and out the back screen door.

It was hot and windy outside, with the acres of grass behind the house rumpling and tangling together. The few things on the line—Simon's bathing suit and Janie Rose's crinoline and Sunday blouse—were being whipped about by the wind so that they made little cracking sounds. While Joan unpinned Janie's things, Simon wandered nearby snapping the heads off the weeds.

"Simon," she called to him, "what kind of sandwich you want?"

"I ain't hungry."

"I'll just make you a little one. And go call your mama and daddy; they have to eat too."

"I wish *you* would."

"Come on, Simon."

He shrugged and started toward the house, still walking aimlessly and kicking at things. "All right," he said. "But I'll tell them it's your fault I came."

"They won't mind you coming."

"You think not?"

He banged the screen door behind him. After he was gone Joan stood in the yard awhile, clutching Janie's things against her stomach, feeling the dampness soak into her stocking feet. She wished she could just walk off. If it weren't for Simon, she would; she would go find some place to sit alone and think things out. But her feet were growing cold, and there were sandwiches to make; she shook her hair off her forehead and started back toward the house. The closer to the house she came the quieter the wind sounded, and when she stepped back into the kitchen there was a sudden silence in her ears that felt odd.

She put the things from the clothesline into the closet, and then she returned to the kitchen and leaned against the refrigerator while she planned a meal. The room was so cluttered it made thinking difficult. Small objects lay here and there, gathering dust because no one had ever found a place for them. The kitchen windows were curtainless, and littered with lost buttons and ripening tomatoes. And the wall behind the stove was covered with twenty or thirty drawings, Scotch-taped so closely together they might have been wallpaper. Most of them were Simon's—soldiers and knights and masked men with guns. His mother thought he might be an artist someday. Scattered among them were Janie Rose's drawings, all of the same lollipop-shaped tree with hundreds of tiny round apples on it. She said it was the tree out back, but that was only a tiny scrubby tree with no leaves; it had never borne fruit and wouldn't have borne apples even if it had, since it was some other kind of tree. Once her mother said, "Janie, honey, why don't you draw something *else*?" and Janie had run out crying and wouldn't come down from the attic. But the next day she had said she would draw something different. She came into the kitchen where they were all sitting, carrying a box of broken crayons and a huge sheet of that yellow pulpy paper she always used. "What else *is* there to draw?" she asked, and her mother said, "Well, a house, for instance. Other children draw houses." Then they all hung over her, and she drew a straight up-and-down line and a window, and then a green circle above it with lots of red apples

on it. Everybody sat back and looked at her; she had
drawn an apple tree with a window in it. *"Oh,* my,"
she said apologetically, and then she smiled and began
filling in the circle with green crayon. After that she
never tried houses again. She labored away at apple
trees, and signed them, "Miss J.R. Pike" in the corner, in large purple letters. Simon never signed his,
but that was because his mother said she would recognize his style anywhere in the world.

When Simon came downstairs again he had changed
into his boots; he was trying to make the floor shake
when he walked. "Daddy's coming and Mama ain't,"
he said. "She ain't hungry."

"Did you ask if she wants coffee?"

"She didn't give me a chance. She said go on and let
her rest."

"Well, run up again and ask her."

"No, sir," Simon said. He sat down firmly in one of
the chairs.

"Just run up, Simon—"

"I won't do it," he said.

Joan thought a minute, and then she said, "Well, all
right." She reached out to smooth his hair down and
for a minute he let her, but just barely, and then
shrugged her hand away.

"Daddy wants just a Co-Cola," he told her.

"He's got to have more than that."

"No. He said—Hey, Joan."

"What."

"I got an idea."

"All right."

"Why not you and me go *out* and eat. You like that?"

"We can't," Joan said.

"We could go to that place with the chicken."

"We have to stay home, Simon."

"I would pay for it."

"No," Joan said, and she touched one upright piece of his hair again. "Are you the one that doesn't like using other people's forks? That makes twice in two days you've had that idea."

"Well, anyway," said Simon. But he must have been expecting her to say no; he sat back quietly and began drumming his fingers on the table. Above them was the sound of Mr. Pike's footsteps, crossing the hall and beginning to descend the stairs, and Joan remembered why she was in the kitchen and went back to the refrigerator. She opened the door and stared inside, at shelves packed tightly with other people's casseroles. At the kitchen doorway her uncle said, "I only want a Coke, Joan," and came to stand beside her, bending down to peer at the lower shelves.

"You have to eat something solid," Joan told him.

"I can't." He straightened up and rubbed his forehead. He was a lean man, all bones and tough brown skin. Ordinarily he did construction work, but for the month of July he had been laid off and was spending his time the way Joan did, helping Mr. Terry get his tobacco in. Years of working outdoors had made his face look stained with walnut juice, and his eyes were squinted from force of habit even when he wasn't in the sun. They were narrow brown slits in his face, the same shade as Simon's, and they were directed now at Joan while he waited for her to speak.

"There's a chicken salad here from Mrs. Betts," said Joan.

"No, thank you."

"The kind you like, with pimento."

"No."

"Now, eat a *little* something," she said. "I could be perking coffee for you to take Aunt Lou, if you'd sit down a minute."

"Oh, well," he said.

He sat down awkwardly, across from Simon, giving his Sunday pants a jerk at each knee to save the crease. "How you been getting along?" he asked Simon.

"Okay."

"Not giving Joan any trouble."

"No, sir."

"He's been just fine," said Joan. She set the salad out and laid three plates on the table. Her uncle studied his own plate seriously, hunching his shoulders over it and working his hands together.

"I'm glad to hear it," he said finally. When Joan looked over at him he said, "About Simon, I mean. James and Ansel feed you okay, boy?"

"No, sir."

"Well. Joan, Dr. Kitt left a prescription for your aunt but I don't see how I can go into town and leave her. I wonder, would you mind too much if—"

"I'll see to it after we eat," Joan said.

"All right."

He accepted his chicken salad wordlessly, keeping his eyes on Joan's hands as she dished his share out. When she had passed on to the next plate, he said, "Thank you," and the words came out hoarse so that he had to clear his throat. "Thank you," he said again. Even then his voice was muffled-sounding. In the last three days he had been talking steadily, always mumbling something into Mrs. Pike's ear to keep her going. It was probably the most he had talked in a lifetime. Ordinarily he sat quiet and listened, with something like awe, while his wife rattled on; he seemed perpetually surprised and a little proud that she should have so much to say.

When Joan had sat down herself, after filling the others' plates and passing out forks, she said, "Eat, now." She looked at the other two, but neither of them picked up his fork. "*Come* on," she said, and then Simon sighed and tucked his paper napkin into his collar with a rustling sound.

"This feels like Sunday-night supper," he said.

"It does."

"Not like afternoon. Why're we eating in the afternoon? What the *day* feels like, is Wednesday."

"Wednesday?"

"Feels like Wednesday."

"Why does it feel like—?"

"She blames it on herself," said Mr. Pike.

"What?"

"It breaks my heart. She keeps saying how she was hemming Miss Brook's basic black at the time—I never *have* liked that Miss Brook—and Janie Rose comes up and says, 'Mama,' she says, 'I'm going off to—' and Lou just never did hear where. Miss Brook was going on about her bunions. 'Lou,' I told her, I said, 'Lou, *I* don't think that would have—' but Lou says that's how it come to happen. She *never* let Janie Rose play with those Marsh girls. Never would have let her go, if she had known. But she was—"

"Never let her ride no tractors, either," said Simon. "Shakes a girl's insides all up."

"Hush," Joan told him. "Both of you. There's not even a dent made in that chicken salad."

Her uncle picked his fork up and then leaned across the table toward her. "She *blames* herself," he said.

"I know."

"She keeps—"

"*Eat*, Uncle Roy."

He began eating. His fork made steady little clinking sounds on the plate, and he chewed rapidly with the crunchy sound of celery filling the silence. When he was done, Joan put another spoonful of salad on his plate and he kept on without pause, never looking up, making his way doggedly through the heap of food. Simon stopped eating and stared at him, until Joan gave his wrist a tap with her finger. Then he started eating again, but he kept his eyes on his father. When Mr. Pike reached for the bowl and dished himself another helping, still crunching on his last mouthful, chewing without breathing, like a thirsty man drinking water, Simon looked over at Joan with his eyes round above a forkful of food and she frowned at him and cleared her throat.

"Um, Mrs. Hammond phoned today," she said. "She's a very *cheering* person, Uncle Roy; maybe Aunt Lou could talk to her later on. I told her to call back in a day or—"

"Remember Janie Rose?" Simon asked.

His father stopped chewing. "Remember *what*?" he said.

"Remember how she did on the telephone? Never answering 'Hello,' but saying, 'I am listening to WKKJ, the all-day swinging station,' in case WKKJ was ever to call and give her the jackpot for answering that way. Only you know, WKKJ never *did* call—"

"Simon, I *mean* it," Joan said.

"Lou is breaking my heart," said Mr. Pike.

"Wouldn't you feel funny, if you was to call someone that answered like that? 'I am listening to—' "

"It wasn't her *fault*," Mr. Pike said. "Janie never

asked for no special attention, like. She just kind
of—"

"God in heaven," Joan said.

The doorbell rang. It made a sharp, burring noise,
and Joan stood up so quickly to answer it that her chair
fell over backwards behind her. She let it stay. She escaped from the kitchen and crossed the parlor floor,
smoothing her skirt down in front of her, making herself walk slowly. Behind the screen, standing close together with their faces side by side and peering in, were
the Potter sisters from next door. They stepped backwards simultaneously so that Joan could swing the door
open, and then Miss Faye entered first with Miss Lucy
close behind her.

"We only stopped by for a minute," said Miss Faye.
"We wanted to bring your supper."

"Well, come on in," Joan said. "Really, do. Come
out to the kitchen, why don't you."

"Oh, I don't think—"

"No, I mean it." She took Miss Faye by one plump
wrist, almost pulling her. "You don't know how glad I
am to see you," she said.

"Well, if you really think—"

They walked on tiptoe, bearing their covered dishes
before them like sacred offerings. When they reached
the kitchen door, Mr. Pike stood up to greet them and
his chair fell backwards too, so that the room with its
overturned furniture looked stricken. "Why, Miss, um,
Miss Lucy," he said. "And Miss Faye. I declare. Come
in and have a—" and he bent down and pulled the chairs
up by their backs, both at the same time. "Sit down,
why don't you," he said.

Joan drew up the chair from beside the stove, and
Miss Lucy sat down in it with a sigh while Miss Faye

went to sit beside Simon. "We only mean to stay a minute," said Miss Lucy. She plopped the bowl she was carrying down on the table in front of her and then sat back, sliding her purse strap to a more comfortable position on her wrist. The Potter sisters always carried handbags and wore hats and gloves, even if they were going next door. They were small, round women, in their early sixties probably, and for as long as Joan had known them they had had only one aim in life: they wanted to have swarms of neighborhood children clamoring at their door for cookies, gathering in their yard at the first smell of cinnamon buns. And although no one came ("Children nowadays prefer to buy Nutty Buddies," Miss Faye said), they still went on baking, eating the cookies themselves, growing fat together and comparing notes on their identical heart conditions. It was those heart conditions that Miss Faye was discussing right now. She was saying, "Now, you and Lou know, Roy, how much we wish we could have climbed that hill today. If there was *any* way, the merest *logging* trail, we would've got there. But as it was, it would just have meant more tragedy. You know that."

And Mr. Pike was saying, "Well, I know, I know," and nodding gently without seeming to be listening. There was chicken salad on his chin, which meant that both the Potters kept staring tactfully down at their gloves instead of looking at him. Joan passed him a paper napkin, but he ignored it; he sat forward on his chair and said, "It surely was nice of you to come. Nice to bring us supper."

"It's the *least* we could do," said Miss Lucy. She looked around her, toward the kitchen door, and then lowered her voice. "Tell me," she whispered. "How is she now? How's Lou?"

"It just breaks my heart," said Mr. Pike.

"Oh, my."

"Not a thing I can do, seems like. She just sits. If she would stop all this *blaming* herself—"

"They all do that," said Miss Faye.

"She said Janie was the one she never paid no mind to."

"Will you listen to that."

"Never gave her a fair share."

"If it's not one reason it's another," Miss Lucy said. "I've seen that happen plenty of times."

"Maybe if you talked to her," said Mr. Pike. He pushed his plate away and straightened up. "You think you could just run up there a minute?"

"Well, not *run*, no, but—"

"I didn't mean that," he said. "No, you can take the stairs as slow as you want to. But if you two would talk to her a minute, so long as you don't mind—"

"Why, we don't mind a bit," said Miss Faye. "We'd be proud." She reached up to set her flowered hat straighter, as if she might like to put an extra hat on top of the first one for such a special visit. And Miss Lucy pulled gloves to perfect smoothness, and then folded her hands tightly over her purse.

"I just don't like to trouble you," Mr. Pike said.

"You stop that, Roy Pike."

They rose simultaneously, with their backs very straight. But even making the trip across the kitchen they walked slowly, preparing themselves for the stairs. "Be careful," Joan told them. "Just see they don't get out of breath, Uncle Roy."

"I will."

But Simon was frowning as he watched them leave. "Hey, Joan," he said.

"Hmmm?"

"When they go up to bed at night, it takes them half an hour. They take two steps and then rest and talk; they bring their knitting along."

"Well, that's kind of silly," said Joan.

"Could they crumple up and die on our stairs?"

"No, they could not," she said. "It would take more than that."

"How do you know?"

"I heard Dr. Kitt tell them so. They just shouldn't get too out of breath, is all, or run in any marathons. He said—"

"I got an idea," Simon said.

"What?"

"Listen." He stood up from his place at the table and came around to face her, with his hands hitched through his belt loops. "How about us going to a movie," he said. "That Tarzan movie."

"We're not supposed to."

"Well, I got to get out," he said.

She looked down at him, considering. His face had a thin, stretched look; patches of flour still clung to it like some sort of sad clown makeup and his hair stuck up in wiry tangles. "Well, I do have to get Aunt Lou's prescription," she said. "Would you comb your hair first?"

"Sure."

"All right, we'll go."

"Right now?"

"If you want to."

He nodded, but with his face still wearing that strained look, and turned to go upstairs and then turned back again. "I'll wash downstairs," he said.

"There's no soap here."

"I don't care."

He turned on the water in the kitchen sink and splashed his face, and then he reached spluttering for the dishtowel. "My allowance money's all the way upstairs," he said. "I'll pay you back tomorrow, if you'll lend me the money."

"All right."

She went into the living room, with Simon following, and handed him a comb from her pocketbook. While he was combing his hair she went upstairs for her shoes. Mrs. Pike's door was open now. She was lying on her bed, with her head propped up on two pillows and the sisters beside her talking steadily, and when Joan walked past, her aunt followed her with her soft blue eyes but only vaguely, as if she weren't seeing her, so Joan didn't stop in to say anything. She put on her shoes and picked up a scarf and went downstairs, where Simon was waiting with his hand on the newel post and his face strained upward.

"What're they doing?" he asked her.

"I don't know."

"Are they crying?"

"I don't think so."

"Well. I *would've* gone upstairs," he said. "You know."

"I know."

"Did you think I wouldn't?"

"No." She sighed suddenly, looking back toward the stairs. "*I* don't know how to comfort people," she said.

"Well."

They went out the front door, across the porch, and down the wooden steps. It was beginning to get cool outside. Joan could hear tree frogs piping far away, and the wind had died down enough so that the sound of cars on the east highway reached her ears. She clasped her hands behind her back and followed Simon, cutting across the road and through the field toward town.

"Remember I've got heels on," she called.

"I remember."

"Remember that makes it hard walking."

He slowed down and waited for her, walking backwards. Behind him and all around him the field stretched wide and golden, with bits of tall yellow flowers stirring and glimmering like spangles in the sunlight. And when Joan came up even with him, so that he turned and walked forward again by her side, she could look down and see how his hair, bleached lighter on top, took on a varnished look out here and the little line of fuzz down the back of his neck had turned shiny and golden like the field he was walking in. "Right about here . . . ," he said, but the wind started up just then and blew his words away.

"What?" she asked.

"Right about here is where I lost that ball. Will you keep a lookout for it?"

"I will."

"Do you reckon I'll ever find it?"

"No."

"I don't either," Simon said.

But they walked slowly anyway, keeping their eyes on the ground, kicking at clumps of wild wheat to see what might turn up.

3

"*H*old still," James said. He bent over and peered through the camera. No one was holding still. Line upon line of Hammonds, from every corner of the state, littered the Larksville Hammonds' front lawn, sitting, kneeling, and standing, letting arms and legs and bits of dresses trail outside the frame of his camera. Whole babies were being omitted; they had crawled to other patches of grass. Yet the grown-ups stood there with their dusty blue, look-alike eyes smiling happily, certain that they and their children were being saved intact for future generations. James straightened up and shook his head.

"Nope," he said. "You've moved every whichaway again. Close in tighter, now."

He waited patiently, with his hands on his hips. For five years he had been going through this. Every year there was a picture of the Hammond family reunion to be put in the Larksville paper, and another two or three for the Hammonds themselves to choose for their albums. By now he was resigned to it; he had even started enjoying himself. He smiled, watching all those hordes of Hammonds close in obligingly with sideways steps while their eyes stayed fixed on the camera. Moving like that made them look like chains of paper dolls, bright

49

and shimmering in the heat. Eyelet dresses and seersucker suits blurred together; their whiteness was blinding. James shaded his eyes with one hand, and then he
said, "Okay," and bent down over his camera again.
But someone else was moving. It was Great-Aunt Hattie in the front row; she had started coughing. She was
sitting in a cane-bottom chair, with children and ani-
mals tangled at her feet and the grown-ups forming a
protective wall behind her. When she began her coughing fit, they closed in still tighter in a semicircle and
the oldest nephew leaned down with his head next to
hers. The coughs grew farther apart. After a minute the
nephew raised his head and said, "She's sorry, she
says." The others murmured behind him, saying it
didn't matter. "Swallowed down the wrong throat,"
said the nephew.

Someone called out, "Give her brown bread." And
someone else said, "No, rock candy will do it." But
the aunt spread her old hands out in front of her, palms
down and fingers stretched apart, signifying she was
better now and wanted to hear no more about it. "Back
in your places," James said, and the twenty or thirty
Hammonds closest to him drifted back to their original
positions and made their faces stern again. Mothers
looked anxiously down the rows, gripping their neighbors' arms and peering around them to make sure their
children were at their best, and fathers hooked their
thumbs into their belts and glared into the lens. "Hold
it," James said. When he snapped the picture there was
a little stirring through the group, and everyone relaxed. "That's the second," he called to the hostess.
"You want another?"

"One more, James."

While he was fiddling with the camera people began

talking again, still standing in their set places, and some lit cigarettes. He peered through the view-finder at them. If this were any other picture he would snap it now, catching them at their ease, but family pictures were different. He liked the way they stood so straight in jumbled, self-conscious rows, and molded themselves to make a block of tensed-up faces. "I'm ready," he warned them, and they did it again—closed their mouths and narrowed their eyes and set their shoulders. He snapped the picture that way. Then he said, "That's all," and watched the children as they shook themselves and scattered off to play.

The hostess walked up to him, trailing white lace, sinking into the ground at every step in her high-heeled pumps. "There's one more I want, James," she said, and then stopped and let her eyes wander after her youngest child. "Joey, you *know* not to ride that dog," she called.

"Yes, ma'am."

"I want you to photograph Great-Aunt Hattie alone," she told James. "She's getting old. Can you do that?"

"If she's willing," said James.

"She's not."

"Then maybe we should—"

"Now, don't you worry," said Mrs. Hammond. "I'll talk her around. They're serving up the ice cream over there. You go and get you some, and when you're through I'll have Aunt Hattie ready. Hear?"

"Well, okay," James said. But Mrs. Hammond hadn't stayed to hear his answer.

He folded his equipment up and put it on the porch, out of the way of the children. Then he went across the yard to the driveway, where the others were standing in line for ice cream. They looked different now, quick-moving and flexible, with the paper-doll stiffness gone. In a way James was sorry. Some of the best pictures he had were these poker-straight rows of families, Hammonds and Ballews and Burnetts; he kept copies of them filed away in his darkroom, and sometimes on long lonesome days he pulled them out and looked at them a while, with a sort of faraway sadness coming up in him if he looked too long. He might have seen any one of those families only that morning in the hardware store, but when he looked at their faces in pictures they seemed lost and long ago. ("I just wish once you'd take a *giggly* picture," Ansel said. "You make me so sorrowful.") Thinking about that made James smile, and the girl in front of him turned around and looked up at him.

"I'm thinking," he told her.

"That's what it looked like," she said. Her name was Maisie Hammond, and she lived across town from here and sometimes came visiting Ansel. She thought Ansel was wonderful. James was just considering this when she said, "How's that brother of yours?" and he smiled at her.

"Just fine," he said. "He's home reading magazines."

"Well, say hello to him." She moved up a space in line, still facing in James's direction and walking backwards. Standing out in the sunlight like this she was pretty, with her towhead shining and her white skin nearly transparent, but Ansel had always said she was homely and only out to catch a good husband (it was rumored James and Ansel came from an old family). Whenever she came visiting, Ansel turned his face to the wall and played sicker than he was. That was how he planned to scare her off, but Maisie only stayed longer then and fussed around his couch. She liked taking care of people. She would fetch pillows and ice-water, and Ansel would wave them away. When she was gone, James would say, "Ansel, what you want to treat her like that for?" But by that time Ansel had fooled even himself, and only tossed his head on the pillow and worried about how faint he felt. To make it up to Maisie now (although she wasn't aware there *was* anything to be made up), James stepped closer to her in the line and said, "Maisie, it's been a good two weeks since you've been by."

"Two *days*," said Maisie. "Day before yesterday I was there."

"I never heard about it."

"You were off somewhere. Taking care of some arrangements for the Pikes."

The man ahead of her left with his Dixie cup of ice cream, and Maisie turned forward again and took two cups from the stack on the table. "Here," she said. She passed him a fudge ripple, with a little paper spoon lying across the top of it. "The children got to the strawberry before us."

"That's all right," said James. "I don't like strawberry."

He followed her back across the lawn, preferring to stick with her rather than interrupt the little individual reunions that were going on among the others. When she settled on the porch steps, fluffing her skirt out around her, he said, "You mind if I sit with you?" She shook her head, intent on opening her ice cream. "I'm going to take a picture of your great-aunt," he said.

"Oh, her."

"Do you like sitting out in the sun like this?"

"Yes," she said. But she looked hot; she was too

thin and bird-boned, and being the slightest bit uncomfortable made her seem about to topple over. James was
used to Joan, who was unbreakable and built of solid
flesh.

When he had pried the lid off his own ice cream, and
dipped into it with his paper spoon, he said, "It's sort
of melty-looking." Maisie didn't answer. She was staring off across the yard. "Better eat yours before it turns
to milk," he told her.

But Maisie said, "Ansel was laying down, when I
went to see him."

"He does that," said James.

"I mean laying still. Not doing anything."

"Well, it was nice of you to come," he said.

She shrugged impatiently, as if he hadn't understood
her. "You were out doing something," she told him.
She seemed to be starting all over again now, telling
the story a second time. "You weren't around."

"I was helping Mr. Pike with some arrangements,"
said James.

"That's what Ansel said."

"I'm sorry I wasn't around."

"Well. When I came in I said, 'Hey, Ansel,' and
Ansel didn't even hear me. He was just laying there. I
said, 'Hey!' and he jumped a foot, near about. He was
a million miles away."

James was making soup out of his ice cream. He had
it down to a sort of pulpy mess now, the way he liked
it, and then he looked up and saw Maisie wrinkling her
nose at it. He stopped stirring and took his first bite.
"Ansel's a great one for daydreaming," he said with
his mouth full.

"He wasn't daydreaming."

"Oh."

"He was crying, near about."

"*Ansel?*"

"Well, almost," said Maisie. She sat forward, with the ice cream still untasted in her hand. "I said, 'Ansel, *what's* the matter?' But he never did say. His eyes were all blurry."

"You got to remember Janie Rose," James said. "It was only three days ago."

"Well, I thought of that. But then I thought, no, Janie wasn't all that much to him. She was right bothersome, as a matter of fact. We had her over for supper just a month ago, her and her family; we gave them chicken. Mama forgot about Janie being vegetarian. Janie said, 'This chicken's *dead*,' and her daddy said, 'Well, I *hope* so,' and everybody laughed, but Mama's feelings were a little hurt. Though she went to the funeral and all, just like anyone else. I said, 'Ansel, is that what's bothering you? Janie Rose Pike being taken?' But the way he was acting, I don't think that was the real reason."

"His feet hurt him sometimes," said James.

"This is *serious*, James."

"I'm being serious."

"Anyway," Maisie sighed, and she took the first mouthful of her ice cream. It bothered him, the way she ate it; she chewed, slowly and carefully, even though the ice cream was nothing but liquid now. When she had swallowed, she said, "All he would talk about was dying. He said he could see how it would all turn out; they would mourn him like they mourn Janie Rose, not sad he died but sorry they hadn't liked him more. He'd rather they be sad he died, he said."

"Oh, now," said James. "He's been on that for days. It'll pass."

"Will you listen? I can't hardly sleep nights, for thinking about it. I keep wondering if he's all right."

"Of course he's all right," James said.

But Maisie was still hunching over, frowning into space. Her ice cream was forgotten. A child ran by, chased by another child, grabbing Maisie's knee for support as he pivoted past her, and Maisie only brushed his hand away absentmindedly. "Those times he goes away," she said finally, "those times he starts to get better and then goes off drinking for a night and can't be found till morning. He'll die of it."

"He won't die," said James. "He could lead a life like any other man, if he wasn't so scared of needles."

"He *might* die," Maisie said. "What if one of those nights of his, he don't come back?"

But James was getting tired of this. "Look," he said firmly. He swallowed the last of his ice cream and said, "Ansel only goes so far, you notice. Only enough to worry people. You ever thought of that?"

"What? Well, if that isn't the *coldest* thing. How do you know how far he'll go?"

"I just do," James said. "I been through this."

"Can you say for *sure* how far he'll go?"

"I been through it *hundreds* of times."

"I believe you don't even give it a thought," said Maisie. "That's what Ansel said. He said, 'What does *James* care—' "

"Well, we've got to be clearheaded about this," James said.

"You're clearheaded, all right." She jabbed her spoon into her ice cream and left it there, standing straight up in the middle of the cup. " 'What does James care,' he said, and then just lay there with his eyes all blurry—"

"I do everything I can think of," said James.

"Oh, foot."

"I try everything I know."

"Then tell me this, if you do so much all-fired good. Can you say that never, never once in all your life, have you thought about Ansel's going off and letting you be someday?"

"Well, for—"

"Never thought how nice it would be to live on your own for a change, just one little old TV dinner to pop into the—"

"I try *every*thing I *know*!" James shouted, and then noticed how loud his voice was and lowered it. "I mean—"

But Maisie just folded in the rim of her Dixie cup with all her concentration, as if her mind was made up. Then she rose and said, "Well, I'll be seeing you." Her skirt was rumpled in back, but she didn't bother smoothing it down. When she walked away James stood up, from force of habit, and waited until she was half-way across the yard before he sat down again. Inside he felt slow and heavy; he was chewing on his lower lip, the way he did when he didn't know what to say. All the way across the yard he watched her, and turned his empty ice cream cup around and around in his hands.

In front of him some children were playing statues. An out-of-town boy was flinging the others by one arm and then crying, "Hold!" so that they had to freeze there, and when he came to Janice Hammond, who was the littlest, he swung her around so hard that she spun halfway across the lawn and landed against Mrs. Hammond, who was heading over toward James. "Hold!" the boy said. Mrs. Hammond looked down at Janice, who was clutching her around the middle. She said, "*Oh*, Janice," tiredly, and was about to pull away, but the other children stopped her. "No, Janice has got to stay that way," said the out-of-town boy, and Mrs. Hammond seemed too tired to argue. She stood still, rising above Janice's circled arms like the figure of someone passively drowning, and called out, "James, we're ready with Aunt Hattie."

"Where is she?" he asked.

"Over there. Standing up. We wanted her to sit but she says no, she'll do it standing. Die with her boots on. She doesn't like cameras." She came to life suddenly and disentangled herself from Janice, ignoring the other children's protests. "She's fading," she said. James looked over at Janice, surprised, and Mrs. Hammond caught his look and shook her head. "Aunt Hattie, I mean," she said. "Just fading away."

"I'm sorry to hear that," said James. He gathered up his equipment and came after her. "She looked all right to me."

"Well, she fades out and then in again."

They circled a little group of women, all standing in identical positions with folded arms while they watched the children playing statues. "I don't like doing this if she don't want me to," James called. "Some people just have an allergy to cameras."

But Mrs. Hammond smiled brightly at him over her shoulder and kept walking. Out here on the grass the sun was still hot, and the back of Mrs. Hammond's powdered neck glistened faintly. She had the same brittle little bones as her niece Maisie, only covered now with a solid layer of flesh. James looked away from her and shifted his equipment to the other shoulder. "Right here would be a good place," he said. He hadn't really looked around; he just wanted to stop and not do anything any more. The heaviness inside was weighing him down. He set the camera on its tripod and then leaned on it, with his chin propped on his hand, and Mrs. Hammond said, "You all right?"

"I'm fine," James said.

"You look kind of tired."

He straightened up and tucked his shirt in. There was Great-Aunt Hattie, only a few yards away now, being led gingerly by Mrs. Hammond. Aunt Hattie looked neither to the right nor to the left; she seemed to be pretending Mrs. Hammond wasn't there. The closer they got to the camera, the farther away her eyes grew.

"Right here would be a good place," said Mrs. Hammond. "Don't you think so, James? In front of the roses?"

"Fine," James said. He had started adjusting his camera and wasn't really looking now. But when he raised his eyes again he saw that the old woman had been placed directly in front of a circular flower bed; she seemed to be rising from the middle of it, like an intricately sculptured garden decoration. James smiled. "I've changed my mind," he said. "I don't think she should have those flowers behind her."

"They're so pretty, though," Mrs. Hammond said sadly.

"Well. But I think she should have just grass behind her. You mind moving over, Miss Hattie?"

"I have just one thing to say," Miss Hattie said suddenly.

"Ma'am?"

"Don't push me. You can tell me where to go, but don't push me around."

"Oh, I won't," said James.

"The *last* time I had my picture taken—"

"I think he wants you to move over," Mrs. Hammond said. "Could you step this way, dear?"

The aunt stepped stiffly, jerking her chin up. "I was saying, Connie," she said, "the *last* man that took my picture was in need of an anatomy lesson. I told him so. He came right up to me and pushed my face sideways but my shoulders full-front, and my knees sideways but my feet full-front, so I swear, I felt like something on an Egyptian wall. You should have seen the photograph. Well, I don't have to tell you how it looked. I said—"

"If I were you I'd let my beads show," said Mrs. Hammond. "They're such nice ones."

"Well, just for that I won't," snapped Aunt Hattie. She raised her hands, heavy with old rings, and fumbled at the neck of her crepe dress until she had closed it high around her throat, hiding the beads from sight. "Now *no* one can see them," she said, and Connie Hammond sighed and turned to James with her hands spread hopelessly.

"I try and I try," she told him, and he looked up from fiddling with his camera and smiled.

"Why don't you go on and see to the others," he said, "and I'll call you when I'm through. I bet you haven't even had your ice cream yet."

"No. No, I've been so busy. Well, I might for just a minute, maybe—" She trailed off across the yard, looking relieved, and the last part of her to fade away was her voice, which still flowed on and on.

"She's putting on weight, don't you think?" Aunt Hattie asked.

James had the camera ready now, but he was waiting because he wanted the picture to be just right. He bent

down and cleared away a dandelion from one of the
tripod legs, and then over his shoulder he called, "You
comfortable like that? Don't want to sit down?"

"No. I'll stand."

Connie Hammond wouldn't like that, but James was
glad. To him Aunt Hattie looked just right this way—
standing against a background of bare grass, holding
her shoulders high to hide the beads and jutting her chin
out at him. She had terrified high school students for
forty years that way, back when she taught Latin I. People still told tales about her. She had declined her nouns
in a deafening roar and slammed her yardstick against
her desk on the ending of every verb. While students
could lead other teachers off their subjects just by asking how they'd met their husbands, Miss Hattie had
only strayed from Latin once a year, at Christmastime,
when she read aloud from a condensed version of *Ben
Hur*. James could picture that. He wished he had her in
a classroom right now, to photograph her the way she
stood in his mind. But all he had was this wide lawn,
and he would have to make do with that. He stood there,
pressing a dandelion between his fingers and squinting
across at her. "That's right," he told her. "That's what
I want."

She shifted her feet a little. "How many prints you
plan to make of this?" she asked.

"Ma'am?"

"How many copies."

"Oh. As many as you want."

"Well, I want *none*," she said. "I'd like to request
that you make the one picture asked of you and have
that be that."

"Oh, now."

"Connie can have one, if she wants it so much. But

that's because I don't like her. Nothing she could *do* would make me like her; I just constitutionally don't. Danny can't have one.''

"Danny who?'' he asked. "Raise your chin a little, please.''

"Danny Hammond. Is there anyone in this world whose last name isn't Hammond?'' She raised her chin but went on talking; James leaned his elbow on his camera and waited. "Danny I put up with,'' she said. "How long will they hide him away from me?''

"Danny *Hammond*? Why, I saw him only last—''

"*You* saw him. You saw him. But do you think *I* do? They rush him away the moment I come around; he looks back over his shoulder all bewildered. He's only seven.''

"Could you turn more toward me?'' asked James.

"They think he insulted me last Valentine's Day.''

"Oh, I don't think Danny would—''

"Made me a present. None of these easy-breaking things from the gift shop. Made me a ceramic salt-shaker in school, and it was the exact shape of my head, with even the wrinkles painted in.''

"That's nice,'' said James.

"Do you know where the salt came out?''

"Well, no.''

"My nose. Ho, out my nose. Two little holes punched for nostrils, and out came the salt. Can you picture Connie's face?''

James laughed. "I sure can,'' he said.

"Well, of course she hadn't *seen* the thing, prior to my unwrapping it. She thought it was a bobby-pin holder or something. She said, 'Danny *Hammond*!' and made a grab for it, but I was too quick for her. I meant to *keep* it; it's not often I get such a personal present.

But Connie rushed him off like I would eat him and there I sat, all alone with my saltshaker. No one to thank.''

"Maybe you could—"

"I still use it, though."

"Ma'am?"

"The saltshaker. I use it daily."

"Well, I would too," said James.

"Then you see why he shouldn't have my picture."

That stumped him; he had to consider a minute. (If Miss Hattie Hammond was fading out, should he not just let it pass and agree with her?) But Miss Hattie seemed the same to him as ever, as sharp as a rock against the green of the lawn. "I don't see what you mean," he said.

"Ah well."

"I don't understand what pictures have got to do with it."

"Not much," she said. "But they're photographing me because I'm old, you know. They think I'm dying. (I'm not.) They think they'll have something to remember me by. But pictures are merely one way, Mr. Green. Should a person that I *like* have a picture of me?"

"I wouldn't let it worry me," said James. "I find no one ever looks at pictures anyway, once they get hold of them."

"*I* don't want Danny remembering just a picture. Remembering something flat and of one tone. What is ever all one way?"

"Well," James said. He frowned down at his fingers, sticky now with dandelion milk. "Well, *plenty* of—"

"Photographs," said Miss Hattie, "are the only thing. Don't interrupt. Everything else is a mingling of things. Photographers don't agree, of course. Why else would they take pictures? Press everything flat on little squares of paper—well, that's all right. But not for people that you'd like to stay *interested* in you. Not for Danny Hammond.''

''Now, wait a minute,'' said James, but Miss Hattie held up her hand.

''I already know,'' she said. ''*I* know photographers.''

James grinned and bent over his camera again. ''As far as things that're all one way,'' he called, ''I can name—''

''No. Not a thing, not a person, Mr. Green. Take your picture.''

He gave up. Through the frame of his viewfinder he saw her standing just the way he wanted her, old-fashioned-looking and symmetrical, with her hands across her stomach and her mouth tight. Her face was like a turtle's face, long and droopy. It had the same hooded eyes and the same tenacious expression, as if she had lived for centuries and was certain of living much longer. Yet just in that instant, just as his hand tightened on the camera and his eyes relaxed at seeing the picture the way he had planned it, something else swam into his mind. He thought of Miss Hattie coughing, in the center of that family reunion—not defiant then but very soft and mumbling, telling them all she was sorry. He frowned and raised his head.

''Well?'' said Miss Hattie.

''Nothing,'' James said.

He bent down again, and sighted up the haughty old turtle-face before him and snapped the picture. For a minute he stayed in that position; then he straightened up. ''I'm done,'' he said.

''I should hope so.''

"I'll get one copy made, for Mrs. Hammond."

"I'm going in then. I'm tired."

"All right," he said. "Goodbye, Miss Hattie."

"Goodbye."

She nodded once, sharply, and turned to go, and James watched after her as long as she was in sight. Then he stared down at his camera. Just to his right Connie Hammond materialized—he caught a fold of lace out of the corner of his eye—but he didn't look at her.

"Well, now!" Mrs. Hammond said brightly. She was out of breath and looked anxious. She came around in front of him and went to stand where Miss Hattie had stood, with her eyes intent on the ground, as if by tracking down the print of Miss Hattie's Wedgies she could suddenly come to some understanding of her. "I'm sure it'll come out good," she called over her shoulder.

"Well."

"What's that?"

"Yes, I'm sure it will," James said. He folded up his tripod and gathered the rest of his equipment together. "I'm leaving now," he told her.

"Oh, are you?"

"I'll have the pictures ready in a day or two."

"That'll be fine," said Mrs. Hammond. But she was still staring at the ground and looking anxious; she didn't turn around to say goodbye.

James's pickup truck was parked on the road at the edge of the lawn. He circled around the children, being careful to stay clear of the ones playing statues. Their game was growing rougher now. Little Janice Hammond was frozen in the exact stance of a baseball pitcher, her right arm drawn back nearly out of joint, and even her face was frozen—she was grimacing wildly, showing an entire set of braces on her teeth. But she unfroze just as James passed her; she shook out her arms and smiled at him and he smiled back.

"I want to come out *pretty* in them pictures," she said. "You see what you can do about it."

"I'll see."

He placed the camera on the leather seat of the pickup and then went around to the driver's side and climbed in. It was like an oven inside. First he started up the motor and then he rolled down his window, and while he was doing that he caught sight of Maisie Hammond. She was standing high up on the lawn, waving hard to him and smiling. He waved back. This time when the heavy feeling hit his stomach he didn't shrug it off; he sat turning it over in his mind, letting the motor idle. As long as he sat there, Maisie went on waving. And when he had shifted into first and rolled on down to the bottom of the hill, he looked in the rear-view mirror and saw her still waving after him. He thought suddenly that she must be having two feelings at once—half one way and half another. Half angry at him, and half sorry because she had told him so. And now she had to keep on waving.

He looked down beside him at the camera, where Miss Hattie was so securely boxed now in her single stance. But the fields he drove through shimmered uncertainly in the sunlight; the road was misted with dust, and he was driving home now not knowing if he wanted to go there or not, not knowing for sure what he thought about anyone. All he could do was put the heavy feeling out of his mind, and let only the road and the fields alongside it occupy his thoughts.

4

That Sunday, Joan began thinking about Simon's hair. She started out by saying, "Simon, tomorrow morning first thing I want to find you in that barber's chair," but Simon said, "Aw, Joan, I don't want to go downtown." Since that movie yesterday he had changed his mind about town; he hadn't even asked to eat in a restaurant today, and Joan could see his point. Going downtown meant people murmuring over him and patting his head, asking Joan in whispers, "How is he taking it? Is his mother coming out of it?" while Simon stood right next to them, his chin tilted defiantly and his eyes on their faces. Little boys who were usually his friends circled him widely, looking back over their shoulders in curious, half-scared glances. They had never seen someone that close to funerals before, not someone their own age. When Simon and Joan were coming out of the movie theater a member of Mrs. Pike's church had stopped smack in front of them and said to her friend, "Oh, that poor little boy!" Her voice had rung out clearly and hung in the air above them, making other people stop and stare while Simon pulled on Joan's hand to rush her home. She could understand it if he had never went downtown again.

So instead of insisting, she said, "Well, all right. But we've got to cut your hair at home then. Today."

"It's not so long," he said.

"Curls down over your ears."

"Well, we've got nothing to cut it with."

"Scissors," Joan reminded him. "Your mother's sewing scissors. *Anything.*"

"Okay. Tomorrow, then," said Simon. "Bright and early."

"Tomorrow's a tobacco day; I won't be here. You know that."

"*Other* boys have hair *lots* longer."

"Orphans do," said Joan. "Will you fetch the scissors?"

He slid off the couch, grumbling a little, and went for his mother's sewing basket. It sat in one corner of the living room, gathering dust, odds and ends of other people's clothing poking out of it every which-way. (Mrs. Pike was a seamstress; she made clothes for most of the women in Larksville.) The materials on the top Simon threw to the floor, making a huge untidy pile beside the basket, and he rummaged along the bottom until he brought up a large pair of scissors. "These them?" he asked, and walked away from the basket with that heap of material still lying beside it. Joan let the mess stay there. She followed Simon into the kitchen, a few steps behind him, with her eyes on the back of his head. Where it had been pressed against the couch his hair was as matted as a bird's nest. It would take a sickle to cut all that off.

In the kitchen she found an apron and tied it around his neck, to keep the hair from tickling, and then she had him sit on the high wooden stool beside the kitchen table. He revolved on it slowly, making the seat of it squeak, while Joan looked him over and debated where to start. "I don't know where you *got* all that hair," she told him. "When was the last time you went to the barber's?"

"I don't know."

"It couldn't have been all that long ago."

"You sure you know how to cut hair?" Simon asked.

"Of course I do."

"Whose have you cut?"

"Well, my own," Joan said.

He stopped revolving and looked at her hairdo. "It's a little choppy at the ends," he told her.

"It's supposed to be."

"Will mine come out like that?"

"I surely hope not."

"If it does, what will we—"

"Now, Simon," Joan said, "I don't want to hear any more about it. Let's just get it over with."

He sighed then and gave in, but with his shoulders squinched up and his neck drawn into itself as if he thought she might slip and cut his head off. His hair grew in layers, lapping downwards like hay on a haystack. When Joan cut too much from one of the sun-yellowed upper layers it sprang straight up, choppy and jagged-edged, and she quickly pressed it down again and shot a look at Simon to see if he had noticed. He hadn't. He sat slumped on the stool, idly swinging one boot and gazing out the window. The only sound now was the steady snipping of scissors.

Out in the back yard Joan could see her uncle—just his head and his crumpled blue shirt. He was tilting back on an old kitchen chair in the sunshine, with one hand resting absently on Nellie's neck. That was the way he had been sitting all day. When Joan called him for his meals he came in docilely and ate everything set before him, and then he went out back again. Twice he had gone upstairs to see his wife, but that had taken only a minute; he must have given up trying to talk to her. Even Joan had given up. When she went to her aunt's bedroom, to where she was lying on her back with the covers pulled up around her, and asked her to come down for a bite to eat, her aunt only said, "No," and closed her eyes. Saying that one word seemed to take all the strength she could muster; Joan didn't dare argue with her. In the back of her mind she kept trying to think up little plots, planning ways to get her aunt interested in something, but she wasn't the kind of person who could do that. The most she could do was try and take care of the house for a while, and feed Mr. Pike and Simon. Even that was hard; she had never learned how to keep house.

The top part of Simon's hair was cut now. She squinted at it, not sure if this was how it was supposed to be or not. It seemed a little homemade-looking. But then she shrugged and began on the shaggy part along the back of his neck. She could always even it up later on.

Outside, Ansel called, "Is anybody home?" His voice was thin and wavered in the wind. Simon gave a sudden start and turned his head, so that Joan nearly gouged him in the neck. "Hold *still*, Simon," she said, and Ansel called again, "Is anybody home?"

"It's him," Simon said.

"Who do you mean? It's Ansel."

"I know. It's him."

"Just stop wiggling," said Joan. She raised her voice and called out, "We're out here, Ansel."

"Out where?"

"Out *here*."

"Well, is someone going to come and let me in?"

"It's not locked," Joan said, and returned to her cutting. She didn't like Ansel and had never pretended to; he could open his own doors. When he came ambling out to the kitchen, walking in that shuffling way of his and stooping to get through the doorway, she didn't even turn around to look at him. "How are you," she said, making it a statement.

"Oh, not so bad, I guess."

"Turn a little to the left, Simon."

"Hey, Simon," Ansel said.

Simon frowned at his boots.

"*Hey*, boy."

"He's having his hair cut," said Joan.

"Ah, I see. That makes it impossible for him to speak."

"Will you have a seat?"

"I might," he said. He pulled out one of the chairs from the table and sat down, facing Joan and Simon. He was looking better than usual today. The yellowish pallor of his face had faded and he sat nearly erect, with his arms folded across his chest. When he saw Simon frowning at him he smiled his dippy smile and said, "What's the matter with the barber, boy?"

"What?"

"Barber sick?"

But Simon only shrugged and didn't answer. Joan said, "I'm cutting his hair myself this time."

"I see that."

"I'm using the sewing scissors."

"I see."

That seemed to leave nothing more to be said. Joan

hesitated a minute, with the scissors in mid air, and then she said, "Turn around, Simon."

"Are we done?" Simon asked.

"Almost. I want to think what to do about the front part of it."

"Where's Mr. and Mrs. Pike?" said Ansel.

"Uncle Roy's out back."

"Where's *Mrs*. Pike?"

Joan was frowning at Simon's hair, trying to figure out how to begin on that front shock. Any way she managed it, it was almost sure to end up looking like bangs. She snipped gingerly at one piece and held what she had cut off up to the light to examine it. Then she said, "Ansel, what're you here for?"

"Who, me?"

"Didn't James tell you not to bother her? Where *is* James?"

"He's taking pictures of the Hammonds."

"Didn't he tell you not to come around here?"

"Well yes, he did," Ansel said. "He *suggested* that I not. But I was sitting reading on the couch and it occurred to me: I thought I might just wander over and see how you all are doing."

"We're doing fine," said Joan. She snipped off another piece of hair.

"Joan, you're ruining that boy."

"It'll turn out all right."

"Well. I was sitting reading a *Guideposts*," Ansel said, "and after that two outdoor-type magazines, and then I read them again. I would've read them a third time, if I hadn't come on over here. I read even the smallest inch-long ads for worm farms; I read the list of editors at the front and the entire information about the subscriptions. Then I thought I might come and see you."

"Simon, maybe you better get a mirror," Joan said. "I'm not sure what you're going to think of this."

"Aw, I don't care," said Simon. "Is it done?"

"You go look in a mirror and *see* if it is."

Simon stood up and little rags of hair fell around him, spilling off the apron around his neck. When he walked out of the room he trailed fuzz in a long path behind him.

"He won't thank you for this," Ansel said.

"I don't think it's so bad."

"Twice before, I started to come," Ansel said. "I got up and headed for the door and then I thought, 'No.' I cut my fingernails. I cleaned out my wallet. Then I thought I might as well come over. I thought—"

When he talked he had a way of leaning slightly forward and placing his fingertips together, as if words came hard to him and he had to consider. Yet in reality the words came flooding from him; it always made her feel swept away and drowned, with so many useless words spilling around her. Sometimes she could even get interested in what he said, but she never lost that drowned feeling. While he talked she stood silently by the stool, keeping her face blank and idly snipping at thin air with her scissors, but inside she was thinking, I wish you would *go*. The pale thinness of his face irritated her. She thought about all the long evenings of three long years, with James sitting next to her on the porch and never taking one step forward, never asking for more than tonight's kiss and tomorrow's date and never mentioning marriage or a family or any of those other things she was sitting there waiting to hear. And the reason for it all was Ansel, who hung limp and heavy in his brother's living room and expected to die any day, although actually he was stronger than any of them. He had that flood of words, after all, and that sad dippy smile, and that way of placing his fingers together as if asking people to be patient while he fumbled for what to say. "I thought I would come offer sympathy and then leave again," he was saying, and Joan snapped, "Well, you've offered it. Are you leaving?"

"Huh?" Ansel said. He looked up, bewildered. "Joan, I ain't even seen your Aunt *Lou* yet—"

Simon came in, with his hair plastered down by water. "It looks kind of like I expected it to," he said.

"You don't like it?"

"Well, yes. It'll grow out."

"I could trim it around the edges a little more," Joan said.

"No, that's all right. Thank you anyway."

"Or maybe tomorrow you could—"

"Hush!" Ansel said. He sat up straight, listening, and when the other two turned toward him he pointed at the ceiling. "Footsteps," he said.

It was the slow, clapping sound of Mrs. Pike's mules, crossing the upstairs hallway. "She's only going over to the bedroom," Joan said, but then the sound continued to the stairs, and Ansel said, "She's coming down." He stood up, preparing to meet her. Joan reached out and touched his arm. "Let her be," she said. "Why don't you go home?"

"I wanted to say hello."

"Do it some other time."

"No, I want—"

The footsteps descended slowly, like a child's—both feet meeting on the same step, then another hesitant

step downwards. Joan left the kitchen, with a wave of
her hand toward Ansel to show that he should stay there.
He did, which surprised her a little. She crossed through
the parlor alone and came to stand at the bottom of the
stairs, looking up. Her aunt had just barely reached
the halfway point. She was holding on to the railing
and gazing steadily at Joan, her face blank without its
makeup, her dark yellow hair straggly and uncurled,
and her plump body wrapped in a chenille bathrobe.
The grayness of her made her blend into the dark stairwell. She said, "Joan," and her voice came out blurred
and gray also, without expression.

"What?" Joan said.

But her aunt didn't answer. She continued down the
stairs laboriously, and when she reached the bottom she
would have gone straight into the kitchen except that
Joan took hold of her by one arm.

"Don't you want to sit in the parlor a while?" she
asked. "I'll bring coffee."

"No."

"*Ansel's* out there in the kitchen."

"No."

Mrs. Pike went on walking, not pulling away from
Joan but just walking off, so that Joan had to drop her
arm or follow her. She dropped it. Her aunt said, "No,"
again, as if some new question had been raised, but
Joan was trailing behind her now in silence, frowning
at Mrs. Pike's back. Her back was soft and shapeless,
and folded in upon itself at the waist where her sash
was tightened. When she walked the hem of her robe
fluttered out and Joan could see the dinginess where it
had dragged across the floor.

Ansel was standing, ready to greet her. He said,
"Mrs. Pike, I been waiting to see you," and Mrs. Pike

said, "Ansel," and crossed to one of the kitchen chairs. Over by the window Simon stood with his back to her, his hands jammed awkwardly in his pockets and his chopped-at, straggly head wearing a stiff and listening look.

"I only came to tell you how I feel," Ansel said gently. "Then I'll leave."

"Where is Roy?" asked Mrs. Pike.

"Out back. You want I should get him?"

"No."

Mrs. Pike was sitting craned forward a little, with her hands on her stomach as if it hurt her. After a minute Ansel sat down opposite her, but Joan remained standing and Simon stayed by the window. Mrs. Pike didn't look at any of them. "I thought I would come downstairs a little," she said.

"That's the way," said Ansel. "You shouldn't sit alone."

"I wasn't sitting."

"What I actually came to say," Ansel said, "was how bad I feel about all this. That's all I wanted to tell you. I told James, I said, 'It's like the tragedy has struck at our own lives. I know just how she feels,' I said. I said—"

"No," said Mrs. Pike.

"Ma'am?"

But Mrs. Pike only looked away then, toward the screen door. Behind her, Simon picked up the cord of the paper window shade and began tying knots in it, small tight knots running up and down the length of the cord.

"What was you saying no for?" Ansel asked.

Mrs. Pike didn't answer.

"Was you saying I *don't* know how you feel? Mrs.

Pike, I know how you feel better than you do yourself. I been through this before.''

"Ansel," Joan said, "You've offered your sympathy now. I think you'd better leave.''

"But I've got so much I want to *say* to her—''

"I came down to eat," said Mrs. Pike, "but I don't think I will.''

Joan turned away from Ansel and looked down at Mrs. Pike. She said, "Why, Aunt Lou, there's all kinds of things to eat in the icebox. Everyone's been bringing things.''

"No," her aunt said.

"I know that when my mother died," said Ansel, "everyone kept trying to snap me out of it. They said that mourning has never brought the dead back. But it's only right to mourn; it's only natural. People have their faults but when they're dead you mourn them, and you expect to be mourned yourself someday.''

"Janie Rose didn't have no faults," said Mrs. Pike.

"No, ma'am, of course she didn't. When my—''

"We don't know how it might have turned out. She was a little chubby but not, you know, really fat. She might have slimmed down some later on. I never *said* to her she was fat. I don't know what she *thought* I said but really I didn't. Never a word.''

"When my mother died," said Ansel, "I thought of all the bad things I ever said about her. I got in a real swivet about it. She was a fine woman, but scared of everything. Wouldn't stand up against my father for us. When some sort of crisis was going on she had a way of sort of humming underneath her breath, slow and steady with no tune, and sewing away at someone's overalls without looking up. My father was—''

Joan came over and stood between Ansel and Mrs.

Pike, bending down low so as to make her aunt look into her face. "I want you to eat something, now," she said. "There's a stew. Would you like that?"

"No."

"There's a whole icebox of things."

"No."

"My father was not what you'd call a man of *heart*," said Ansel, placing his fingertips together. "Very strict. We always kept two goats around the place, to eat off the underbrush—"

"Isn't it funny," Mrs. Pike said, "that no one sent roses. Roses are a very normal flower, yet nobody sent them. Everything but, in fact."

"It's a little hot for good roses," Joan said.

"In the spring, when the goats had kids," said Ansel, "we would fatten them up for eating. Only by the time they were fat they'd be good pets, and we would beg for my father not to kill them. We would cry and make promises. But my mother sat humming (though she loved those goats the best of all and had names for every one of them) and my father always killed them. Only there was one thing that made up for that—"

"Ansel," Joan said, "Will you go home?"

"Wait a minute. When my mother brought a roasted kid in, or any part of it, holding it high on a wooden platter with potatoes around it, she always dropped it just in the doorway between the kitchen and the dining room. It never failed. The meat on the floor, and the potatoes rolling about like marbles and leaving little buttery paths behind them. 'Pick it up,' my father always said, but she would begin talking about germs and never let us eat it. I haven't *yet* tasted a piece of roasted goat. I think about that often now; it makes up for that humming, almost. I'm sorry I ever—"

Someone knocked on the front door. Joan said, "Ansel, will you go see who that is?"

"Why, Joan, it's *your* house."

"I don't care; just go."

"I'm not *well* enough to go bobbing up and down for people," said Ansel. But he rose anyway, moving slowly like an old man and holding his chest. "Who is it?" he called.

"Is that you, Ansel?"

It was James, with his voice sounding loud and steady even though he was still outside the house. Hearing him made Joan straighten up and feel suddenly more cheerful, and Simon turned around and let the window-shade cord slip out of his hand. "Ansel, what are you doing here?" James called.

"What're *you* doing here?"

"I'm looking for you. I been looking all over."

James had let himself in now, seeing that Ansel wasn't advancing to the door very quickly. He crossed the parlor in long strides, and appeared in the kitchen entrance with his hands on his hips.

"I'm taking you home for supper," he told Ansel. "I'm sorry about this, Mrs. Pike."

Mrs. Pike only gazed at him unblinkingly, without appearing to hear him. Joan said, "I wish you would, James."

"Come on, Ansel."

"Supper in the after*noon*?" asked Ansel.

"It's getting on towards sunset."

"Well, I don't feel so good, James. I'm not hungry."

"What's the matter with you?" James asked.

"My head is swimming."

"You been resting enough?"

"Well, yes. But after lunch this blackness started floating in, and then a little later this, um—"

Joan leaned back against the table, watching. She had never seen James actually *listen* to all this before; it seemed strange, and she couldn't figure out why he was doing it. The more James listened, the more Ansel's symptoms expanded and grew in detail; even his face looked paler. But James kept on nodding, saying "Hmm," every now and then. Finally he said, "I'll put you in bed. You can have your supper on a tray, if you want."

"Oh, I think I'll just stay here and—"

"It's time to go, Ansel."

Ansel sighed and let himself be led toward the doorway by one elbow. To Mrs. Pike he called, "I hope you're feeling better, ma'am. I'll be back tomorrow, maybe, or the next day—"

"Come on," James said.

They stopped trying to be graceful about it. James gave Ansel's arm a good tug and Joan followed close behind, almost on Ansel's heels, to hurry him out. After her came Simon, with his face looking small and curious under his ragged haircut. Mrs. Pike didn't go with them. She sat quietly in her chair, with her hands still pressed to her stomach, and it wasn't until the others were all the way into the parlor that she spoke.

"*Nobody* knows," she said distinctly.

Ansel wheeled around, fighting off Joan's and James's hands, and shouted, "*What's* that?"

Mrs. Pike didn't answer.

"Let's go," James said.

"I just want to tell you," Ansel shouted toward the kitchen, "I know better than you can *imagine*, Mrs. Pike. You're just sorry now you weren't nicer to her,

but I know how it feels to *really* miss someone. I remember—''

Both James and Joan stopped then, looking first at
Ansel and then back toward the kitchen. But all they
heard was the creaking of a chair, as if Mrs. Pike had
changed positions. And that seemed to show Ansel what
they had been trying to tell him all along: that Mrs.
Pike wasn't listening right now, and that nothing he
could say would do her any good or any harm. So he
shrugged and let himself be led the rest of the way out.
When Joan stepped back a pace, indicating that he
should go first and that she was staying in the house,
he nodded good-bye to her gravely.

"One thing I'd like to make clear, Joan," he said.
He was facing her squarely, acting very formal and dig-
nified. "I *do* know," he told her.

"All right," Joan said absentmindedly.

"I *remember* how it feels. My memory's excellent."

"I believe you."

"Clutters my mind at night, it's so excellent."

James pulled him gently.

"When I want to sleep, it does. Clutters my mind."

"All right, Ansel," James said.

He led him on out to the porch. When he passed Joan
she could smell the smoky, outdoors smell of James's
and he bent closer to her and said, "If you need anything, I want you to tell me."

"I will."

"And when you can get away, come over and see
us."

"I will."

She stood in the doorway with her hand on Simon's
shoulder and watched after them—Ansel tall and thin
and leaning against James, who was solider and could

bear his weight. She heard Ansel say, "Right through my temples it is, James. A sort of spindle of dizzy-feeling, right through my temples."

James said, "We'll lie you down. You feel tired?"

"Naw. I was thinking—"

"You sure now," James said.

"Huh?"

"I want you to tell me."

"Tell you what?" Ansel asked.

But James didn't answer that. And Joan, listening with a frown because it was so strange to her, felt suddenly lost and uncertain. She retreated into the parlor again, letting the screen door swing slowly shut behind her. But there was no one to listen to what was bothering her. Only Mrs. Pike, staring at the wall in the kitchen, and Simon beside her with his funny new haircut.

5

"Now, I can have my ideas," said Missouri, "and you can have yours. Mind what you're doing there, Miss Joan. First off, I don't believe in sitting. I have never believed in sitting. Minute a person sits his mind gives way. Will you *watch* what you're *doing*?"

Joan sighed and handed her the next bunch of tobacco leaves. It was Monday afternoon, late in the day but hot, and even here under the shade of the pecan trees she could feel the sweat trickling down between her shoulder blades. Beside her stood three other women— two handing to Mrs. Hall, who was the fastest tobacco-tier in the county, and the other helping Joan do the handing to Missouri. Missouri was huge and black, and every move she made was a wide slow arc, but she could tie nearly as fast as Mrs. Hall. She stood at the end of her rod with her broad bare feet spraddle-toed in the dust, and first she yanked a handful of leaves from her daughter Lily and then from Joan, wrapping each handful to the rod with one sure circling of the twine so that the leaves hung points-down and swinging. If Joan or Lily was too slow with the next hanging she would click her tongue and stand there disgusted, holding the twine taut in her fingers, and when the leaves were ready she would take them with an extra hard yank and bind them so hard that the twine cut into the stems. Now it was Joan who was slow (they were down to the last of this tableload, and she was having trouble finding a full handing of leaves) and Missouri made her clicking sound and shifted her weight to the other foot.

"What it is," she called down the table to Mrs. Hall, "I bind *across* the stick. You bind on the same side, and I declare I don't see how. With Miss Joan on the left, I take her leaves and bind them on the right, and backwards from that with Lily. You follow my meaning?"

"Yes, and I think it's just as *inefficient*," Mrs. Hall said. She stopped her tying to brush a piece of wispy blond hair off her face. "That's three inches wasted motion every bunch you tie, Missouri."

"Ha. Fast as *I* move, who cares about three inches."

"It adds up. You see if it don't."

"Ha."

She yanked Joan's bunch from her and lashed it to the rod. That finished up the stick; it looked now like one long chain of hanging green leaves, with the rod itself hidden from sight by the thick stems that stuck up on either side. "You!" she said without looking, and Jimmy Terry raised himself from the side of the barn and set down his Coke bottle. By the time he had ambled over to Missouri she had lifted the stick from its notched stand and stood making faces because of the weight of it, holding it very carefully so as not to crush the leaves. "Watch it, now," she said, and thrust it at him, and he started back to the drying-barn while she bent to take another rod and lay it in the notches. "I was saying something," she said. She tied the white twine around the end farthest from her and then snapped it off at a length of five feet or so, while Mrs. Hall stopped tying to watch her. (Mrs. Hall spent every day of every tobacco season trying to figure out how Missouri snapped off her twine ahead of time without measuring it.) "I was talking about sitting," Missouri said, grandly ignoring Mrs. Hall. "This table is *bare*, Lord; when they going to bring us more? Now, when you sit, your blood sort of sits along with you. It don't go rushing around your brain no more. Consequently, it takes that much more time to get rid of some sad idea in your mind. The process is slowed considerable. Whereas if you hurry your blood *up* some . . . There is a sizable amount of people could benefit from what I know. I could just go on and on about it. But do you get what I mean up to now?"

"Well, so far," Joan said.

"Good. Now, what started me on that—well, I do say. Took you long enough."

She was looking off toward the dirt driveway, where the men were just coming with the mule. Behind the mule was a huge wooden sled piled high with tobacco leaves, and it must have been heavy because the mule was objecting. He had stopped trying and began to amuse himself by blowing through his nose at the flies circling his head, and when Mr. Terry slapped his back he only switched his tail and gave an extra hard wheeze through his nose. Mr. Terry pulled out a bandanna and wiped his face.

"You stop that and bring him here," Missouri commanded. "We're out of leaves and getting paid for standing here with our arms folded."

"Well, I wouldn't want *that*," Mr. Terry said, but he went on wiping his face with his back to the mule. He was an easygoing man; it was a wonder to the whole countryside how he ever got his tobacco in. Behind the sled was James Green, filling in for the day because Mr. Pike was at home with his wife, and he wasn't doing anything about the mule either. His face was dark from the sun and glistening, and his hair hung in a wet mop over his forehead. When he saw Joan he grinned and waved, but he didn't look as if he gave a hang whether that mule *ever* moved, so Missouri heaved a huge sigh and laid down her twine.

"I never," she said, and circled the long picnic table where the women were standing and headed for the mule. "Jefferson, you no-good, you," she told the mule, "you going to keep us waiting all day?"

"*That's* not Jefferson," Mr. Terry said. "That's my brother Kerr's mule, Man O'War. He's only a distant cousin to Jefferson."

"I don't care who he is." She reached up and grabbed the mule by one long ear, as if he were a little boy, and pulled in the direction of the table. The mule followed, sighing sadly. "In the end, it's the women that work," Missouri told him. "Stand still now, you hear?"

"I wish it *was* Jefferson," said Mr. Terry. "He was some good mule, old Jefferson."

"He sick?" Missouri asked.

"Nah. Dead."

"That's why this one is doddering around so, then. They know, them mules."

"Mr. Graves shot him down," Mr. Terry said. He and James were both at work now, lifting armloads of leaves from the sled and carrying them over to the table. "He says he has the right, because Jefferson kicked his boy."

"Nah, that ain't so. Only if Jefferson *killed* the boy,

outright. Takes more than that to kill Sonny Graves. Sonny ain't dead, is he?''

"Oh, no.''

"Well, you go on and sue then. Go on and do it.''

"Well,'' Mr. Terry said. He took the mule and turned him around, and when he slapped him this time the mule headed back toward the fields with the empty sled skittering behind him. "We'll let Saul take care of him,'' Mr. Terry told James. To the women at the table he called, "That was the last load, there. Me and the men are going to cut out and have a beer up at the house.''

"Don't you give Lem more than one,'' Missouri said. "You know how he gets.''

"Well.''

He headed toward the house, wiping his face again with the bandanna, and James turned and said, "You yell when you're ready to go, Joan.''

"All right,'' Joan said.

When the men had left there was a different feeling in the air, blanker and stiller. The smell of sweat and mule and hot sun had drifted away, and for a minute the women just stood looking after them with their faces expressionless. Then Missouri said, "Well,'' and she and Mrs. Hall took their places at their rods again and the others turned to the new heap of leaves on the table.

"That James stays out in the sun much more, he's going to change races,'' Missouri said to Joan.

"I guess he might,'' Joan said.

"He's a good man. Though a bit too quiet—don't let things show through.''

"No.''

Missouri waited, still without going back to her work. Finally she said, "Just where is he from?''

The others looked up. Joan said, "Oh . . . from around here he says."

"Well, so are we all," said Missouri. "But what *town*?"

"He doesn't talk much about it."

"*That's* kind of peculiar," Mrs. Hall called. "You ever asked him?"

"He's not *wanted* or nothing, is he?" said Missouri.

"No."

"You never know. I'd been married two and a half years before I found out Lem had been married before. Mad? I tell you—"

"If I were you I'd ask him," Mrs. Hall said.

"Well, I did," said Joan. She was beginning to feel uncomfortable. "He *told* me where he was from but it was just an ordinary town, like Larksville—"

"Then why don't he say so?"

"Well, you know Ansel," Joan said.

"There's an odd one."

"He doesn't like for James to talk about it. He's afraid James'll send him back."

"Good thing if he did," said Mrs. Hall. "You ever been invited to meet their family?"

"Well, no."

"They had some kind of falling-out," Missouri's daughter Lily said. Everyone looked at her, and she said, "Well, that's what Maisie Hammond said."

"Maisie Hammond don't know beans," Missouri said. "Haven't you learned not to listen to gossip?"

"If I was you, Joan," said Mrs. Hall, "I'd just march right up and ask him. I'd say, 'James, will you take me to meet your family?' Just like that, I'd ask."

"No," Joan said.

They went on watching her, waiting for her to say

more, but she didn't. She concentrated on grouping the
leaves together by the stems, a small cluster at a time,
so that they lay flat against each other, and then she
held them out to Missouri and waited patiently until
Missouri gave up and started tying again. Each time
Missouri took the leaves from her there was a funny
numb feeling in Joan's fingertips, from the leaves sliding across layers and layers of thick tobacco gum on
her skin. Tobacco gum covered her hands and forearms,
and it had worked in between the straps of her sandals
so that there was black gum on the soles of her feet.
Tonight when she walked barefoot through the house
she would leave little black tracks behind her. She
rubbed the tip of her nose against a clean spot on the
back of her hand, and Missouri clicked her tongue at
her to tell her to hurry. "I want to get *home*," she told
Joan, and Joan swooped down on another bunch of
leaves and handed them to her. In her sleep she would
see tables full of tobacco leaves, stack upon stack of
yellow-green leaves with their fine sticky coating of fuzz
and their rough surfaces that reminded her of old
grained leather on book covers. Whenever she told her
aunt about that, about dreaming every night of mules
and leaves and drying barns, her aunt thought she was
complaining and said, "Nobody *asked* you to do it. I
even told you, I said it right out, I didn't want you doing
it. Secretaries don't work tobacco, honey." But then
Joan only laughed and said she liked seeing leaves in
her sleep. "There's lots worse I could dream of," she
said, and Mrs. Pike had to agree.

 Missouri had started talking again, now that she saw
Joan wasn't going to answer any more questions. "Let's
get back to sitting," she said. "What led me to speak
of it was, your working and all so soon after that, uh,

tragedy occurred. Now, honey, don't you mind Mrs. Pike. I know her, she feels like even James shouldn't of come. Feels like it shows disrespect. But look at it head-on and—"

"Well, not disrespect," Mrs. Hall called across. "Not that, exactly. But I see Lou's point. *I* wouldn't have come today, Joan. I don't mind telling you."

"What would I do at home?" Joan asked. "Sit?"

"Exactly what led me to my discussion," said Missouri. "What *sitting* does, is—"

"You could have stayed around and helped out," Mrs. Hall said. "Made tea and things. A person needs company at a time like this. And James there, why, he is very close to being Janie's cousin-in-law, or once removed, or whatever you call it—"

Once again they all looked at Joan, but she went on grouping leaves and they sighed and turned back to the table.

"*Any*way," said Mrs. Hall, "with his own brother on the verge of—"

"Well, this is sort of pointless," Joan said. "You just think one way, and me another. I don't think she wants any more than her own husband there, and that's what she's got. And Simon too, if she wants him."

"Ain't *that* a funny thing," Lily said suddenly. "Up to last week, it was Janie *Rose* she never paid no attention to—"

"You hush," Missouri said. "This is Miss Joan's *relatives* we're talking about."

"Well, I know that. Now, won't it Simon she used to brag on all the time? Won't it Simon that was spoiled so rotten he—"

"Hush."

"My feet are killing me," said Mrs. Hall.

Her second hander, the pale one named Josephine, looked down at Mrs. Hall's feet and gave one of them a gentle kick with the toe of her sneaker. "With me it's sneakers or barefoot," she said. "What you wearing leather shoes for?"

"Because I'm older than you. I have to look decent." She snapped off her twine and turned to the barn. "Boy!" she called.

"Will you look?" said Missouri. "She's a stick and a half ahead of me, and you two are poking along. Hurry it up, Lily."

Lily handed her the next bunch and then stretched, raising her thin black arms an enormous length above her head. To show her disapproval Missouri jerked her string with a twanging sound, and one of Lily's leaves fell out of its bunch on the stick and landed in the dust. "Oh, Lord," Missouri said. She handed her string to Joan and bent to pick up the leaf, holding the small of her back with one hand. A pink slip strap slid down over her shoulder. "Four hours ago it was four o'clock," she said when she retrieved the leaf. "Now it's four thirty. When'll it ever be five?"

"Won't help you if it is," called Mrs. Hall, "so long as you've still got leaves on your table."

"Well, I can't help it if they loaded the most leaves on me." She pulled her strap up again and took the end of the twine away from Joan. "I was saying something," she said. "I have that fidgety feeling, like I wasn't finished."

"Sitting," Joan reminded her.

"Sitting? Oh, sitting. My lord, how long I been *on* that? Well, anyway." She snapped her fingers at Lily, who was gazing open-mouthed at a pecan tree, and Lily jumped and handed her another bunch of leaves.

"Originally," Missouri said, "I was getting around to a remedy for Mrs. Pike. Well, now I've gotten to it. Mrs. Pike is going to have to start working again."

"Working?" Lily said. "*I* didn't know Mrs. Pike worked."

"Will you *hush*?" Missouri switched the twine to her left hand and reached across to slap Lily's arm. "I don't know where you spend all your time, Lily," she said. She took up the twine in her right hand again and snatched Joan's leaves from her. "Well, it so happens she does work. She's a seamstress. Teen-iney stitches and a Singer for her machine work. Miss Joan can tell you. Most of it's altering things, but she makes things from scratch also. Reason you might not know," she told Lily, "is she does it at home. Works in. A lot of right important people go there. Mrs. Lawrence, the judge's wife, does—saw her drive up to the door once. Do you see what I'm getting at, Miss Joan?"

"Well, yes," said Joan. "You're saying this would snap her out of it. But being a seamstress is like working in a beauty shop—you have to carry on a conversation. And Aunt Lou just isn't capable right now."

"Of *course* not," said Mrs. Hall. "Why, she just don't have the heart to do that. Will you *look* at you people?"

"I got the answer," Mrs. Hall's first hander called. "I don't see why you are all worrying." She kept on handing as she spoke, thrusting precisely neat bunches at Mrs. Hall with lightning speed. "It's like when you've been sick," she said. "They have to walk you around by the elbow a while. Well, Mrs. Pike needs to be walked around too, only in the talking sense. Joan here only works every other day; she can spare the time. She can greet the customers and tell them the news and all, so's they won't even notice how quiet Mrs. Pike is. Then by and by Mrs. Pike'll start to get interested in what Joan is talking about. She'll begin uncurling and saying a few words herself. That's why she was such a favorite before, Mrs. Pike was; she could talk up a storm."

Missouri was watching her with her mouth open. "Charleen," she said, when Charleen had finished speaking, "you are just as silly as you look, Charleen. You must think Miss Joan is some kind of a walking newspaper. Do you? She don't say two words in a day, Joan don't. Customers would drop off like apples in the fall, and Mrs. Pike would have one more reason not to get a grip on things."

"Silly yourself," Charleen muttered, and bent closer over her pile of leaves.

"Mrs. Pike's no worse than my sister Mary was," said Mrs. Hall. "When Mary's oldest died she sat on the porch seven days and seven nights and it rained on her. I thought she'd *mold*, before we got her in again. Mrs. Pike is at least talking some."

"Not much," Josephine said. She was scraping tobacco gum off her hands with a nail file while Mrs. Hall tied a knot at the end of her stick. "I went up to her at the burying and, 'Mrs. Pike,' I said. 'I surely am sorry.' And you know what she said? She said, 'This is where Simon's bedroom was going to be.' I tell you, it scared me."

"Well, they were going to build a house there," Mrs. Hall said. She slammed another stick in the stand. "I say they should have put Janie Rose by the church, but that's a individual matter."

Missouri took off her straw hat and began fanning

her face with it. "You can rest," she told Joan and Lily. "We're even now. Boy?"

"Yes'm."

"Well, come on and get it."

Joan and Lily leaned back against the table, half sitting on it, and Missouri tilted her head back so that she could fan her neck. "Sun's about gone," she said, "but still working. What was it I was thinking, now? Lily?"

"Well, I'm sure *I* don't know," Lily said.

"Hush. Wait, now—oh." She stopped fanning herself, clamped her hat on her head again, and bent for another rod. "Stop that standing around," she commanded. "Charleen, I take it back."

"What?"

"What I said. I take it back. You only half silly."

"Oh, why, *thank* you."

"Only half as silly as you look. Stand up straight, Lily, you're a mess. What's that all over your hands?"

"It's tobacco gum, what you think?"

"Oh." She snapped off her length of twine, with Mrs. Hall watching closely, and reached for Joan's leaves. "I'm a little vague, but I'm thinking," she said. Then she frowned into space for a while. Finally she said, "Growing old surely do damage a person."

"Well, is *that* what you've been getting ready to say?" Mrs. Hall asked irritably.

"*Oh* no," Missouri said. "It was something entirely different. I was working up to something."

"You were talking about Aunt Lou," Joan reminded her.

"Well, I know I was. If you all would just let me—"

"Personally," said Mrs. Hall, "I think this is a lot of fuss for nothing. You think it's something wrong if

Mrs. Pike sticks to herself a few days. Well, something *is* wrong. Somebody died. And that's all I'm going to say.''

"It's just as well," said Missouri. "You keep distracting my mind."

"Why, Missouri—"

"You *said*," Missouri reminded her, "you said that was all you was going to—"

Mrs. Hall sighed and turned her back, muttering something but not attempting to argue any more, and Missouri nodded to herself several times. "There now," she said. "Now, what was I—?" But when Lucy clicked her tongue in exasperation, exactly like her mother, Missouri waved her free hand at her to tell her not to speak. "Now I remember," she said. "Growing old surely do—Well. Anyway. Now, of course we're not saying anything's wrong with Mrs. Pike. Sure she's sad. Going to go right on being that way, always a little sad to the end of her days. But that don't stop us from trying to make her feel better; that's just natural. We all got reasons. Maybe we want to stop remembering the dead ourselves. Or a host of other reasons."

She bent down and slapped a fly on her leg. "Oh, you," she said to the fly, and then reached out for Joan's leaves. Joan was holding the leaves too high and far away, and Missouri had to snap her fingers at her. "*Come* on," she said. Joan came to life and handed the leaves over.

"*Any*how," said Missouri. "Now I've lost my place again. Where was I?"

"Mrs. Pike," Joan said.

"Mrs. Pike? Oh, her. Well, no, I was passing on to someone else. What's-his-name. What's his name?"

"*Mr.* Pike?" Lily suggested.

"Just hush. Though he's in this too, of course. No, just hush—Simon. That boy of theirs. You know him, Joan?"

"He's my cousin," said Joan.

"Oh, yes. Yes. Simon. Going to go to pieces if things go on this way. Do you see now what I'm getting at?"

"Well, no."

"It's as plain as the nose on—Boy? Come on, now, quit that poking. I'm saying it's Simon should be in her beauty shop with her."

"In her—?"

"I mean in her sewing shop. Look what you done now, got me all confused. Well, that's who you want."

"You mean he should entertain the customers," Joan said.

"That was my point."

"Well—"

"He's the only one can help now. Not hot tea, not people circling round. Not even her own husband. Just her little boy."

"I don't see how," said Joan.

Missouri made an exasperated face. "*You* don't know," she told her. "You don't know how it would work out. Bravest thing about people, Miss Joan, is how they go on loving mortal beings after finding out there's such a thing as dying. Do I have to tell you that?"

She snapped her twine tight and held it there while she watched Joan scrape up the last of the leaves. "I despise finishing the day on half a stick," she said.

"Well, I'll be," said Charleen. She leaned back against the table, shaking her head and watching Mrs. Hall tie the end of her stick. "I never. Was *that* what you did all this talking to say?"

"It was," said Missouri.

At the other end of the table, Mrs. Hall suddenly looked up. "That's true," she said slowly, but when they turned toward her she only shook her head. "That's true," she said again, and lifted her tobacco rod gently from its notches and handed it to the waiting boy.

6

James was halfway through his second beer before he saw Joan coming toward him. He was sitting on Mr. Terry's porch, leaning back against the side of the house in a folding chair and lazily listening to the other men talking, and his beer can was making a cold wet ring on his knee. There were four other men there, all sitting just like he was in a line against the house. Maybe if Joan hadn't come he would have sat with them till supper, just to rest up from the long day's work and let the breeze dry his damp shirt. But then Mr. Terry said, "If you'll look out yonder—" and James raised his eyes toward the fields and saw Joan padding down the dirt driveway in bare feet with a sandal swinging from each hand. "Out yonder to the east is what I mean to cultivate year after next," Mr. Terry went on. He had been saying that for as long as James had known him. "I aim to extend the alfalfa a bit. No sense in letting good land grow wild, I say." James only nodded, not really listening. He squinted his eyes so as to see better—Joan was still far away—and watched how she picked her way so quickly and gently along the dusty wheel-tracks. Her head was bent, so that her hair fell forward and nearly hid her face. Way behind her were the other women, going in the opposite direction toward town, and once they turned back and waved at Joan but she didn't see them. The women bobbed on, farther and farther, until all that showed of them was their bright dresses between the tobacco rows and two huge black umbrellas shading Lily and Missouri from the sun.

"I also been thinking about the eight acres out back," said Mr. Terry. "They're Paul Hammond's, but he's not using them."

"No," James said.

"You listening?"

Joan had reached the edge of the Terrys' front yard. She crossed onto the grass, sliding her feet a little as if she liked the coolness of it, and Mr. Terry stopped talking and the others sat forward and took their hats off.

"Hey, Joan," said Mr. Terry.

"Hey." She stopped at the bottom of the steps and smiled up at them. "Lem," she said, "Missouri sent you a message. She said to come right on home."

Lem tipped back again in his chair, shaking his head. "Must be a mistake somewheres," he said. His eyes were faraway and dreamy, and the others laughed softly.

"Well, anyway," said Joan. "I came to see if you're ready to go yet, James. Or do you want to stay on a while."

"No, I'm ready."

He finished his beer in one gulp and stood up. Down at the end of the porch, Howell Blake looked up from cleaning his fingernails with a pocket knife and said, "You coming tomorrow?"

"Depends on Roy Pike, I guess. Looks like he'll be sitting with his wife a while."

"Well, just so's *one* of you makes it," said Mr. Terry. "You tell Roy I know how it is. *You* tell him, Joan."

"I will."

James went down the steps toward Joan, and she
switched one sandal to the other hand so that he could
take her free hand in his. Both of them were coated
with tobacco gum. The gum had lost its stickiness by
now but it still clung to their skin in heavy layers, so
that it was like holding hands with rubber gloves on.
He kept hold of her anyway, and turned partway back
to nod at the others. "See you tomorrow, I guess," he
said. "I or Roy, one."

"Okay. So long."

"So long."

They crossed the yard together and then they were on
the dirt driveway again, heading toward the gravel road.
When James looked down, he could see the dust rising
in little puffs around Joan's toes every time she took a
step. Her toes were gum-covered too, and the dust had
stuck to them like a layer of sugar frosting.

"I have to have a bath," Joan said, as if she had been
following his eyes.

"No. I like you this way."

"I'm serious. You have to have one too, and then we
can sit outside and cool off."

"Okay," James said. He pulled her along faster, because he liked the idea of just the two of them sitting
out on the porch a while. But Joan slowed him down
again.

"I have to put on my sandals to walk fast," she said.
"Do you want me to?"

"No, that's all right."

But she bent down anyway, and James stood waiting
while she slid her feet into the sandals. She was wearing
bermudas and a faded blue shirt with the tails out, and
when a breeze started up it ballooned out the back of
her shirt and made her look humpbacked. He put one

hand on the hump. It vanished, pressed flat by the weight of his hand, and he could feel the ripple of her backbone through the thin cloth of her shirt. It seemed to him he knew Joan's clothes by heart. He could tell the seasons by them, and if she bought something new, he felt uneasy and resentful toward it until it had become worn-looking. When spring came he never really felt it until those old cotton shirts had come out again, though for days he might have known about the bits of green on the trees and the flowering Judas buds by the side of the road. He smiled down at Joan now and she straightened up and looked at him, not knowing anything about what was going on in his mind.

"What're you thinking?" she asked him.

"Nothing."

They turned onto the gravel road, holding hands again. A station wagon drove past, clanking and rattling as if it would fall apart before their eyes, and Joan waved at whoever was driving but James didn't look up. He was concentrating on the gravel beneath his feet, and on steering Joan into the sandiest part of the road. Finally he said, "I've got an idea."

"What?"

"How about coming over and cooking supper tonight? We could sit out and eat it on the porch."

"You know I can't cook."

"Well, hot dogs is all right."

He dropped her hand and put his arm around her, so that he could feel her shoulder moving against his rib cage as they walked. They were going very slowly now; he had stopped caring if they never got anywhere at all. He would like to go down this road indefinitely, with everything around him shining and wearing a clean, finished, end-of-the-day look. The sun picked things up slantwise, and the fields were very still in between the gusts of breeze. When they rounded the bend and their house appeared, long and shabby with its tin roof batting the sunshine into their eyes, it seemed surprising and out of place. Both of them slowed down still more to stare at it. Then Joan said, "Well, I'll race you home."

"Now?"

"Come on."

She started running, moving in bursts of uneven speed and letting her hands stay open instead of doubling them into fists the way most people did. Beside her, James ran at a slow easy pace because he didn't want to leave her behind. When he ran like this he was scarcely breathing hard, but Joan was out of breath and laughing. They reached the edge of the yard, and she stopped to tuck her shirttails in. "You weren't even trying," she told him. "That was no race."

But he reached out for a tall blue spiky flower and presented it to her gravely, as if she had won, and she accepted it.

"When you coming over?" he asked.

"In an hour or so. I have to take a bath and see that the others eat."

"Can you leave your aunt?"

"I'll see how she is," Joan said. She bent over suddenly and clapped her hands together, with the stem of the flower between them. "Hey, Nellie," she said. "That you?"

The bushes beside the lawn rustled and the dog poked just her head out, her nose pointed upwards. "Where you been?" Joan asked her. She made little coaxing motions with her hands. For a minute James watched, and then when it looked as if Nellie would be a long

time making up her mind to come he turned toward the
house.

"I'm going on in," he called.

"All right. Come on, Nellie."

James crossed the yard and climbed the steps at his
end of the porch. In the seat of Ansel's chair was a
rumpled magazine, which he picked up to take inside
with him. "I'm home, Ansel," he said in the doorway.
But Ansel didn't answer, and his couch was bare. "Hey,
Ansel?"

On the coffee table was Ansel's entire collection of
seashells, all laid out neatly with the hollow sides up.
This must have been one of his bored days, spent wandering aimlessly through the house with an occasional
pause to glance over some possession of his before he
grew tired of it and began wandering again. But he hadn't
been flipping through James's photographs, the way he
usually did on those days. And he wasn't in the kitchen,
or up in his room. "Ansel?" James called once more,
and his voice rang out into a waiting, ticking silence
that worried him.

He went outdoors again. Joan was still in the yard,
sitting on her heels and patting Nellie. When she saw
James she said, "You're supposed to be in the tub by
now," but James only shook his head.

"I can't find Ansel," he said.

Joan stood up then and came over to the porch. "He's
probably just gone visiting," she told him. "Did you
look for a note?"

"*Ansel* don't leave notes."

"Well, he'll be back."

"I don't know. I want you to check your aunt's for
me; I don't like bothering her."

"All right." She turned and made a kissing sound at

Nellie, who danced after her toward the porch. "It's time for your supper," Joan told her, and then led her through the Pikes' door by snapping her fingers high above Nellie's head. After they disappeared into the house James stayed out on the porch, waiting to see if Joan had found his brother. If she had, she would need help coaxing him out. He had a sudden clear picture of Joan backing out the door again, snapping her fingers at Ansel to lead him forward the way she had led Nellie. He smiled, and then relaxed and swung one foot up onto the porch railing.

But when Joan came she came alone. "He's at the Potters'," she said, before James could ask. "Uncle Roy said he came calling, but Simon wouldn't let him in. He went on to the Potters."

"Well, maybe I'll just check," said James.

"Oh, he's all right, James. What's got into you lately?"

"I just want to make sure," he told her. "I wish you'd come with me. If I go alone I'll *never* get out, once they start to talking."

"Well, all right."

She came over to stand beside him, and he knocked on the Potters' door. There was no screen on it, because they didn't need one; they kept the inner door shut. Summer and winter their part of the porch had a closed, unbreathing look, and they had long ago paid James two dozen cinnamon buns for taking the baggy old screen door off its hinges and carting it out back. When James knocked there was first a faint movement of the paper shade—they had to make sure who it was—and then there was the sound of two bolts sliding back. The door cracked open; Miss Faye poked her round face out.

"Why, James," she said.

"Hello, Miss Faye."

"And Joan too. Both of you together. Joan, honey, don't you look fresh and outdoorsy today. I was saying to Miss Lucy just a—well, step on inside, step in."

"Actually," James said, "I just wanted to see if you had Ansel here."

"Ansel?" She had the door wide open now, and was throwing back one arm to show that they were welcome. James kept trying to peer past her, hoping to see Ansel, but the way the Potters' house was arranged made it impossible. They had set up a labyrinth of tall black folding screens with needlework flowers on them, so that the house was divided into a dozen or more tiny rooms. No matter how James craned his neck around Miss Faye, all he saw was the screen behind her and more screens behind that. "Oh, Ansel," Miss Faye was saying. "James, I worry about that boy. I was saying just a while ago; I said—are you coming in? Don't stand outside; come on in."

"We've only got a minute," Joan said gently. "Is Ansel here?"

"Well, let's see." She stepped further back, leaving them the whole doorway to enter through, and after a minute the two of them came in. Who could tell what might be hidden in this maze of screens? The air was dark and stale, from being separated into so many cubicles in a tightly closed house. And there was a thick feeling to the walls that must have come from the heavy tapestries, because every place else in this house was shell-thin. When they were inside, Miss Faye shut the whole world behind them out; she said, *"Now,"* and slammed the door and slid the two locks into place.

James frowned (it made him uneasy, being locked in this way) but Joan only looked amused.

"You were going to tell us if Ansel's here," she reminded Miss Faye.

"Yes. Yes, I was saying—Lucy? Lucy, are you coming to say hello?"

They heard Miss Lucy's footsteps, sounding very faint and taking a long time to weave in and out among the screens. First she came close and then went farther away again, and suddenly she popped out right behind Miss Faye. She wore a huge white apron with jokes about outdoor barbecues printed all over it.

"Lucy, look who's here," said Miss Faye.

"Well, isn't this nice?" Miss Lucy came towards them with both hands outstretched, making James wonder, just as he always did, what he was supposed to do when she reached him—hug her?—but Joan saved the day by stepping up and taking both Miss Lucy's hands in her own. "You're looking just as *healthy*," Miss Lucy told her, and then gave a little giggle and shook her tight cap of curls. "We've had so much company today that I'm getting all—"

"Well, that's really what we came to talk about," said James.

"Aren't you going to sit down?"

"We wanted to ask—"

"You *have* to sit down." She began backing around the first screen, still holding Joan's hands. James glanced over at a puffy plush chair, with its layers and layers of antimacassars, and then shook his head.

"I'm sorry," he said, "but it looks like Ansel isn't here, and that's what we came about."

"*Oh* yes. Yes, he was here."

"When?" James asked.

"At three o'clock today, on the nose. No, more like three fifteen. I forget, Faye . . ."

"It was three twenty exactly," said Miss Faye. "It was my turn to wear the brooch-watch today. I had looked down at it, while checking to see if my blouse was clean, just before I answered the door. And it was Ansel at the door. Will you sit down, please?"

"That was nearly two hours ago," James said.

"No, you're wrong, James."

"Well, it's way past five."

"Oh, it was nearly two hours ago that he *came*, all right. But it was more recently that he left, because he stayed to have a jam braid."

"Well—"

"Also a glass of milk. I said, 'Ansel, we've got to get some meat on your bones.' So did Miss Lucy. She said so too. Ansel said, 'Oh, Miss Faye, I just don't know.' He was feeling sad."

"What about?" asked James.

"He didn't say. Well, you know how he is. Some days the world is just too much for him. That's how he put it. 'Miss Faye,' he said, 'some days the world is just too much for me.' He told Lucy that too. 'Miss Lucy,' he said, 'some days the—' "

"Did he say where he was going?"

"Why, home, I reckon."

"I have to leave," James said.

"Oh, now. You only just—"

"I'm sorry, Miss Faye. Come on, Joan."

He reached the door before Miss Faye could, and he slid the bolts back himself, with Miss Faye's hands fluttering anxiously above his. Then he shot out on the porch, not even trying to be polite about it. Joan followed, but with her head turned toward the Potters, her voice drifting back to them as she tried to smooth everything over. "I'm sorry we have to leave this way," she said, "but I know you see how it is—" and the Potters made thin, sad little sounds to show that they did.

"Just please come back," Miss Faye told them, and James nodded tiredly and let the door swing shut. The two bolts slid back into place.

When they were outside again James just stood there, trying to think where to begin. Joan didn't seem worried at all. She said, "I got tobacco gum all over Miss Lucy's hands."

"That's too bad," James said absently.

"She was staring at her hands all funny-like; that's how I noticed. Little bits of black were sticking to them."

James turned around and looked at her. "Will you *listen*?" he told her. "I can't find Ansel."

"I'm sorry, James." She grew serious, and came over to stand beside him. "He'll come back," she said.

"I don't know."

"He always has before."

"Well, I just don't *know*," James said. He knelt to tie his shoe and then stayed that way, looking down the porch to see who might be coming along the road. No one was in sight. "We don't know *what* might have happened," he said.

Joan squatted down beside him and said, "Well, he's come back every other time, James."

"You already said that."

"I just meant—"

"I *know* he comes back. I been through this a hundred times. If I didn't even go looking for him, he'd come back. But I can't be a hundred percent sure of that.''

Down the road came a red hen, strutting importantly, sticking her neck far out as if she were heading someplace definite. As she walked she talked to herself, in little conversational clucks. James and Joan watched after her until she had disappeared.

"Somehow I can't get what Maisie said off my mind," James said finally. "How would I feel if just once he went too far? There'd be no one to blame but me, if that happened.''

"Maisie who?'' Joan asked.

"Maisie Hammond.''

"Well, if you *did* go after him, you know how it'd be. You ever seen Ansel standing on a street corner waiting for you? He goes somewhere you'd never think to look, James. You go up and down town all night searching for him, waking every drinking man to ask him if he knows, and where does it get you? You always end up right here, waiting for him to decide to come back.''

"I like to think I looked,'' James said.

"I know that.'' She stood up again, and the cotton smell of her shirt floated past him. "I can see it better than you can,'' she told him. "I don't like him. I can see easier than you how he will always come back.''

"You can't see.''

"Look,'' Joan said. "What's got into you? Things were getting better for a while. You weren't fussing over him, and he had almost stopped wandering off. Why have you started acting this way?''

He stared down at her feet, long and dirty in sandals that had molded themselves to the curl of her toes. Her feet made him so angry that he almost didn't answer her. But then she looked down at him, with her face worried and unsure, and he said, "I don't know."

"Well, there's got to be some reason."

"Will you stop asking me that? *You* don't have a brother."

"Maybe not," Joan said, "but there is nothing I like or understand about you going to look for Ansel all the time. If he wanted he could have done a full day's work today, and been off at a dance right now."

"No, he couldn't."

"Yes, he could. He could be dancing and you and I could be going someplace. We could be doing something. We could be someone besides an old familiar couple that'll be courting when they're seventy and the town's fondest joke. Are you listening?"

"No," James said.

He got up off his knees and went down the porch steps. Bits of tobacco gum and dust from the floorboards clung to the knees of his pants, but he didn't brush them off. The sunset glowed red and dull across the roof of the pickup. "Don't bother fixing supper," he called.

"I wouldn't *think* of fixing supper."

He stopped and looked back at her. She was standing at the edge of the porch now, with her arms folded and her feet planted solidly apart. "I wish you'd wear some real *shoes* once," he said.

"What?"

"I'm sick of those sandals."

"Well, I'm sick of everything," Joan said.

Her voice was flat now, and only sad-sounding. It made him look back at her one more time, but by then she had turned away and was walking down the porch. "Joan?" he said. She went on walking, not answering.

From behind, her folded arms gave her a thin, round-shouldered look, and she stepped in that gentle way she had, with her bare pointed heels rising and falling delicately across the long gray porch.

7

At night, when everyone was in bed, the house seemed to belong to one family instead of three. The separate sleeping-sounds mingled and penetrated through all the thin walls, and by now James could identify each sound exactly and where it came from. He knew Miss Faye's snore, as curlicued and lacy as she herself was, and the loud, honking sound that Mr. Pike made. He knew Miss Lucy's rat-a-tat on the walls, first on Mr. Pike's wall when the snoring grew too noisy and then on his own wall if he talked in his sleep. He thought it must be a thimble she tapped with. Because there was a big room's width between his end of the house and the Pikes' end, he wasn't sure of the softer sounds there—Simon's snoring, for instance, or Mrs. Pike's. And he had always wondered if Joan snored. But he had heard Janie Rose's nightmares often enough. They came through loud and clear, drifting up from the open window of her tacked-on bedroom downstairs. "*That's* not something you should be doing," she would say reasonably. And then, "Daddy, would you come *quick*?" and the floundering thuds across the floor as Mr. Pike began groping his way toward her voice in the dark. But if Simon talked in his sleep, he must have talked quietly. All James heard of him was in the morning, when they tried to wake him and he bellowed out, "Oh, *fine*, I'll be right there! I already got my socks on. Ain't this some day?"—yet all the while sound asleep, and just trying to fool people. Sometimes Mr. Pike shouted too. He would have too many beers on a Saturday night and throw all the pillows out the window. "Ninety-nine point two percent of all the people in the southern *states* die of smothering," he would roar to the night, and then Miss Lucy would rap on the wall. Miss Lucy never slept at all; James was convinced of that. She spent her time policing the area. On nights when Ansel was restless, when he tossed around on his old wooden bed across the room from James (he wouldn't sleep in the other bedroom, for fear of waking alone and finding his feet numb), and when he kept calling, "James, how long has this night been going *on*?" Miss Lucy would tap very gently and ask if Ansel wanted her hot water bottle. "No, ma'am," James always said, and Miss Lucy would go back to her quiet, patient pacing. Sometimes James had a great urge to go see what she was wearing. He pictured her in a twenty-pound quilted robe with lead weights at the bottom, like the ones sewn into curtains, because it dragged so loudly across the floor at every step she took. But once he had had a horrible nightmare, right after eating two pizzas. He had shouted out, "My *God*!" and awakened shaking, with the terrible sound of his own shout still ringing in his ears. Then Miss Lucy had tapped and called, "Why, *it's* going to be all right," and the horror vanished. He had lain back down, feeling comforted and at home, and now it never annoyed him to hear Miss Lucy's bathrobe dragging.

In the Potters' bedroom the clock struck four, whirring and choking before each clang. James lay tensed,

counting the strokes, although he already knew how
many there would be. He had slept only in patches all
night, and even in his dreams he was searching streets
full of people for the thin stooped figure of his brother.
In the last dream it had been a year ago—that time they
had called from ten miles away to tell him Ansel had
been run over, but neglected to add it was only a bicycle that had done it. After that he couldn't sleep at
all. He thought of all the things that had happened to
Ansel in the past, the really serious things, and all the
things that might be happening to him tonight. When
the clock had stopped whirring he found that he was
frowning into the darkness so hard that the muscles of
his forehead hurt. Then, as if that clock had been some
sort of musical introduction, a faraway voice began
singing outside:

>   There's sunshine on the mountains,
>   And spring has come again. . . .

James sat up and pulled back the curtain. Outside it
was pitch black, with a handful of small stars scattered
like sand across the blue-black sky. The trees beyond
the field were only hulking dark shapes, and not one
light glimmered from the town behind them.

>   My true love said she'd meet me,
>   But forgot to tell me when.

He climbed out of bed and untwisted the legs of his
pajamas. At his bedroom wall there was one sharp tap,
questioning (he had learned to read Miss Lucy's thimble language), and he called, "It's all right, Miss
Lucy." She resumed her pacing again, with her robe

trailing her footsteps like a murmuring companion. James shot out of his room, still buttoning his pajama top, and went downstairs in the dark. The voice was nearer now.

> I was walking down the track, Lord,
> With a letter in my hand,
> A-reading how she'd left me
> For that sunny Jordan land.

The front door was open but the screen was hooked shut. James pushed the hook up, jabbing his finger, and swung the screen door open. Then he walked across the porch barefoot, with the cold rough grain of the wooden floorboards stinging the soles of his feet. Around his ankles the cuffs of his pajamas fluttered and ballooned and nearly tripped him (they were Ansel's, and too long); he bent to roll them up. Then he descended the steps, scowling into the dark as he tried to see. He was halfway down the path before he stopped, more by sensing someone in front of him than by seeing him. Ahead of him was a long tall shape, swaying gently, smelling of bourbon. The voice was so close now that James could feel its breath.

> Oh, there's sunshine on the hills, Lord,
> And the grass is all of gold. . . .

His reedy roice was piercing, but the thinness of it made it seem still far away. James stepped closer. "Ansel," he said.

> My love has gone and left me,
> And I'll cry until I'm old.

"Ansel," James said again.

"I'm singing, please."

"Come on in."

He took Ansel by the arm. It was stone cold; he could feel the bone underneath. When he pulled Ansel toward the porch Ansel came, but lifelessly and with the shadow that was his face still averted. "People keep asking you in nowadays," he told the dark. "They got a thing about it."

"Careful," said James. "We're coming to the steps."

"The *Potters* downright *lock* you in. Slide little bits of machinery around. You mind if I finish my song?"

"I certainly do."

"I might just finish it anyway. Where you taking me, James?"

"In," said James, and half lifted him up the first step. Ansel was as limp as a rag doll. His limpness made James realize suddenly how angry he was at Ansel, after all this worrying and waiting; instead of guiding him so carefully, he felt like giving him a good shove into the house and having done with it. "Get on in," he said, and took his hand away from Ansel's arm. Ansel gave him a deep lopsided blow and entered first.

"Certainly nice of you to ask me," he told James. "Certainly are a *hospitable* man."

"If you're hungry, Ansel—"

"I'm starved."

"Cook up some eggs," said James, and began making his way across the dark living room toward the stairs. Behind him Ansel said, *"Hey,* now—" but James paid no attention. The way he felt, he couldn't even make a cup of coffee for Ansel; he had been worrying for too long, and all he wanted now was sleep. Already he was unbuttoning the tops of his pajamas, preparing to go back to his bed.

"Don't you have food waiting?" Ansel asked.

"Nope."

"Don't you even *care* if I come back?"

"You know how to fry an egg."

"Well, I'll be," said Ansel, and sat down suddenly on something that creaked. "I take it back, James. What's so hospitable about you?"

The stairs were narrow, and James kept stubbing his toes against them. He touched the wall to guide himself, feeling the ripples and bubbles of the wallpaper as he slid his fingers along it. Behind him Ansel said, "You mad at me, James?" but James didn't answer. He could already hear the tapping sound that was coming from upstairs. Miss Lucy must be worried.

"I reckon you're wondering where I was at," Ansel said, and there was another creak when he stood up again. "You always *do* wonder." He banged into something, and then his footsteps wavered uncertainly toward the stairs. "You're taking all my places from me. Once I tell you, I can't go back no more. How long you guess it'll be before I've used up every place there is?" He was climbing the steps behind James now. His voice rang hollowly through the stairwell. For a minute James paused, listening to him coming, and then he continued on up and reached the top, with his hand still on the wall so that he could find his room. "It's all a question of time," Ansel said sadly. "Time and geography."

"If you're coming to sleep in *my* room," James told him, "you'd better shut up that talking."

"Well, I only want to explain."

"I'm sleepy, Ansel."

"I only want to explain."

James kept going, heading in the direction of Miss Lucy's tapping thimble. He could hear Ansel's hands sliding along behind his now on the wall, and then the sliding sound stopped and there was a click as Ansel snapped the hall light on. For a minute the light was blinding. James screwed his eyes up and said, "Oh, Lord—" and Ansel turned the light off again, quickly and guiltily. "I just thought," he said, "as long as we had electricity—"

"It's four a.m., Ansel."

"What're you, wearing my pajamas?"

"Go to hell, will you?"

"I never," said Ansel, but James was past listening. He was in the bedroom now, and on his way to bed he reached out and knocked on Miss Lucy's wall for her to stop that tapping. She did. He eased himself down between the sheets, which were cold already and messy-feeling. When he was lying flat he closed his eyes and wished away the figure of Ansel, standing like a long black stick and swaying in the bedroom doorway.

"I wisht I knew what was wrong with you," Ansel said. "You angry with me, James?"

"Yep."

"I only went out for a walk."

"You usually end up half dead after those walks. It's me that's got to nurse you back."

"Well, wait now," Ansel said. "I can explain. All you need to do is listen."

"How can I listen when I'm asleep?" asked James, and turned over on his side with his face to the window. He could hear Ansel's feet shuffling into the room, and he knew by the soft thumping noise that he had reached the other bed and was sitting on it.

"I tried and I tried," Ansel told him. "I went to the

Pikes' first off, but Simon don't like me any more. I
went to the Potters', and they locked me in and re-
quested news of my hemoglobin. What could I do? At
the tavern I said, 'Charlie,' I said, 'I got a problem.'
But all Charlie did was sell me hard liquor under the
counter; he didn't listen to no problem.''

Ansel's shoes were dropped on the floor, first one and
then the other. There was a small whipping sound as
he flung his tie around a bedpost. Even with his eyes
shut James could picture his brother, how he would be
leaning toward James with his shoulders hunched and
his hands flung out as he talked, even though he knew
he couldn't be seen. "Go to sleep, Ansel," he muttered, but Ansel only sighed and began unbuttoning his
shirt with tiny popping sounds.

"This all has to do with Janie Rose," he told James.
"Are you listening?"

"No."

"Just about everything has to do with Janie Rose these
days. I don't know why. Looks like she just kind of
tipped everything over with her passing on. Janie don't
like gladioli, James."

James didn't answer. A button flew to the floor and
then circled there for an endless length of time, and
Ansel stamped one stocking foot over it and shook the
whole house. James could feel the floorboards jar beneath his bed. There was a long silence; then Ansel
bent, with a small puff of held-in breath, and scraped
his fingers across the floor in search of the button.

"Got it," he said finally. "All today, I was so sick
and tired. I had looked at that picture of the Model A
too long. I don't know why I do things like that. Then
I thought, well, I'll just go up the hill and pay my
respects to Janie Rose. I'll go slow, so as not to get

overtired. And I did. I stopped a plenty on the way. But when I got close I saw her flowers, how they had got all wilted. I thought: I wisht I'd brought some flowers. I thought: I wisht I'd brought some bluets. You listening, James?''

James gritted his teeth and stayed quiet.

"There's four names for bluets I know of. Bluets, Quaker-ladies, pea-in-the-paths, and wet-the-beds. You can count on Janie Rose; she called them wet-the-beds. Well, she had problems herself in that line. But what I thought was: I wisht I'd brought some bluets. I *didn't* think: I wisht I'd brought some wet-the-beds.''

"Oh, Lord,'' James said tiredly. He turned his pillow to the cool side and lay back down on it.

"Now, bluets are not good funeral flowers. Too teeny. But Janie Rose is not a funeral *person*. Usually it's only the good die young. Consequently I thought: I wisht I'd—''

James raised his head and shouted, "Ansel, will you *hush*?'' and on his wall there was the sudden sound of frantic tapping. "I don't want to hear,'' he told Ansel more quietly, and then lay back down and forced his mind far away.

"I'll just get to the point,'' Ansel said. "I have to tell you this. James, there are *gladioli* on Janie's grave.''

James heard a zipper slide down, and after a minute a pair of trousers were tossed shuffingly across the floor. Then Ansel's socks dropped one after the other beside his bed, in soft crumpled balls, and James heard them fall and winced because his ears seemed raw tonight.

"Janie Rose *despises* gladioli,'' said Ansel.

James said nothing.

"She hates and despises them. Believes they're witches' wands, all frilled up. She told me so.''

James opened his eyes and rolled over. "Funerals are
for parents," he said. "Ansel, Janie Rose is dead."

He waited, frowning. Out of the corner of his eye he
could see the white blur that was Ansel in his underwear, standing before the bureau with his skinny arms
folded across his chest. Finally Ansel said, "I know."

"She's dead."

"I know all about it. Nevertheless, she despises gladioli."

"The funeral is not really for her," James said, and
rolled over again to face the wall. "It don't make any
difference to her about those gladioli."

"*Oh* now," said Ansel. "*Oh* now." He crossed to
his bed, heavily. "It's hard to bury people, Jamie.
Harder than digging a hole in the ground."

"Will you go to bed?"

"They keep popping up again, in a manner of speaking."

James dug his head into his pillow.

"I remember Janie Rose's religious period," Ansel
went on comfortably. "It was a right short one, wouldn't
you know. But she took this tree out back, this scrubby
one she was always drawing flattering pictures of. Ded-
icated it to God, I believe; hung it with tin cans and
popcorn strings. Didn't last but a week; then she was
on to something new. The birds ate the popcorn. But
those tin cans are still rattling at the ends of the branches
when a wind passes through, and Mr. Pike sits out back
all day staring at them. Thought he had placed every
last bit of her in a hole in the ground. Ha."

James reached behind him for the sheet and pulled it
up over his head, making a hood of it. The rustling of
the sheet drowned out everything else, and then when
he was still again the sounds couldn't come through to

him so clearly. The creaking of Ansel's bedsprings when he sat down was muffled and distant, and his voice was thin-sounding.

"I ought to studied botany," he was saying. "Don't you think? All I know about flowers, I ought to studied botany."

James lay still, and stared at the dark vines running up the wallpaper until his eyes ached.

"With Mama it was lilies," said Ansel. "Lord, she hated lilies. All she wanted, she said, was just a cross of—"

"We won't go into that," James told the wallpaper.

"We don't go into *nothing*. Getting so the only safe topic around here is the weather. Well, I was saying. Just a cross of white roses, she wanted. No lilies. And you know what they sent? You know what?"

He waited. The silence stretched on and on. James's arm, pressed beneath his body, began to go to sleep, but he didn't switch positions for fear of breaking the silence. He wiggled his fingers gently, without making a sound.

"Well, they sent lilies," Ansel said finally. "I thought you would have guessed. If you'd been there, I wouldn't have to be telling you all this. But I called you. I called you on the phone and said, 'James,' I said, 'will you kindly come to Mama's funeral?' I called you long distance and person-to-person, Caraway to Larksville. But you never answered me. Just hung up the telephone, neat and quiet. If I was the persistent type, I'd be asking still. I'd ask it today: 'James, will you kindly come to Mama's funeral?' Because you never have answered, never once, not once in all these years. I'll ask it now. James, will you kindly—"

"No, I won't," said James.

Across the room there was a little intake of breath,
quick and sharp, and over behind the Potters' wall the
measured pacing suddenly began again, with the
weighted bathrobe sighing behind it. Ansel lay down
on his bed.

"There's two kinds of sin," he said after a minute.
His voice was directed toward the ceiling now, and
sounded dreamy. "There's general sin and there's private sin. General sin there's commandments against, or
laws, or rules. Private sin's a individual matter. It's
hurting somebody, personally. You hear me? Listen
close now; this is essential. What I chose was a general
sin, that they'll be a long time forgiving. I did all that
drinking, and ran around with that girl that everyone
knew was no good. But what you chose was a private
sin, that they'll *never* forgive. They got hurt personally
by it—you forever running away, and telling them finally what you thought of them and leaving home altogether. Then not coming to the funeral. Think they'll
forgive *that*? No, sir. Me they will cry over in church
and finally forgive, someday. But not you. I'm a very
wise man, every so often."

James didn't say anything. Ansel raised himself up
on one elbow to look over at him, but he stayed within
his hood of sheets. "James?" Ansel said.

"What."

"You don't care *what* I say, do you?"

"Yes," James said.

"Don't it bother you sometimes? Don't you ever think
about it? Here we are. You walked off from them without a backward wave of your hand, and I got thrown
out like an old paper bag. Don't it—"

"Got *what*?" James asked.

"What?"

"You got *what*?"

"Got thrown out, I said, like an old—"

"You never got thrown out," said James.

"I did. Daddy said I was an alcoholic; he said I was—"

"He never said that."

"Well, almost he did. He said, 'Leave this house,' he said. 'You and your drinking and that girl in red pedal pushers, I never want to see you again.' That's what he told me."

James raised himself slightly from beneath the hood of the sheet. He peered across the dark room toward Ansel and said, "Don't you give me that, Ansel."

"What?"

"You *left*. You left, I left. Tell it that way."

"Well, what difference does it make? Who cares?"

"I care," said James. "Do *I* make excuses for leaving? Run out on him or don't run, but don't make it easy on yourself; don't tell me he *kicked* you out."

"Well," Ansel said after a minute, "I was drinking all that—"

"You don't even like the taste of it," said James.

"I do too."

James lay back down and pulled his sheet closer over him, and Ansel's voice rose louder. "It has a *won*derful taste," he said. And then, "Well, maybe he didn't exactly throw me out, but anyhow—"

Up on the tin roof, rain began. It started very gently, pattering in little sharp exclamation points that left spaces for Ansel's voice. "James?" Ansel said.

"Hmm."

"There's one thing I don't get, James. It was *you* they liked best. The others weren't nothing special, and I was so runny-nosed. I had a runny nose from the moment I was born, I think, and pinkish eyes. One time I heard Daddy say, 'Well, if there's ever a prize for sheer *sniveliness* given, he'll take it,' and Mama said, 'Hush now. Maybe he'll grow out of it.' They didn't think I heard them, but I did.''

''They didn't mean that,'' said James.

''You know they did. But *you* they liked; why did you leave? Why didn't you come to the funeral? I said, 'Daddy,' I said, 'you want I should ask James to Mama's funeral?' 'Which James is that?' he asks. 'James your *son*,' I tell him. And he says, 'Oh. Oh, why, anything you want to, Ansel.' This was when I was still home and they had hopes I would change my ways; they let me do some things I wanted. I called and said, 'James, will you kindly come to Mama's funeral?' Then he asked what happened. 'Ansel,' he said, 'did you invite that person you had mentioned previously?' And I said no, figuring it was better that way. Daddy said, 'He wouldn't have come. He was born that way,' he said, 'lacking our religion. There was no sense asking him.' ''

The rain grew louder. Now it was one steady booming against the sheets of tin, and all of Ansel that could be heard was his words; the quality of his voice was drowned out.

''I'm going back there sometime,'' he was saying. ''They'll forget, and I'll go back. I crave a religious atmosphere.'' He lay back down and James nodded to himself, thinking maybe he would be sleepy now. ''Churches here are somewhat lacking, I think,'' Ansel went on. ''Quiet-like. At home it was better. Mrs. Crowley spoke in tongues. There was things that bound you there. A red glass on the windowsill in the choir loft, with something brown rising above it like the head of a beer. I think now it was wax, and the glass was a sort of candle. But before I thought it was a sort of brown fungus, some kind of mold just growing and growing. Do you remember, James?'' He waited a minute. *"James?"* he said, and now his voice rose even above the roaring of the rain.

"No, I don't,'' James said.

"Sometimes I think your mind is just a clean, clean slate, James.''

"I keep it that way,'' said James.

"You do. I bet when I go back you won't even miss me. I'll go and bring presents. A natural-bristle hairbrush for each sister and a table game for Claude, and a French briar pipe for Daddy. Flowers for the grave and a set of them new, unbreakable dishes to go in the kitchen. A conch shell with the crucifixion inside to make up for that one you dropped, and a crane-necked reading lamp . . .''

The rain roared on, and James listened to that with all his mind. He thought it was the best sound he had heard all day. The heavy feeling was beginning to fade away, and the rain was lulling him to sleep.

". . . a new swing,'' Ansel was saying, "though none of us would use it now, I reckon. Before, it was a tire we swung on. It was all right and it went high enough, but there wasn't no comfortable way to sit in it. Inside it, your legs got pinched. Straddled above it, you'd be dizzy in no time what with all that spinning. 'Stop!' you'd say, and cling like a monkey on a palm tree while everybody laughed . . .''

8

On Tuesday morning, Mr. Pike was the second person awake. He arrived in the kitchen wearing his work clothes and carrying a nylon mesh cap, and when he sat down at the table he sat heavily, stamping his boots together in front of him and scraping the chair across the linoleum. "I'm picking tobacco today," he told Joan. Joan was at the stove, peering into the glass knob on top of the percolator to see what color the coffee was. When her uncle made his announcement she said nothing, because she was thinking of other things, but then she turned and saw him looking at her expectantly.

"I'm sorry?" she said.

"I'm going to pick tobacco," he repeated.

"Oh. All right."

But he still seemed to be waiting for something. He folded his big bony hands on the table and leaned toward her, watching, but Joan couldn't think what was expected of her. She picked the coffeepot off the stove and carried it over to the sink, in order to dump the grounds.

"We need the money," her uncle said.

Joan shook the grounds into the garbage pail, holding

127

the coffee-basket by the tips of her fingers so as not to get burned.

"Well, *some*time I got to start work," he said.

"Of course you do, Uncle Roy."

"Things are getting worse and worse in this house. I thought they'd get better."

"Pretty soon they will."

"I wonder, now."

He watched as Joan set his cup of coffee before him. She handed him the sugar bowl but he just stared at it, as if he'd never seen one before.

"Sugar?" Joan prodded him.

He shook his head, and she set the bowl down at his elbow.

"It's no good sitting in a *room* all my life," he said.

"Drink your coffee," Joan told him. She poured a cup for herself and then sat down opposite him hitching up the knees of her blue jeans. Her eyes were still foggy from sleep and things came through to her blurred, in shining patterns—the blocks of sunlight across the worn linoleum, the graduated circles of Mrs. Pike's saucepan set hanging on the wall, the dark slouched waiting figure of her uncle. When she stirred her coffee with a kitchen knife that was handy, the reflection of the sunshine on the blade flashed across the wall like a fish in a pool and her uncle shifted his eyes to that. He watched like a person hypnotized. She set the knife down and the reflection darted to a point high on the wall near the ceiling, and he stared upward at it.

"You going to want sandwiches?" she asked.

He didn't answer. She took a sip of her coffee, but it was tasteless and heavy and she set the cup down again. "Putting my foot down," her uncle mumbled. Joan drew lines on the tablecloth with her thumbnail. Out-

side a bird began singing, bringing back all the spots
and patches of restless dreams she had had last night,
in between long periods of lying awake and turning her
pillow over and over to find a cool place. Ever since the
rain stopped those birds had been singing. She rubbed
her fingers across her eyelids and saw streaks of red and
purple behind them.

"In regard to sandwiches," her uncle said suddenly,
"I don't want them. I'll come home for lunch."

"All right."

"*Least* I can do."

"All right."

"What's the matter with *you*?" he asked, and reached
finally for the sugar bowl. "You mad I'm picking tobacco?"

"No, I think it's the best thing you could do. Don't
forget to tell James he won't need to work today."

"I thought you'd do that," said Mr. Pike.

"You can."

"You're not working today; you can spare a minute."

"No, I'd rather you do it."

"*Oh* now," Mr. Pike said suddenly. "You two have
a fight?"

Joan took another sip of coffee. It still had no taste.
A hummingbird swooped down to the window and just
hung there, suspended like a child's bird-on-a-string,
its small eyes staring curiously in and its little heart
beating so close and fast they could see the pulsing
underneath the feathers. Mr. Pike gazed at it absently.

"I never *did* hold with long engagements," he said.

"What?"

"Longer the engagement, the more time for fights.
Shouldn't allow it, Joan."

"I'm not engaged," Joan said shortly. "And anyway,

it's none of *my* doing.'' Her uncle looked away from the hummingbird and frowned at her.

''I don't know about that,'' he said. ''And I'll tell you. Some men need a little shove.''

''I don't believe in shoving.''

''Only way, sometimes. I ever tell you how I came to marry your aunt?''

''I'm not in the mood for that,'' said Joan.

''I was only going to mention.''

''No, I don't want to hear,'' she said, and pictured suddenly her aunt, no longer young, lying so still upstairs. ''*You* go tell James,'' she said.

''Aw, Joan.''

''Someone has to.''

''Aw, Joan, you know how it is. I'll go over and there will be Ansel, all talkative and cheerful. Cheerful in the morning—can you feature that?''

''Maybe he's still asleep,'' Joan said.

''Ansel? No. I heard him come in long after midnight just singing away, and I reckon he sang all night and is singing still. Where's Simon?''

''In bed.''

''Been days since I seen that boy. Send *him* over.''

''He won't go either.''

''Look,'' said Mr. Pike. He stood up, jarring the table, and the hummingbird flew away without even preparing to go. ''I can't see Ansel today,'' he said. ''I don't know why but he gets under my skin nowadays. Will you *please* go?''

''Oh, all right,'' Joan said.

''All right, that's settled. Thank you very much.''

He sat down again, and Joan went back to looking at the patterns in the kitchen. Everything she saw made her homesick, but not for any home she'd ever had. The sunlight on the linoleum reminded her of something long ago and lost; yet she had never lived in a house with a linoleum kitchen, never in all her memory. She kept staring at the design of it, the speckled white floor with bars of red and blocks of blue splashed across it, and the sun lighting up the dents and scrapes made by kitchen chairs. Finally she looked away and into her uncle's frowning, leather-brown face, but her uncle only said, "We need the money," so she looked away again. Her coffee had cooled, and the surface of it was greasy-looking. She drank it anyway.

When her uncle was through with his coffee he pushed the cup toward the center of the table and rose, clamping the mesh cap on the back of his head. "You can take care of things here, I guess," he said.

"Yes."

"I'll be running along, then."

He clomped off toward the front of the house, swinging his boots in that heavy way that Simon always tried to copy. His steps made the whole floor shake. She heard the screen door swing open with a twang of its spring and then slam shut again, rattling on its hinges. Then the clomping continued across the porch, and she waited for the extra-heavy sound of his boots descending the wooden steps to the yard but it didn't come. "Joan?" he called.

"What."

"*Joan!*"

She rose and went out front, wondering why men always had to shout from where they were instead of coming closer. Her uncle was standing on the edge of the porch with his back to the house and his cap off, scratching the back of his head. "What is it?" she asked him, and he turned toward her.

"Well, I already informed your aunt," he said, "but I'm not certain she heard."

"Informed her about what?"

"About my working. But I'm not certain she heard. Will you tell her again?"

"All right," said Joan.

"Say we need the money, tell her. Say I'm sorry."

"All right, Uncle Roy."

"I can't sit looking at *trees* all my life."

"No, I know," said Joan, and reached out to give his shoulder one gentle push so that he would turn and leave. He did, still frowning. Then halfway across the yard he slapped his cap back on his head and thrust his hands in his pockets and began walking more briskly, getting ready to go out into the world again. Joan watched after him till he was out of the yard, and then she went down toward the Greens' end of the porch.

Ansel was in his window, chewing sunflower seeds. He looked very happy. He spit the hulls out on the porch floor and then leaned over, his hands on the windowsill and his elbows jutting behind him like bird wings, and tried to blow the hulls all the way across the porch and into the yard. Joan wished he would fall out. She stood over him with her hands on her hips and waited until he had straightened up again, and then she said, "Ansel."

"Morning, Joan."

"Ansel, will you give James a message?"

"If I can remember it," said Ansel. "My health is poorly this morning. Seems to be growing worse and worse."

"Doesn't look to me you could *get* much worse," Joan said.

"At least you noticed. James just don't even care. He's in an ill mood today."

Joan gave up on him and stepped over to the door and knocked. For a minute Ansel stared out his window at her, puzzling this over; then he shrugged and withdrew. He came to the door and opened it with a flourish.

"Morning, Joan," he said.

"Where's James?"

"Ain't seen you in a long time. James? He's in the back yard, emptying out the garbage."

"Will you tell him he doesn't have to work today? Make up your mind, now. If you're planning to forget I'll just do it myself."

"Oh, I'll tell him," Ansel said. "Come in and set, why don't you. Old James'll be back any minute."

"No, thank you," said Joan.

"Well, suit yourself." He yawned. "Saw your uncle go off to work this morning," he said. "Seems kind of soon for him to be doing that, don't it?"

"No."

"Well, I just thought I'd point it out." He yawned again and fished another sunflower seed from the packet in his hand. The shirt he had on was James's, she saw. It was a dark red plaid and hung too loosely on him. She stared at it a minute and then, without a word, turned and went back up the porch. "Hey!" Ansel called after her, but Joan was inside her own parlor by now, letting the door slam shut behind her.

Upstairs, Simon was sound asleep, with his pajamaed legs sprawled and all his covers kicked loose from the foot of the bed. Joan went over and touched him gently, just on the outflung, curled-in palm of his hand. He

stirred a little and then mumbled and turned away from
her.

"Get up, Simon," she said.

"I *am* up. I am."

"Come on."

"I'm half dressed already. I got my—"

"Simon."

He opened his eyes. "Oh light," he said, and Joan
smiled and sat down on the bed beside him.

"I got something I want to talk over," she told him.

"Okay."

"You listening?"

"I just can't find any clean jeans," he said, and
closed his eyes and was asleep again. Joan picked up
his hand and shook it, but it hung loose and limp.

"Simon, this is about your mother," she said.

"I'm listening."

"I think your mother should start working today."

He turned over and squinted at her, through foggy
brown eyes. "What at?" he asked.

"At her sewing. I want you to stay around and help
with the conversation, all right? Missouri says I'm no
walking newspaper."

"What?"

"Will you help me out?"

"Oh, why, sure," Simon said, and would have been
asleep again if Joan hadn't pulled him to a sitting position. He stayed there, slumped between her hands,
with his head drooping to one side. "I was in this
boat," he said.

"Come on, Simon."

"Then we started sinking. They told me I was the
one that had to swim for it. Do you believe that'll happen someday?"

"No," said Joan, and pulled hard on him till he was standing beside the bed.

"They say everything you dream will happen," Simon told her. "It's true. Last year I dreamed Mama would find out about me smoking and sure enough, that night at supper there was my half-pack of Winstons lying beside my plate and Mama staring at me. It came true."

He bent down to examine a stubbed toe and Joan stood up, preparing to go. "You come down when you're dressed," she said.

"I don't have any clean jeans to wear."

"That's just something you said in your sleep. You have lots of jeans."

"No, really I don't," Simon said. "No one's been doing the laundry."

Joan crossed to his bureau and pulled open his bottom drawer. It was bare except for a pair of bermudas. "Oh, Lord," she said. "I forgot all about the laundry."

"I told you you did."

"Well, wear bermudas till this afternoon, why don't you. By then I'll have you some jeans."

"Have my *knees* show?" Simon asked.

"What's wrong with that?"

"Boys don't *have* their knees out any more. You ought to know that."

"Well, la de da," said Joan, and rumpled the top of his hair. "Wear a pair of *dirty* jeans, then."

"They'd all call me sissy if my knees showed."

"All right. Hurry up, now."

She closed the door behind her and went downstairs. In the parlor she sat down on a faded plush footstool and reached for the telephone, which sat on a table

beside her. She hooked the receiver over her shoulder
and then opened the telephone book to the very back,
where there was space for frequently used numbers.
The page was filled to the bottom, and looked messy
because of so many different handwritings. Mr. Pike
had listed the names of bowling pals in a careful,
downward-slanting script, and Simon had scrawled the
names of all his classmates even though he never talked
to them by telephone, and Janie Rose had printed names
in huge capitals that took two lines, after asking several
times how to spell each one—the four little Marsh girls,
each listed separately, and the milkman who had once
brought her a yellow plastic ring from a chicken's leg,
which she had worn every day until she lost it. Mrs.
Pike's handwriting was small and pretty, every letter
slanting to the same degree, naming off her steady customers one by one with little memos to herself about
colors and pattern numbers penciled in lightly beside
them. Joan went down the list alphabetically. Mrs. Abbott, who never talked. Mrs. Chrisawn, who was in
such a black mood most of the time. Davis, Forsyth,
Hammond . . . She stopped there. Connie Hammond
was always good to have around during a tragedy. She
brought chicken broth whether people wanted it or not,
and she knew little things like how to make a bed with
someone in it and what to say when no one else could
think of anything. As far as Joan was concerned, having
a person talk incessantly would be more harm than help;
but her aunt felt differently. Her aunt had actually sat
up and answered, the last time Connie Hammond came.
So Joan smoothed the phone book out on her knees and
dialed the Hammonds' number.

Mrs. Hammond was talking to somebody else when

she answered. She said, "If that's not the *worst* thing—" and then into the phone, "Hello?"

"Mrs. Hammond, this is Joan Pike," said Joan.

"Why, Joan, honey, how *are* you?" Mrs. Hammond said, and then softened her shrill voice to ask, "How's your poor aunt?"

"Well, that's what I wanted to talk to you about," said Joan. She spoke at some distance from the receiver, in case Mrs. Hammond should grow shrill again.

"What's that you say?"

"I said I wanted to *talk* to you about that. Aunt Lou is just miserable."

"Oh, my." There was a rustling sound as Mrs. Hammond cupped her hand over the receiver and turned away. "Lou Pike is just *miserable*," she told someone. Her hand uncupped the receiver again and she returned, breathless, to Joan. "Joan, honey, I told Mr. Hammond, just last night. I said, I haven't ever *seen* someone take on so. Well, of course she has good reason to but the things she *says*, Joan. It wasn't her fault; it was that noaccount Ned Marsh who did it. How he manages to drive even a *tractor* recklessly is more than I can—"

"Um," Joan said, and Mrs. Hammond stopped speaking and snapped her mouth shut audibly, to show she had been interrupted. "Um, she hasn't even gotten up today. She's still in bed. And Uncle Roy's at the tobacco barns—"

"The where?"

"Tobacco barns. Working tobacco."

"Why, that man," said Mrs. Hammond.

"Well, he can't just sit staring at the *trees* all—"

"He could comfort his wife," Mrs. Hammond said.

"She won't listen. So I was thinking, as long as he's away today—"

"Men are like that," Mrs. Hammond said. "Work is all they think about."

"As long as he *is* at work," Joan said firmly, "I think maybe Aunt Lou should start working too."

"Working?"

"Working at sewing. Missouri said—"

"Mrs. *who*?"

"Mrs.—never mind. Wait a minute." Joan switched ears and leaned forward, as if Mrs. Hammond could see her now from where she stood. "Mrs. Hammond," she said, "I know how good you are at helping other people."

"Oh, why, I just—"

"I know you could help Aunt Lou right now, if anybody could. You could bring that dress she was working on, that—was it purple?"

"Lilac," said Mrs. Hammond. "Princess style."

"That's the one."

"Lou said it would add to my height a little, a princess style would."

"That's right," Joan said. "That's the one."

"Especially since it has up-and-down pinstripes."

"Yes. Well, I was thinking. If you could just bring it over and get her to work on it for you, just take her mind off all the—"

"You might be right," said Mrs. Hammond. "Why didn't I think of that? Why, the day before the funeral, when I came—*you* remember—I did feel she was doing wrong to sit so quiet. I said so. I have always believed that baking calms the nerves, so I said to her, 'Lou,' I said, 'why don't you make some rolls?' But she looked at me as if I'd lost my senses. After all, I'd just *brought* two dozen, and a cake besides. Yet I felt she ought to be doing something; that's what I was trying to tell her. You just might be right, Joan.''

"Well, then," said Joan, "do you think you could come over sometime today?"

"I'll come over right this minute. I just wouldn't feel at rest until I had. You say your aunt's still in bed?"

"She was a minute ago," Joan said.

"Well, you try and get her up, and I'll be there as fast as I can find the dress. I'll be there, don't you worry.''

"All right," Joan said. "It certainly is nice of you to come, Mrs. Hammond.''

"Well. Goodbye, now.''

"Goodbye.''

Joan hung up and sat back to rub her ear, which felt squashed. Now that all that was settled, the next step was to get Simon downstairs. He would have to back her up in this.

Simon was standing in front of his mirror when Joan came in. He was wearing blue jeans but no shirt, and scratching his stomach absently. "Hey," Joan said, and he jumped and looked up at her. "Find yourself a shirt," she told him. "Connie Hammond's coming."

"Aw, gee, Joan. Mrs. *Hammond*?"

"She'll be here any minute. Come on, now. It's a special favor to your mother.''

"I bet she'll never notice," Simon said, but he pulled a bureau drawer open. Joan closed the door and went on to her aunt's room.

Mrs. Pike was sitting up against two pillows, fat and soft in a gray nylon nightgown. She had her hands folded across her stomach and was looking vaguely at the two points her feet made underneath the bedspread.

"Good morning," Joan said, and Mrs. Pike raised her eyes silently and peered at her as if she were trying to pierce her way through mist. But she never answered. After a minute her eyes passed on to something else, dismissing Joan like the wrong answer to a question she had asked. Joan came to stand at the foot of the bed.

"Aunt Lou," she said, "would you like to get up?"

Her aunt shook her head.

"Mrs. Hammond's coming. Do you want her to find you in bed?"

"No," said Mrs. Pike, but she didn't do anything about it. She settled lower into the pillows, with her eyes worrying at the wallpaper now, and in so much dim clutter she appeared to be sinking, overcome by the objects around her. Under Joan's feet were cast-off clothes, everywhere, everything her aunt had been persuaded to put on in the last few days. She had stepped out of them and left them there, returning wearily to her gray nightgown. Mr. Pike, on the other hand, had made some effort at neatness. He had laid his clothes awkwardly on the back of the platform rocker, where they rose in a layered mountain that seemed huge and overwhelming in the half-dark. On the bureau were hairbrushes and bobby pins and old coffee cups with dark rings inside them. The sight of it all made Joan feel caved in and despairing, and she went over to raise the window shade but the light only picked up more clutter. "Aunt Lou," she said, "we just have to get organized here."

"What?"

"We have to start cleaning things up."

Her aunt nodded, without seeming to pay attention, but then she surprised Joan by moving over to the edge of the bed and standing up. She stood in that old woman's way she had just acquired—searching out the floor with anxious feet, rising slowly and heavily. For a minute she stood there, and then she shook her nightgown out around her and faltered toward the bureau. "I'm going to clean up," she told Joan.

"That's it."

But all Mrs. Pike did, once she reached the bureau, was to stare into the mirror. She put both hands on the bureau top and leaned forward, frowning into her own eyes. The alarm clock in front of her ticked loudly, and she reached out without looking to set it farther away. "Some people stop all the clocks when someone dies," she said.

"What're you going to wear, Aunt Lou?"

"If Connie Hammond's coming, why, she'll have to turn around and go off again."

"What *dress* are you going to wear?" Joan asked, and the sharpness of her voice made Mrs. Pike sigh and stand up straight again.

"Any one will do," she said. She pulled out a small plastic box from a half-open drawer and began putting bobby pins into it. One by one she scraped them off the top of the dresser, working like a blind woman with careful fingers while she kept her eyes on the mirror. Joan watched, not moving. Each bobby pin made a little clinking sound against the bottom of the plastic box, and each time the sound came Mrs. Pike winced into the mirror. "My *grand*mother stopped all the clocks," she said. "She would also announce the death to each fruit tree, so that they wouldn't shrivel up. But we don't have no fruit trees." Her fingers slid slowly across the bureau top, and when she found that all the bobby pins were picked up she closed the box and set it down again. Then she went back to bed. She tucked her feet down

under the covers and drew the top sheet with great care
over her chest.

"No, wait," Joan said.

"I did what I could, Joan."

Joan went over to the closet and pulled out the first
thing she touched, a navy blue dress with white polka
dots. "Is this all right?" she asked.

"No."

"This, then." And she lifted a brown dress from its
hanger and laid it on the bed without waiting for an
answer. "It's the prettiest one you've got," she said.

Outside, a car screeched to a halt and sent up a spray
of gravel that Joan could hear from where she stood.
She looked out and saw Mrs. Hammond's Pontiac
swerving backwards into the yard with one sharp turn
of the wheel, while Mrs. Hammond herself remained
rigidly facing forward. The car came to rest right beside
James's pickup, within an inch of running over Simon's
bicycle. Then Mrs. Hammond shot out, clutching bits
of cloth and tissue paper to her chest and leaving the
car door open behind her. All she needed was an ambulance siren. Joan leaned out the window and called,
"Mrs. Hammond?" and Mrs. Hammond looked up,
with her face startled and worried-looking.

"Just walk on in and come upstairs," Joan told her.
"Aunt Lou's in bed still."

"Oh. All right."

She bent her head over her armload of cloth and
started running again, and Joan could hear her quick
sharp heels along the porch and then inside, across the
parlor floor and up the stairs. "Oh, law," she was saying to no one. She sounded out of breath.

But Mrs. Pike didn't say a word to all this. She just
lay back against the pillows and folded her arms across

her stomach again, her face expressionless. When Mrs. Hammond burst into the room and said, "Why, *Lou!*" as if Mrs. Pike had somehow taken her by surprise, Mrs. Pike only nodded gently and watched the wallpaper. "Lou?" said Mrs. Hammond.

"She was just now getting up," Joan told her.

"Well, I'll help. That's what I came for." She set her load down on the dresser and peered into the mirror a second, pushing back a wisp of hair, and then she came over to sit on the edge of the bed. Every move she made was definite; now that she was here, the room seemed to lose its swampiness. Her face was carefully made up to cover the little lines around her mouth, and she was packed into a nice summery sheath that Mrs. Pike had made two years ago. The sight of so much neatness made Mrs. Pike sit up straighter and pull her stomach in, even though her face stayed blank.

"I was talking about stopping all the clocks," she told Mrs. Hammond.

"*Oh*, no."

"I've about decided to do it."

"Oh, no. I don't think that's necessary."

But Mrs. Pike said, "Yes. I don't know why I didn't think of it before."

"It depends on the type," Mrs. Hammond said. "Ormolu, for instance, or mahogany—that you would stop. But those are the only kind. Isn't that so, Joan?"

Joan hadn't heard that before, but she said, "Well, yes," and Mrs. Hammond beamed at her and rocked gently on the bed.

"Only if it's *ornamental*," she told Mrs. Pike.

"Oh. I didn't know that."

"You wouldn't stop a Baby *Ben* or anything."

"No."

"Do you want to get up?"

"Connie, I just can't," Mrs. Pike said. "I just don't have it in me. You're going to have to go off again."

"Oh, now." Mrs. Hammond shook her head and then began examining the room, as if anything Mrs. Pike said was to be expected and she was just planning to wait till it was over. "This place could use a bit of cleaning," she said. "Also, if I was you I'd add some patches of color to it. You know? I put an orange candlestick in Mr. Hammond's brown den and it just changed the whole atmosphere. He don't like it, but you'd be amazed at the difference it makes."

"I don't care about any of that," Mrs. Pike said distinctly.

"Now, Lou."

"I just want to sleep a while."

"After you make up my lilac dress, I'll let you sleep all you like," said Mrs. Hammond. "I need it for a party."

She stood up and went over to the bureau, where she pulled open the top left drawer as if she knew by instinct where Mrs. Pike kept her underwear. From a stack on the right she took a nylon slip and held it up to the mirror. "Oh, my, how pretty!" she said, and tossed it in the direction of the bed. Mrs. Pike caught it in her lap and stared at it.

From across the hall came the clattering sound of Simon's walk, closer and closer. He had his boots on now. When he reached his mother's door he walked on in without knocking and said, "I'm ready." Then he stood there at the foot of the bed, tilting back and forth in that awkward way he had and keeping his hands jammed tightly in his pockets.

"What're you ready for?" Mrs. Hammond asked interestedly.

"To be sociable at the sewing," Simon told her. "Would you like to know what was the cause of that fight Andy Point's mama and daddy had?"

"In a minute I would," said Mrs. Hammond. "Right now I'm trying to get your mother out of bed."

For the first time, Simon looked at his mother. He looked from under bunched eyebrows, sliding his eyes over slowly and carefully. But she wasn't watching. He kicked at one leg of the brass bed, so that a little jingling sound rose among the springs. Then he said, "Well, I'll be down getting me some breakfast," and sauntered out again. Mrs. Hammond looked after him and shook her head.

"Something is seriously wrong with that boy's hair," she told Mrs. Pike.

"No."

"How long you going to keep on like this, Lou?"

Mrs. Pike looked down at her hands and then shook her head, as if that were her secret. "Are you *sure* not to stop the clocks?" she asked, but Mrs. Hammond didn't answer. She had picked out the rest of Mrs. Pike's underwear, and she tossed it on the bed and then reached out to pull her gently to a sitting position. "That's it," she said. To Joan she said, "You go along and get that boy a decent breakfast. I'll have her down in a minute."

It didn't look to Joan as if they'd *ever* be down, but she was glad to leave the room. She shut the door behind her and descended the stairs quickly, taking two steps at a time, trailing her fingers along the railing. When she reached the kitchen Simon had already taken out the makings for a peanut butter and mayonnaise sandwich. He was running his thumbnail around the edge of the mayonnaise label, making little ripples in it. "Would you like some milk coffee?" she asked him, but he only shook his head. He stopped playing with the label and opened the jar, and Joan handed him a knife.

"From now on, I'm going on no more boats," he said. "I take *stock* in dreams."

"That's kind of silly," said Joan.

"I know when I been warned."

He slapped mayonnaise on top of peanut butter and clamped the two slices of bread together. Then he began to eat, starting with the crust and working his way around until all he had was a small crustless square with scalloped edges. When that point was reached he looked relieved, because he hated crusts. He took a bite out of what was left and began talking with his mouth full.

"Instead of staying here," he said, "I just might go on over to Billy's house. His daddy gave him a chemistry set." He looked up at Joan, but she didn't say anything. "I might do that instead of staying around here talking," he told her.

"Well, suit yourself," said Joan.

"*Mama'd* never notice."

"Sure, she would."

"I bet not."

Joan went over to the cupboard and took down a huge plate, a green glass one that looked like summer and river-water. She began laying out cookies and cakes on it, choosing from boxes that neighbors had brought, while Simon watched her and chewed earnestly through a mouthful of peanut butter. When Joan was finished she stepped back and looked at the cake plate with her eyes squinted a little.

"Aunt Lou does it better," she said.

"Oh, I don't know."

"She puts it in a design, sort of."

"One thing," said Simon, "she don't ever lay out that *much*. Not with just one customer, she don't."

"That's true."

"She uses that little clear sparkly plate."

"Well, it's too late now," Joan said. She picked up the plate and carried it out to the parlor, where she set it on a lampstand by the couch. Then she swung her aunt's sewing machine out into the middle of the room. It was the old kind, run by a treadle, set into a long scarred table. From one of the drawers underneath it she took her aunt's wicker spool box, and while she was doing that she heard the slow careful steps of Mrs. Pike beginning across the upstairs hall. *"That's* it," Mrs. Hammond was saying, *"That's* it." The kitchen door swung open and Simon came out, chewing on the last of his sandwich, to stand at the foot of the stairs and gaze upward. "Mama's coming down," he told Joan.

"I see she is."

"First time she's come before noon. How long have I got to stay here?"

"You don't have to stay at all."

"Well, maybe I will for a minute," said Simon. He swung away from the stairs and went to sit on the couch, and Mrs. Pike's feet began searching their way down the steps. "That's it," Mrs. Hammond kept saying. Joan pulled a chair up to the sewing machine and then stood waiting, with her face turned toward the sound of those heels.

When Mrs. Pike appeared she was dressed more neatly than she had been in days. Her brown dress was freshened up with a flowered handkerchief in the pocket, and her hair was combed by someone who knew how. The only thing wrong was that she had lost some weight, and her belt, which had had its eyelets torn into long slashes from being strained across her stomach, now hung loose and stringy a good two inches below the waist of the dress. Mrs. Hammond was following close behind her to pull the belt up from in the back, so that at least it looked right in front, but it kept slipping down again. "Doesn't she look *nice*?" Mrs. Hammond asked, and both Joan and Simon nodded.

In Mrs. Hammond's other hand was the bundle of cloth and tissue paper. She escorted Mrs. Pike to the chair Joan had ready and then she set the bundle down on the sewing table beside her, saying, "There you are," and stepping back to see what Mrs. Pike would do. Mrs. Pike didn't do anything. She looked at the lilac cloth as if she'd never seen it before. "Well, now," said Mrs. Hammond, and began opening out the bundle herself. "If you'll remember, you cut this out back in May, before all that business about Laura's wedding came up, and I haven't tried it on since. Joan honey, do you want to bring your aunt some coffee and a roll?"

"I'm not hungry," said Mrs. Pike.

But Joan escaped to the kitchen anyway, while Mrs. Hammond went on talking. "I've been on a tomato diet for three weeks," she was saying, "all in honor of this princess-style dress. So now, Lou, I want you to pin it on me again. Don't make it an inch too big, because I want to lose five *more* pounds, Lord willing—"

Joan took two cups and saucers down and set them on a tray. Then she poured out the coffee, taking her time because she was in no hurry to get back to the parlor. When the last possible thing had been seen to, she picked up the tray and carried it out.

"The older you get," Mrs. Hammond was saying, "the harder the fat clings." She had patches of lilac pinned on over her regular dress now, but she was more or less doing it herself. Mrs. Pike just kept smoothing down the already pinned-on patches, running her fingers along the cloth with vague fumbling motions. "There's only four pieces," Mrs. Hammond reminded her. "Plus the pocket. Where's the pocket? You remember that's one reason we decided on this. You could whip it up in a morning, you said. Do you remember?"

In the silence that followed the question Joan set the coffee down by the cake plate and passed the two cups over. Her aunt's she put on the table, and Mrs. Hammond's she placed on the chair arm, but neither woman noticed. Mrs. Pike seemed fascinated by the little wheel on her sewing machine. Mrs. Hammond was waiting endlessly, with her hands across her breasts to keep the lilac cloth in place. She seemed to be planning to keep silent forever, if she had to, just so that one question of hers could be answered. But Mrs. Pike might not even have heard.

Then Simon said, "Um, why Andy Point's parents won't *speak* to each other—" and Mrs. Hammond looked up at him. "Why they sit in their parlor in chairs faced back to back," he said, "all dates back to Sunday a week. Least that's what Andy says. But I couldn't hardly believe it, it was such a little thing that set them fighting."

"It's nearly always little things," said Mrs. Hammond. Mrs. Pike nodded and took a packet of pins out of her spool box.

"They were on their way to church, see," Simon said. "Andy was along. They made him come. When suddenly they passed this sign saying, 'Craig Church two miles, visitors welcome,' Mrs. Point she said, 'Why, I never have seen *that* before.' Just being conversational. And *Mr.* Point says, 'Well, I don't know why not. It's been there a year or more,' he says. 'No it ain't,' Mrs. Point says. 'Yes, it has,' Mr. Point says . . ."

"Well, now, isn't that typical," said Mrs. Hammond. She turned slightly, but Mrs. Pike pulled her back again to pin two pieces of cloth together at the waist. Mrs. Pike's mouth was full of pins, and her eyes were frowning at everything her fingers did.

"So anyway," Simon said, "that was what began it. Andy says he never saw such a thing. He says they've even had to order another newspaper subscription, because they wouldn't share the one between them."

"If that isn't the limit," said Mrs. Hammond. "Ouch, Lou."

"Oh, I'm sorry," said Mrs. Pike. Everyone looked toward her, but she only went on pinning and didn't say any more, so Mrs. Hammond took up where she had left off.

"What doesn't make sense," she told Simon, "is Mary Point's *nature*. She's not the type to bear a grudge."

"Oh, it won't her fault," said Simon. "Andy says she had forgot about it. She just went on into church and never thought a thing about it. But then at dinner, Mr. Point wouldn't eat what she had cooked and made himself a sandwich right after. That's a sign he's mad. Mrs. Point said, 'Andy,' she said, 'I'll be. Is your daddy mad about something?' And Andy said, 'Well, I reckon he's mad you said that sign wasn't there.' So she said,

'Oh, I had forgot all about that,' but then it was too late. Now she's mad at him for being mad, and it don't look like it's ever going to end.''

''You haven't lost a pound,'' Mrs. Pike said. She had finished pinning the pieces together now, and she was shaking her head at how tightly they fit.

''I have too,'' said Mrs. Hammond. ''You allow a good inch for the dress I'm wearing underneath it, Lou.'' She acted as if it were perfectly natural that Mrs. Pike was speaking, but right on the tail of her words she shot Joan a meaningful glance. Joan nodded, although privately she didn't feel too sure of anything yet. But Simon kept on bravely, with his hands clutching the edge of the couch and his eyes on his mother, even though it was Mrs. Hammond he was speaking to.

''I asked him,'' he said. ''I asked, 'Andy, how you think you're going to *end* it?' And Andy says, 'Same way it started, I reckon. By accident.' ''

''Well, no,'' said Mrs. Pike, and once again everyone's attention was on her alone. She removed the pins from her mouth and laid them on the sewing table, and then she said, ''It's not that easy. Why sure, one of them might speak by accident. Mary might. Then Sid might answer, being glad she'd spoken first, but by then Mary would have caught herself. She'd feel silly to speak first, and only snap his head off then. It's not that easy.''

''No, you're right,'' said Mrs. Hammond, and Joan thought she would have agreed no matter what her aunt had said. ''You have to think about the—''

The telephone rang. Mrs. Hammond stopped speaking, and Simon leaped over to pick up the receiver. ''Hello?'' he said. ''What?'' He was silent a minute,

"No, I knew about it. I knew, I just forgot. Well, thank you anyway. Bye." He hung up.

"Who was that?" asked Mrs. Hammond.

"Just that station."

"What?"

"Just that radio station. They got this jackpot on. They call you up and if you don't say, 'Hello,' if you say instead, 'I am listening to WKKJ, the all-day swinging station—' "

"*I've* heard about that," Mrs. Hammond said.

"If he'd just called before, boy. It's not *me* who was prepared for them to—"

Mrs. Pike's spool box went clattering on the floor. All the colors of thread went every which-way, rolling out their tails behind them, and Mrs. Hammond said, "Why, Lou," but Mrs. Pike didn't answer. She had crumpled up against her sewing machine, leaning her forehead against the wheel of it and clenching both fists tightly against her stomach. *"Lou!"* Mrs. Hammond said sharply. She looked at Joan and Simon, and they stared back. "Did something happen?"

"I said something," Simon told her.

Mrs. Hammond kept watching him, but he didn't explain any further. Finally she turned back to Mrs. Pike and said, "Sit up, Lou," and pulled her by the shoulders, struggling against the dead weight of her. "What's the matter?" she asked. She looked into Mrs. Pike's face, at her dry wide eyes and the white mark that the sewing-machine wheel had made down the center of her forehead. "What's the matter?" she asked again. But Mrs. Pike only rocked back and forth, and Simon and Joan stared at the floor.

9

All Tuesday morning, Ansel had visitors. The first one was Joan. She mustn't have stayed long because she came and went while James was emptying the garbage, which only took a minute. When he returned Ansel said, "Joan's been here," and then dumped a cupped handful of sunflower hulls into an ashtray and sat down to read the paper.

"What'd she want?" James asked.

"Oh, nothing," said Ansel. He opened the paper out and stayed hidden behind it, and with just one tuft of pale hair on the top of his head exposed to view. "You won't have to work tobacco today," he added as an afterthought.

"How's that?"

But Ansel didn't answer. Ever since he had awakened he had been angry; James could tell by his long silences, but he knew there was no point asking what was wrong. So he went on fixing breakfast, and while he was doing that he figured out that Joan must have come to say her uncle was working today. He flipped over a fried egg that was burning and called, "Ansel?"

"Hmmm."

"Is Roy Pike working today?"

But that was another question he never got the answer to. All he heard was the steady thumping of Ansel's foot (Ansel kept time to everything he read, as if it were a poem) and the crackling of newspaper pages. He didn't try asking again.

The second visitor was Maisie Hammond. She came while Ansel was eating breakfast off the Japanese tray, and when she walked in Ansel said, "Um. Maisie," and went on munching on his fried egg. (It was one of those days when James had brought a tray without being asked, simply because it was more comfortable to eat in the kitchen alone. Ansel had said, "*Well*. I see you've taken up cooking again," which hadn't even made sense.) Maisie was wearing a white summer dress with a full skirt, and she stood over his couch like Florence Nightingale and bent down to inspect Ansel's egg. "What's that?" she asked.

"Fried egg, of course."

"It looks kind of funny."

"It's James's," said Ansel.

"Ah." And she turned around, so that now she could see James where he sat eating in the kitchen. "Hey, James," she said.

"Hello, Maisie."

"Taken any pictures lately?"

"No."

That seemed to end the conversation; she turned back to Ansel. "You mind if I sit on your couch?" she asked.

"I'd prefer the armchair."

"Well."

She settled on the very edge of the armchair, spreading her skirt around her. When she bent her head toward Ansel, with the tow-white hair falling over her face, the morning sun seemed to pass right through her hair. She looked like glass. James studied her through the doorway as he munched on a piece of toast, but she didn't look his way again. "I came to ask you to a picnic," she told Ansel.

"Oh, no. Thank you anyway."

"Aunt Connie's giving it."

"Well, it's nice of you to ask," Ansel said.

"Don't you *want* to come?"

"Oh, I can't. James, I'm through with my tray."

"Put it on the table," said James.

"There's too much other stuff there."

James scraped his chair back and went to the living room, still chewing his piece of toast. By the time he reached the couch, Ansel was already preparing to lie down; he held the tray out in one hand, while he swung his feet up onto the couch.

"Ansel won't come to Aunt Connie's picnic," Maisie said.

"That's too bad," said James. He picked the tray up and went back to the kitchen.

"He just won't be reasoned with," Maisie called after him.

"Maybe he don't feel up to it."

"Will you hush?" Ansel asked. "*I'm* not giving any excuses; why should you?"

James made another trip back for the salt and pepper, which were sitting on the arm of the sofa. As he bent to pick them up, Maisie said, "Will you talk to him?"

"Nothing I can say."

"Why doesn't he ever go places?"

"That's *my* secret," Ansel said. They looked at him. He was lying on his back, with his hands crossed over his chest as if he expected to be laid out any minute, and his eyes were staring upwards, wide and blank. But now that he had their attention, all he did was switch his eyes suddenly to the window overhead and say, "Well, now. Yonder goes a jet."

They both waited, still watching him.

"Little white tail behind it," he said finally.

"Are you in some pain?" Maisie asked.

"Well, yes."

She looked across at James. "Ansel's in pain," she told him. But James just sat down on a wooden chair, still holding the salt and pepper, and stretched his legs out comfortably in front of him. If Ansel began an answer by saying, "Well," there was no use believing him.

"What shall I do?" Maisie asked him.

"I don't know."

"Get him a hot water bottle?"

"Hot water bottle on my *feet* won't help," said Ansel.

"Oh. Is it your feet that hurt?"

"I think it is."

"I declare," said Maisie, and then looked at James again, but he didn't offer any suggestions. Finally she said, "Is that why you won't come to the picnic?"

"No."

"It's not till Sunday, you know. You'd be all better by then."

"I just don't want to come," Ansel said. "But thank you anyway."

Maisie couldn't seem to find anything to say to that. She sat there, twisting at the hem of her white skirt, and James began hitting the plastic salt and pepper shakers together until he had worked up to a good rhythm. He was considering starting some more complicated beat when Maisie said, "Will you *stop* that *noise*?"

James stopped. Outside a car suddenly drove up, making a great racket as it skidded to a stop on the gravel road. Maisie stood up and bent forward a little to peer out the window. "It's Aunt Connie," she said.

"Maybe she's come to invite me personally," said Ansel.

"No, she's going toward Mrs. Pike's."

"She won't stay *there* long. Mrs. Pike wants to be by herself."

"Aunt Connie's very cheering," Maisie said.

"Sometimes. *I'm* very cheering, but you know what happened when I—"

"It's Aunt Connie's biggest party of the summer I'm asking you to," Maisie told him. "That's all. The one where she hires the magician and all."

Ansel sighed and looked at the ceiling. After a minute he said, "The actual place it hurts is right behind the anklebones. The pain is awful."

"The anklebones?"

"Last night I walked too much."

"Where'd you walk to?" Maisie asked.

James frowned at Ansel. He didn't want Maisie to hear about last night, not after the scolding she'd given him. But Ansel wasn't looking at James; he went on, placidly.

"I walked just about everywhere," he said. "I thought, 'I got to get out of here. This is no place for me.' I went everywhere I could think of."

"You shouldn't take such strenuous exercise," Maisie said.

"You have no idea how dizzy I was," Ansel told her. "How swimming in the head I was. I couldn't even pack my things. I had to have a little something first to steady my nerves."

"To—oh," Maisie said, and she shot a glance over at James and narrowed her eyes. "Ansel, you *know* what happens. If you get to drinking, you *see* how you feel."

"It was my mood," said Ansel. "I started walking."

James sat forward and said, "There's a pitcher of Kool-Aid in the icebox. Anybody want some?"

"No," Maisie said. "Where were *you* when all this was going on?"

"I was working," said James. He stood up, before she had a chance to say any more. "I've got to go see Dan at the paper. Take him those pictures."

"Well, goodbye," Maisie said, and turned back to Ansel. James was relieved she had let him go that easily.

In the darkroom he got his pictures together—one fire, one family reunion, two ladies' meetings—for this week's paper. Then while he was hunting for a manila envelope he heard a knock on the door. He straightened up and listened (it might be Joan again) but it was only the Potter sisters, dropping in for their biweekly visit to see how Ansel was. He heard their little chirping voices, with Maisie's voice running flatly behind them. "We brought some Jewish grandmother cookies, the kind you like," Miss Lucy said, and Ansel said, "Why, that's real—" "I'll take them," Maisie said. Maisie was always butting in, James thought. He set down his pictures and came out to the living room, just to say hello, and saw that both the Potter sisters were still standing in the doorway while Maisie sat back in her easy chair with a bag of cookies in her lap. "Why don't you sit down?" he asked them, and then the chirping sounds began all over again, and the sisters came toward him with their hands outstretched. They had on those dressy white gloves of theirs with the ruffles around the wrists. Seeing that made him sad—they looked as if they were expecting so much out of the visit, when all they were going to do was sit on the threadbare plush chairs a minute and then go home again. He said, "It's good to see you, Miss Lucy. Miss Faye. Nice of you to bring the cookies."

"We *like* doing it," said Miss Lucy.

"Will you have a seat?"

Miss Faye took the chair he pointed out to her, but Miss Lucy chose to sit by Ansel on his couch. He didn't object. He was sitting upright now, and when she settled down next to him he only smiled at her. "I *heard* you tapping those walls last night," he said.

"Tapping the *what*?" asked Maisie.

Miss Lucy looked very severe suddenly and tucked her head further inside her high collar. She never mentioned her nightwalking during the daytime. "We came to see if you're well," her sister said, "and to remind you that tomorrow's Wednesday. Time for your shots."

"James already told me," Ansel said.

"Last time you forgot *anyway*. You went visiting."

"That's true, I did," said Ansel, and then he sat back and smiled around the room, looking so happy and pleased with himself that everyone else smiled back. The Potters made little ducking smiles down at their gloved hands, and Maisie smiled with narrow eyes straight into Ansel's face. James stood up; now that people were seated and comfortable he could go.

"I have to see Dan Thompson at the paper," he told the Potters. "Sorry to run off."

"Well, now, have a good time," said Miss Faye.

"Will you remind him of that announcement about our niece's baby?"

"I sure will. See you later."

He went back to the darkroom. Here it was cool and distant-feeling; the voices in the living room were faded. He put the week's pictures in the envelope and then, to prolong his stay in the coolness, he set that down and began filing away the pictures that Ansel had been looking at a couple of days before—the Model A, Ansel on his couch, Joan in the dust storm. When he came to the picture of Joan he stopped and studied it; he thought it might be the best thing he had ever done. Her figure made a straight, black line through a circle of wavery blurs, and her head was bent forward in that way she had when she walked. He didn't know how many hundreds of times he had seen her like that. And facing that photograph head-on, having a tangible picture of the way he saw her in his mind, made him think about the quarrel again. All last night and all this morning, he had been trying not to.

It seemed to him, now that he stopped to consider, that if he wanted things to be smoothed over again it would have to be he who took the first step. Joan wouldn't. She would never change her mind about Ansel or even pretend to, in order to make things easier. He would have to go over and say, "Well, however we feel, I'm sorry that fight happened," or else she would just stay quietly in her own house, playing games with Simon and occupying herself with little private chores until she died. And all over nothing. He tucked her picture back into the file. Mr. Pike was always saying, "Someday, boy, that girl is going to walk off and leave you," and he didn't know how right he was. Last month Joan had packed her things and gone downtown to catch a bus for home, but then she had decided she might as well go to a movie first and by the time the movie was over she had changed her mind and come home again, dragging two big suitcases behind her and hobbling along on her dressup shoes. She had told James about it, laughing at herself as she told it, but James hadn't laughed with her. If she were to go, what would he decide to do about it?

Out in the living room, he could hear Miss Lucy discussing her nephew, who was a missionary in Japan and a great curiosity there because of his red hair. "You ought to see him bow," she said. "They bow all the time, he tells me . . ." James half-listened, drumming his fingers on the steel file drawer.

If Joan were to go, he had only two choices. That was the way he saw it. He could let her be, and spend the next forty years remembering nothing but the way she used to walk across the fields with him from the tobacco barns and the peppermint smell of her breath when she kissed him good night. Or he could go after her and say, "Come back. And will you marry me?" In his *mind* he could say that, but not in real life. In real life he had Ansel, and would have him always because he couldn't walk out on that one, final member of his family that he hadn't yet deserted. And in real life, he could never make Joan and Ansel like each other.

"I'll take Africa any day," Miss Faye was saying. "Africans *know* they need a missionary, but these Easterners are eternally surprised." And Miss Lucy chirped something at the end, but James couldn't hear what she said.

He stood up and rubbed his knees where they ached from being bent so long. Then he picked up the pictures for the paper and left the darkroom. Instead of going out through the front he crossed to the back door, in order to make his escape as quickly as possible. Outside, his eyes searched out those daisies he had been meaning to pick, blowing in the wind and about to be too old. He tucked the pictures under his arm and went deeper into the field, heading toward the tallest ones. It always made him feel silly, picking flowers. He didn't mind doing it (Joan liked daisies far better than bought flowers or any other kind of present), but he didn't like thinking that anyone might be watching. In case someone *was*, he picked very offhandedly—yanking the daisies up nearly by their roots, jumbling them together helter-skelter without looking at them. But while he was rounding the side of the house and heading toward the front yard he arranged them more carefully, and held them up to see if they were all right.

Mrs. Hammond's car was gone; that was one good thing. She must have left while he was in the darkroom. Now all he wanted was for Joan to be the one to answer the door. He knocked and waited, frowning tensely at the screen. For a long time nobody came. Then from somewhere else in the house, Joan called, "Was that a knock?" Her voice echoed; she must have been standing at the head of the stairs.

"It's me," James said.

"Simon, will you let James in?"

Simon came out of the kitchen, dragging his feet. Through the screen, all James saw of him was his silhouette—his spidery arms and legs, his shoulders hunched up as if he were scared of something. Before he reached the door he stopped and said, "You come by yourself?"

"Who would I be bringing?" asked James.

"Oh, no one." And he came the rest of the way to the door and pushed it open. "Joan's upstairs," he said, "putting Mama to bed. She'll be down."

"Your mother got up already?"

"Well, but now she's going back to bed. I said everything all wrong."

"I'll bet you didn't," said James, without being quite sure what he was talking about. He closed the door very softly behind him and went over to a chair. "Is Joan too busy to talk?"

But just then they heard Joan coming downstairs, walking on tiptoe and taking only one step at a time where usually she took two. Simon jerked his thumb toward the sound. "Here she is," he said. When Joan came into view she looked at James blankly a minute, as if she'd forgotten he was here, and then she smiled and said, "Oh. Hello."

"Hello," James said. He stood up and held out the flowers. "I brought you some daisies. I was walking through the field and happened to come across them."

"That was nice," she said, and then frowned at the daisies. James looked at them. They seemed old and draggled now, in a messy little cluster in his hand. "They're not all that special, I guess," he said, but Joan had come out of her thoughts. "I think they're fine," she said. "I'll get a vase."

"Oh, you don't have to get a *vase* for them—"

"Well, of course I do."

She went out into the kitchen, still seeming to walk on tiptoe. Now that James thought of it, there was an uneasy silence about this house. He couldn't tell if it was because of something to do with Mrs. Pike or because Joan was still mad at him, and he didn't know how to ask. He looked across at Simon, who was still standing and staring into space. "Did I come at a bad time?" James asked him.

"Huh?"

Joan came back, carrying a cut-glass vase full of water. He asked her, "Did I come at a bad time?"

"Oh, not really."

"Well, did I or didn't I?"

"It's all right," Joan told him. "Aunt Lou didn't feel well this morning, but she's upstairs now and everything's all right." She took the daisies from him. Her hands when they brushed his were cool and impersonal, and she didn't look at him. "We have to go gradually," she said. "I keep forgetting that. I don't seem to have a *light* touch with anything." Yet her fingers when she arranged the flowers were as light and gentle as butterflies, and the daisies stood up or bent gracefully over the minute she touched them. When she was done they had stopped looking draggled; James was glad now that he had brought them.

"You ought to work for a florist," he told her.

But she set the vase down on a table without even noticing how they looked. She hadn't glanced at them once, all the time she was arranging them. "Mrs. Hammond does," she said. "Have a light touch, I mean. But I'm not sure that's the kind I'm talking about right now."

"I don't know that I follow you," James said.

She shook her head and sat down, as if she had given up on him. "Never mind," she said.

"Mrs. *Hammond* has a light touch?"

"Never mind." She looked suddenly at Simon. "Simon, do you want lunch?" she asked him.

"I just had breakfast."

"Oh."

"*You* have a light touch," James said. "You have the lightest touch of anyone I know."

"Oh, James, *you* don't know."

"Well, I'm trying—" He stopped and glanced toward Simon. It seemed to him Simon looked cold. "Don't you want to sit down?" he asked.

"I'm okay."

"Come on."

Simon shrugged and sat down on the couch. Now that they were all seated here, facing each other and keeping their hands folded in their laps, it seemed more awkward than before. It seemed they should be having a *conversation* of some kind, something that made sense. Not these little jagged bits of words. He tried smiling at Joan but all she did was smile back, using only her mouth while her eyes stayed serious and maybe even angry; he didn't know. "Would you rather I come back another time?" he asked.

"It's all right."

"Well." He sat further forward and looked at his fingernails. "I guess your uncle's working today," he said.

"Didn't Ansel tell you so?"

"In a way he did."

"There's nothing *bad* about it," said Joan.

"Why, no, of course not."

"You have to *do* something. You can't sit around. It's not *fair* to sit around, reminding people all the time—" She stopped, and James looked sideways at her while he kept his head bent over his fingernails. Her voice was so sharp-sounding it made him uneasy, and he didn't know what he was supposed to say to her. But then she said, "Well. So you don't have to work tobacco any more."

"No," James said.

"That's good."

He waited a minute, and then cleared his throat and said, "It'll be a good season, they say."

"Billy Brandon told me that," Simon said suddenly. "Barns are nearly full already."

In his shirt pocket he found a plastic comb, with little pieces of lint sticking to it. By running his index finger across its teeth he made a sound like a tiny xylophone, flat and tinny. Joan and Simon both sat watching him. When he saw them watching he stopped and put the comb back in his pocket. "I guess I'll be going," he said helplessly. "I could come some other time."

"All right," said Joan.

"Do you want me to?"

"What?"

"Do you want me to come back?"

"Oh. Yes."

"Okay," he said, but he still wasn't sure. He stood up and went over to the door, with Joan and Simon following solemnly behind. Then he turned around and said, "I could take you to the movies, maybe, Thursday night. The two of you."

"We'll see," Joan said.

"Do you want to come or don't you?"

"I don't know yet if we can," she said.

"Well, I wouldn't ask so far in advance, but tomorrow night I can't go. I'm going to take Ansel playing cribbage. But Thursday—"

"We'll see," said Joan.

"I *know* I wasn't going to chauffeur him around no more, but lately he's been—Well. We don't have to go into that."

"I'm not going into anything," Joan said.

"Yes, you are."

"I wasn't saying a word."

"I could tell the way you were looking."

"I wasn't looking *any* way. I wasn't even *thinking* about it."

She sounded near tears. James stood there, trying to think of what to say next, but he figured anything he came up with would only make things worse. So he waited a minute, and then he said, "I think I'd better leave. Goodbye."

"Goodbye," Simon said.

He was down the porch steps and halfway across the yard when he heard their door close; Joan had never said goodbye. The only sounds now were from Ansel's window—the birdlike sounds of women laughing, all clustered around his brother, their laughter pealing out in clear happy trills that drifted through the window and hung like a curtain across the empty porch.

10

That afternoon, Joan had a telephone call from her mother. She was upstairs when it came, getting Mrs. Pike out of bed for the second time and finding it a little easier now than it had been in the morning. "What do you want to wear?" she asked, and her aunt actually answered, with only a slight pause beforehand. "The beige, I guess," she said. She waited while Joan lifted it off the hanger. "Can I wear the abalone pin with that?"

"Of course," Joan said. She would have agreed if her aunt had wanted to wear the kitchen curtains. She picked the pin out of the bureau drawer and laid it beside the dress, and then the phone rang. Both of them stopped to listen.

"Hey, Joan!" Simon called.

"I'm up here."

"Someone wants you on the telephone."

"Well, I'll be back," Joan told her aunt, and she went down the stairs very fast, two steps at a time. She didn't know who she was expecting, but when she heard only the ice-cold, nasal voice of the operator she was disappointed.

"Miss Joan Pike?" the operator asked.

"Yes."

"Are you Miss Joan Pike."

"Yes."

"Long distance calling."

"All right," Joan said.

There was a pause, and then her mother said, "Is that Joan?", formally, and waited for Joan to go through the whole business of identifying herself again.

"It's me," said Joan. "Hello, Mother."

"Hello," her mother said. "I called to see how Lou was. Your father said to ask."

"She's getting better," said Joan. She heard her mother turn and murmur to her father, probably relaying Joan's answer. In normal speech her mother had a very soft voice, held in as if there was somebody sick in the next room. But when she returned to the phone her tea-party voice came back, louder and more distinct, the voice of a plump woman who stood very straight and placed the points of her shoes outward when she walked.

"Your father feels bad we couldn't make it to the funeral," she was saying. "He says it's only a sniffle he has, but I don't like the sound of it. Is there anything we can do for Lou?"

"Not that I can think of. The flowers were very nice—Uncle Roy said to tell you."

"Well. We weren't quite sure. Some people have a dislike of gladioli."

"No, they were fine," said Joan.

"That's good. How's Simon?"

"He's all right, I guess."

"Tell him hello for us, now. Tell him—"

Her voice had grown almost as soft as it normally was. Joan could picture her, sitting on the edge of that rocker with the needlework seat, with Joan's father standing behind her and bending cautiously forward to hear what was going on. He was a little afraid of telephones himself; he treated them as though they might explode. She saw how her mother would be smoothing down that little crease between her eyebrows with her index finger, and then letting the crease come back the minute she dropped her hand. The thought of that made Joan miss her; she said suddenly, "I'm tired."

"What?"

"I'm just tired. I want to come home. I don't want to stay here any more."

"Why, Joan—" her mother said, and then let her voice trail off. Finally she said, "Don't you think you should be with Lou now?"

"I'm not helping," said Joan. "She just sits. Every place I look, Janie Rose is there, and I don't feel like staying here. Nothing is right."

"Doesn't Simon need you?"

"Well—" Joan said, and then stopped because her father must have asked to know what was going on. The two of them murmured together a while, her mother's voice sounding faintly impatient. Joan's father was growing deaf; he had to be told twice. When her mother finally returned to Joan, she was sighing, and her voice was loud again.

"You know we'd love to have you," she said. "As soon as you can come. When were you planning on?"

"I don't know. A day or two, maybe. By bus."

"Or maybe James could drive you," said her mother. "We'd love to have him."

"He won't be coming."

"Your father's been asking about him."

"He won't be coming," Joan said firmly.

There was another pause, and then her mother said, "Is something wrong?"

"What would be wrong?"

"Well, I don't know. Shall we expect you when we see you, then?"

"All right. Don't go to any trouble."

"It'll be no trouble. Goodbye, now."

"Goodbye. And thank you for calling."

She hung up, but she stayed in the same position, her hand on the receiver. Out of the corner of her eye she caught sight of Simon. He was leaning against the frame of the kitchen door, eating another peanut butter and mayonnaise sandwich. "Hey," she said, but he only bit off a hunk of sandwich and chewed steadily, keeping his eyes on her face. "That was your Aunt Abby," she told him.

"I know."

"She called to see how everyone is."

He straightened up from the doorframe and came over to her, planting his feet very carefully and straight in front of him. When he had reached her he said, "I hear how you're going there," and waited, with the sandwich raised halfway to his mouth.

"We'll see," said Joan.

"You going by bus?"

"I might not go at all. I don't know yet."

"How long would you go for?"

"Look," said Joan. "I don't know that I'm going. I just think it might be good to get away. So don't tell anyone, all right?"

"Well, all right."

"Not even James."

"All *right*," said Simon. He was good at keeping

secrets; it was an insult to suggest he might tell somebody. "If you do go—" he said.

"I might not."

"But if you do go, can I go with you?"

"Oh, Simon," Joan began, and stopped there because she didn't know what else to say. "Your parents
need you here," she said finally.

"They won't notice."

"Your daddy will. So will your mother, pretty soon."

"No."

"Yes. See, she's coming downstairs now."

He turned and looked toward the stairs. Mrs. Pike
was coming down of her own accord, taking each step
uncertainly but not asking for help. She had pinned the
abalone pin at the neck of her dress, and it was bunching up the material a little. When she reached the bottom of the stairs she looked from Joan to Simon and
back again, as if she were expecting them to tell her
what to do next. Joan went over to her.

"I could fix you a bite to eat," she said.

"I came to sew."

"To sew?"

"I came to sew Connie's dress together."

"Oh," Joan said. She looked around at the sewing
machine, and was glad to see that the dress still lay
there. (Mrs. Hammond had gone away all helter-skelter,
talking to herself, leaving everything behind her.) "It's
all here," Joan told her. "Is there anything else you
need?"

"No. I just want to sew."

"Shall we sit here and keep you company?"

"I just want to sew."

"All right," said Joan, but she waited a minute anyway, and so did Simon. Mrs. Pike didn't look their way

again. She went over to the chair at the sewing machine and lowered herself stiffly into it, and then she picked up the material and began sewing on it. She did it just that suddenly, without examining what she was about to do first or even looking at it—just jammed two pieces of cloth beneath the needle of the sewing machine and stepped hard on the treadle. Finally Joan turned away, because there was nothing more she could do. "Let's go to the kitchen," she told Simon. She steered him gently by one shoulder and he went, but he kept looking back over his shoulder at his mother. When they reached the kitchen he said, "See?" but she said, "Hush," without even asking what he meant. "Maybe we could go for a walk," she said.

"I found my ball."

"What ball?"

"The one I lost. I found it."

"Well, I'm glad to hear it," said Joan. "Is it all beat up?"

"It's fine. You want to play catch?"

"Not really."

"Aw, come on, Joan."

She frowned at him. "We should have taken you to a barber," she said finally.

"Just for fifteen minutes or so? I won't throw hard."

"Oh, all right," she said.

Simon went over to the door and picked up the baseball that lay beside it. It was grayer than before, and grass-stained, but lying out in the field for two weeks hadn't hurt it any. He began throwing it up in the air and catching it, while he led the way through the kitchen and out the back door.

"If we had a big mowed lawn, we could play roll-a-bat," Joan said.

"Roll-a-bat's a baby game."

They cut through the tall grass behind the house, parting the weeds ahead of them with swimming motions and advancing beyond the garbage cans and the rusted junk to a place where the grass was shorter. Janie Rose had set fire to this spot not a year ago, while trailing through here in her mother's treasured wedding dress holding a lighted cigarette high in front of her with her little finger stuck out. James and Mr. Pike and Mr. Terry had had to fight the fire with their own shirts, their faces glistening with sweat and their voices hoarse from smoke, while Ansel leaned out the back window calling "Shame! Shame!" and Janie Rose sat perched in the tin can tree, crying and cleaning her glasses with the lace hem of the wedding dress. Now the weeds had grown up again, but they were shorter and sparser, with black scorched earth showing around them. Joan and Simon took up their positions, one at each end of the burned patch, and Simon scraped a standing-place for himself by kicking down the brittle weeds and scuffing at the charred surface of the soil. "Here goes," he said, and wound up his arm so hard that Joan raised both hands in front of her to ward it off before he had even let go of the ball. Simon stopped winding up and pounded the ball into the palm of his other hand.

"Hey, now," he said. "You going to play like a girl?"

"Not if you throw easy like you promised."

He squinted across at her a minute, and then nodded and raised his throwing arm again. This time the ball came without any windup, cutting in a straight clean arc through the blue of the sky. Joan caught it neatly, remembering not to close her eyes, and threw it back to him underhanded.

"Overhand," said Simon.

"Sorry."

Little prickles of sweat came out on her forehead. She tugged her blouse out of her bermudas, so as to make herself cooler, and almost missed the next ball when it whizzed low and straight toward her stomach.

"Watch it," Simon said.

"You watch it. That one burned my hands."

She threw it overhand this time, and it fell a little short, so that Simon had to run forward to catch it. While he was walking back to his place a screen door slammed behind them, and Joan automatically turned her head and listened to find out what end of the house it had come from. "Coming," said Simon, and just then Joan saw, in the corner of her eye, someone tall in James's plaid shirt, untangling his way through the field and toward Joan. She turned all the way. *"Watch—!"* Simon said, and something slammed into the side of her head and made everything green and smarting. She sat down, not because she had been knocked down but because she was so startled her knees were weak. Beside her, nestled in a clump of grass, was the baseball, looking whiter than she remembered. Her temple began throbbing and she lay all the way down on her back, with the scorched ground underneath her making little crisp brittle sounds. *"Joan!"* Simon was shouting, and whoever wore James's plaid shirt was thudding closer and closer. It was Ansel. She saw that and closed her eyes. In the same moment Simon arrived, with his breath coming fast and loud. He thumped down beside her and said, *"Joan,* oh, *shit,* Joan," which made her suddenly grin, even with her eyes closed and her head aching. She looked up at him and said, "Simon Pike—" and tried to sit up, but someone yanked her back by the shoulders. "*Where* did you—" she began, but then Ansel clapped his hand over her mouth. His hand smelled of Noxzema.

"You lie still," he said. "Don't you sit and don't you talk. I'll call a ambulance."

"An ambulance?" And this time she out and out laughed, and sat up even with Ansel trying to press her back down again. "Ansel," she said, "I *really* don't need an ambulance. I just got surprised."

"I warned you," Simon said. "Oh Lord, people *break* so easy." He settled back on his haunches, clutching his knees, and for a minute it looked as if he would cry.

"Oh, hey, now," Joan told him. She struggled all the way up, letting Ansel keep hold of one of her elbows, and then reached down to give Simon a hand up. When she stood her head hurt more; it was throbbing. She patted Simon's shoulder. "It was my doing," she said. "I turned to see who was coming."

Ansel kept hanging on to her elbow, too tightly. She tried to pull away but he only tightened his grasp and bent closer over her, looking long and pale and worried with his light eyes blinking anxiously in the strong sunlight. "You're coming inside," he told her. "I'll call a doctor."

"I don't *need* a doctor, Ansel."

"Terrible things can happen."

"Oh, for heaven's sake," she said. "I'm not *about* to die on you."

"You never know. You never can—"

She pulled away from him, this time so hard that he had to let her go, and reached out for Simon's hand instead, in case she got dizzier. Simon accepted her hand like a grave responsibility and led her, soberly and silently, toward the house. Ansel followed, panting from all this unexpected exercise.

"We'll go to my house," he said, "where I have iced tea."

"No, thank you."

"I *want* you to go to my house. I feel responsible. And anyway, I'm lonely. James has gone off to Dan Thompson's."

"Oh, all right," Joan said. It was true that she didn't want to go back to that parlor again. They veered toward the Greens' end of the house, with Ansel parting weeds ahead of them and kicking aside bits of rusted car parts so that Joan could have a clear passage. When they reached the back door he held it open for them and ushered them in with a bow, though neither Simon nor Joan paid any attention to him.

"Head on to the front room," he said. "I'll tell you what, Joan: you can lie on my couch."

"Oh, well, Ansel, I don't need—"

"It's not often I let someone do that."

"All right," she said, and went on toward the couch, feeling too aching to argue. The house smelled like James—a mixture of darkroom chemicals and shaving soap and sunshine—and there was a little of that medicine smell of Ansel's there too. She lay back on the couch and closed her eyes.

Ansel brought iced tea, with the ice cubes tinkling in the glasses and a sprig of fresh mint floating on top. It surprised her, because Ansel was used to being waited on himself. She had thought he wouldn't even know where the glasses were. He set the tray down on the coffee table and handed a glass to both Simon and Joan. Then he picked up his own glass and carried it over to the easy chair, where he sat down a little uncertainly, as if he had never sat there before. Maybe he hadn't. "Cheers," he said, and held his glass up high. "In reference to this doctor business, Joan—"

"I feel *fine*."

"But maybe you should see one anyway," said Simon. "You just don't know *what* might have happened."

"Nothing happened. Will you hush?"

She took a sip of iced tea and closed her eyes. It felt good to be cool again. The room was dim and quiet, and the couch was comfortable, and the heat of outdoors had made her feel relaxed and sleepy.

"What else is good," Ansel was telling Simon, "is to drink iced tea with peppermint candy in it. You ever tried that?" His voice was far away and faint, because Joan was half-asleep. She heard him shift his position in the creaky old chair. "You ever tried it?" he asked again.

"No," said Simon. He was still being cautious with Ansel, although Joan couldn't figure out why.

"You ought to have your mother make it for you," Ansel told him.

"She won't care."

"Sure she will. Sure she will."

"We drink mainly Cokes," said Simon.

"This is better."

There was a long silence. Joan reached over to set her glass on the floor, and then she lay down again and put the back of her hand across her eyes to shut the light out.

"James is at Dan Thompson's," Ansel said.

"You told me that," said Simon.

"He just walked out and left me here, alone."

"I don't care."

"If I drop dead today, he'll forget what name to put on the headstone."

"I don't care."

"Ah, well," Ansel sighed, and there was the sound of his stretching in the chair. "There is a collection, in this world," he said, "of people who could die and be mourned approximately a week. If they're lucky. Then that's the end of it. You think I'm one?"

"I don't know," said Simon. "I'm not listening."

"Oh."

There was another pause, and someone's ice tinkled. Ansel's, probably. Ansel said, "I'm going to go away from here."

"Everyone is," said Simon.

"What?"

"Grown-ups can go and not even let on they're going. I wish I could."

"You can come with me," Ansel said.

"Where's that?"

"This town of mine. This place I come from."

"Is it north?" Simon asked.

"North of what?"

"*North* north. Is it?"

"It's south," said Ansel.

"Oh. I want to go north."

"It's all the same. Who you kidding? This town has got a cop that acts like a night watchman. He goes through the town on foggy nights crying out the hours, singing 'Sunshine on the Mountain' and all other sunny songs, middle of the night. Ain't *that* a thing to wake in the night to, boy."

"Yeah," said Simon.

"To wake up after a nightmare to."

"Yeah."

The throbbing in Joan's head kept time to Ansel's words. She wanted to leave now, and stop listening to that thin voice of his going on and on, but the throbbing made a weight on her head that kept her down. She listened dreamily, without interrupting.

"Lately I've been thinking about home," Ansel said. "It was the funeral that did it, somehow."

"You didn't go to the funeral."

"It did it *anyway*. The only problem is, it's hard to know what way to think about it. No telling how it's changed, and I get no letters from there. James does, from our sisters. He writes them once a month, letters all full of facts, but when he gets an answer he pretends he doesn't. I don't know why. I mean he goes on writing but never mentions what their letters to *him* have said, never comments on them. Why do you think he does that?"

"I don't know," Simon said. "This cop, does he sing every night?"

"*Just* about. And there's a feed store that gives away free hats. Big straw hats, with red plumes curling down like Sir Walter Raleigh's. Walk down Sedad Street and it's just an acre of people wearing hats, red plumes bobbing up and down. Merchants wearing hats, farmers wearing hats, everyone but little old ladies wearing hats. Old ladies don't like them hats. You go down to Harper's River and find little boys and colored men fishing in leaky boats, wearing red-plumed hats. Why, you can tell when you're coming home again. You look out the bus window into those country fields and find farmers plowing, wearing hats with red plumes, and the mules wearing them too but with holes cut in them for the ears to stick out. That's how you know you're nearing home."

"How about me?" asked Simon.

"How *about* you."

"If I was to ask, would they give me one too?"

"Why, surely."

"I'll ask, then."

"You do that."

More ice tinkled. Joan's hand had stuck to her damp forehead and she took it away, making a tearing sound, and sighed and turned over on her side.

"What exactly is the name of this town?" Simon asked.

"Caraway, N.C."

"Is there buses to it?"

"Six a day."

"Is there people my age?"

"Is there?" Ansel asked, and he laughed suddenly, a chuckle deep in his throat so that he sounded a little like James. "*Is* there, boy. Well, lots. I ought to know. Another thing. This is something I've never seen in any other town, now: the boys wear one gold ring in their ear."

"*Earrings?*"

"Oh, no. No, this is like pirates wear. Pierce their ears and put one gold hoop through. Everyone did it."

"Did you?"

"My family didn't want me to. Well, I wasn't actually in that particular group, anyway. But James was. He had a hoop, but he took it off finally. Only got one because the family told him not to. Eventually *every*one takes them off, when they're grown up and settled down. You'll hear someone say, 'So-and-so's engaged now. He's got a steady job, and there's no more gold in his ear.' But I never had gold in my ear to begin with."

"Does it hurt?" Simon asked.

"Does what hurt?"

"When they pierce your ears."

"Oh, no. At least, I don't think so. Not for long."

"If I went there, would I wear an earring?"

"Sure you would."

"How long is it by bus?"

Joan felt herself drifting off. The house seemed to be spinning around her, making streaky yellow shimmers of sunshine through her eyelids, but when she found that she wasn't even hearing the others' voices now she pulled herself sharply awake. She opened her eyes and found that she was looking at one of Ansel's shoes, tapping lazily on the floor. "Have I been asleep?" she asked. Simon and Ansel looked over at her. "What time is it?"

"Not yet three," said Ansel. "How's your head?"

"It's fine."

"You sure?"

"Yes. Sorry to disappoint you." She sat up and tucked her blouse in. "Simon, we got to get going," she said.

"Aw, I was just hearing something interesting."

"It can wait."

She let him go through the front door first, and then she turned to Ansel and smiled at him. "Thank you for the use of the couch," she said.

"Nothing to it." He poked his head out the door, past Joan, and looked at Simon. "You be making your plans, now," he said.

"All right."

"Plans for what?" Joan asked.

"Nothing," said Simon.

Joan yawned, and followed him down the porch toward home.

11

"There's not much difference between one person and the next," Ansel said. "I've found that to be true. Would you agree with me?" He raised himself up from a prone position on the couch to look at James, who was sitting nearby with the paper. "Would you?" he asked.

"Well, more or less," said James, and turned to the sports section.

"Course you do. You have to. Is that the Larksville paper?"

"Larksville paper's not out till tomorrow."

"Oh. I thought today was Wednesday."

"It is," said James. "The paper comes on Thursday."

"Oh."

Ansel lay down again and stared thoughtfully upwards, lacing his fingers across his chest. He had been flat on his back all morning, complaining of dizzy spells, and James had been sitting here keeping him company. It was easier that way. Otherwise Ansel would continually think up reasons to call him into the room and things to ask him for. "James," he would call, "what was the name of that old woman who gave sermons on the street corner?" Or, "Whatever happened

183

to that seersucker suit I used to have?" And in the long run James would have to spend just as much time in this room as if he'd been sitting there all along. He yawned now and turned another page of his newspaper, and Ansel switched his eyes back over to him.

"It's a fact, James," he said. "People don't vary a heck of a lot, one from the other."

"You told me that," said James.

"Well, yes, I did. Because it's true. If you will hark your mind back to that Edwards boy, that bucktoothed one that joined the Army—what was his name?"

"I don't know."

"Oh, sure you know. Sure you know. What was his name?"

"Ansel," said James, "I just don't make a point of *remembering* all these things."

"Well, I wouldn't brag about it. Clarence, that was it. Or Clayton; I don't know which. Now, Clarence, he went almost around the world with that Army outfit of his. Almost everywhere. And you know what he said when he got back? He said that every single country he'd been in, one thing always held true: when mothers and children climb into a car to go visiting, the first act a mother undertakes is spitting on a hanky and scrubbing her children's faces with it. Always. Canada, France, Germany—always. If that doesn't prove my point, what does?"

James ran his eyes down the baseball scores. He frowned over them, absentmindedly making a little *tch* sound under his breath when he came upon a score he didn't like. After a while he became aware of the silence, and he looked up to see Ansel watching him with his eyes wide and hurt. "You weren't even listening," Ansel said, and James sighed and folded his paper up.

"I was listening and reading both," he said.

"No. What's it take to make a man listen?"

"Well, I'm sorry. You can tell it to me over again, if you want."

"No."

Ansel turned slightly, so that his cheek was resting on the sofa cushion, and closed his eyes. "I've noticed more and more," he said, "that no one listens when I talk. I don't know why. Usually I think about a thing before I say it, making sure it's worthwhile. I plan it in my mind, like. When I am dead, what will they remember but the things I talked about? Not the way I looked, or moved; I didn't look like much and I hardly moved at all. But only the things I talked about, and what is that to remember when you never even listened?"

"I listen," said James.

"No. Sometimes in one of those quiet periods after I've said something, when no one's saying anything back because they didn't hear me, I look at myself and think, well, my goodness. Am I *here*? Do I even *exist*?"

"Oh, for heaven's sake," said James. He opened the paper again.

"When I am dead, I wonder what people will miss me. You? Simon? Mrs. Pike will wish she'd brought more hot soup. Joan won't notice I'm gone. Will you miss me?"

James read on. He learned all about a boy named Ralph Combs, who was planning to be Raleigh's contribution to the major leagues. He read Blondie and Dick Tracy and Part 22 of the serialized adventure story, and then he noticed the silence again and he lowered his paper to look at Ansel. Ansel was asleep, with one arm flung over his head and his fingers curling in around the sofa arm. His eyelids were translucent and faintly shining, and over his forehead his hair hung rumpled, making him look the way he had when he was twelve. Seeing him that way made James feel sad. He rose and came over to the couch, standing at Ansel's head and looking down at his long pale face tipped back against the cushions. If he hadn't known better, he would have tapped him on the shoulder and said, *"Now* I'll listen." But then Ansel would wake up and be twenty-six years old again, nervously testing himself for new symptoms, beginning some long monologue that he had begun before, changed forever from that scared small brother who could sit a whole evening without saying a word or raising his eyes from the floor. That twelve-year-old would vanish without a trace, leaving not even an echo of himself in the way Ansel smiled or said a certain word. James moved away from the couch and went over to the window.

Because of the way he felt, the view from the window took on a sad, deserted look. Everything was bowed low under the breeze, straightening up for a second only to bow again. Simon's bicycle lay on its side with a drooping buttercup tangled in its spokes. At the edge of the yard the Potters' insurance man was just climbing out of his Volkswagen. (He came every week, because the Potters had to be constantly reassured that their policy really was all right.) He looked tired and sad. While he was crossing the yard he mopped his face and straightened the plastic carnation in his buttonhole, and then on the first porch step he snapped his head erect and put a bright look on his face. After that James lost sight of him. But he could hear the knocking, and the sound of the Potters' door cautiously opening and the bolts being slid back after the insurance man was taken inside. They slid easily in their little oiled tracks.

The quickness of them made James smile, and he could picture Miss Lucy's eager fingers fumbling rapidly at the locks, shutting little Mr. Harding in and the loneliness out for as long as she and Miss Faye could manage. He stopped smiling and moved away from the window.

Back in the kitchen it was even worse. There was one daisy on the counter, a stray one from the field in back, and it was dead and collapsed against Ansel's untouched lunch tray. ("I'm not eating today," Ansel had said. "Do you care?" "Suit yourself," said James.) Out the back window was the half-mowed field, looking bald and straggly. Simon Pike was leaning against an incinerator staring at it all, and while James watched, Simon straightened slowly and began wandering in small thoughtful circles around the incinerator. With the toes of his leather boots he kicked at things occasionally, and he had his shoulders hunched up again so that he looked small and worried. James stuck his head out the window.

"Hey, Simon," he said, "why don't you come in?"

Simon raised his head and looked at him. "What for?" he asked.

"Well, you look kind of lonely out there."

"Aw, no."

"Well, anyway," said James, "I want to take a picture of you."

That made Simon think twice. He stood still for a moment to consider it, with his chin stuck out and his eyes gazing away from James and across the field. Then he said, "What kind of picture?"

"The kind you like. A portrait."

"Well, then, I reckon I might. I'll come in and think about it."

"*That's* the way," said James.

He let Simon come in his own good time, stopping to kick at a bootscraper and wasting several minutes examining some blistered paint on the door. When Simon was troubled about something, this was the way he acted. He circled all around the kitchen without once looking at James or speaking to him, and he picked up several things from counters and turned them over and over in his hands before setting them down again. Then he jammed his hands into his back pockets and went to the window. "Mama's hemming a dress," he said.

"That's good."

"She talks a little, too, but not about any concern of mine."

"Well, you got to give her time," said James. "First thing people talk about is weather and things."

"I know," Simon said. "Daddy is at the fields, and Joan too. It's her tobacco day. Everybody's busy."

"So're you," said James. "You're having your picture taken."

"Yeah, well."

But when James headed toward the darkroom, Simon followed him. "Where are we going to take it?" he asked.

"Outdoors, if you like."

"I'd rather the living room."

"All right," James said. He opened the door of the darkroom and led the way to where his cameras stood. "You got to be quiet, though, because that's where Ansel's sleeping."

"*Now?*"

"It's one of his dizzy days."

"Oh, cripes," said Simon, and he started walking in circles again. He put the heel of one boot exactly in front of the toe of the other, and keeping his balance that way made him fling both arms out and tilt sideways slightly. "It's a bad day for everyone," he said. "I declare." He seemed to be walking on an imaginary hoop, suspended high above the ground.

James had seen the kind of portraits that Simon and Janie Rose liked best—the ones taken against a dead white screen, with the faces retouched afterwards. He favored a homier picture, himself. He left the screen behind and brought only a couple of lamps, not the glaring ones, and his favorite old box camera. "We'll put you in the easy chair," he told Simon. He had given the camera to Simon to carry, and Simon was squinting through the view-finder as he walked. "Do you want to be doing anything special?"

"Yes," Simon said. "I want to be smoking a cigar."

"Be serious, now."

"I am serious. You asked me what I wanted to be doing. Well, all my life I've been waiting to get my picture took with a cigar. I been counting on it."

"Oh, what the hell," said James. He set his lamps down and went over to the living-room mantelpiece. From the old wooden cigar box that had belonged to his grandfather he took a cigar, the fat black kind that he smoked on special evenings when no one was around to complain. "Here you go," he said. "But don't you light it, now. Just get your picture took with it."

"Well, thank you," said Simon. He crossed to the easy chair, giving Ansel a sideways glance as he passed, but Ansel only stirred and didn't wake up. "He don't know what he's missing," Simon whispered. "Me with a cigar, boy."

"It'll all be recorded for posterity," said James.

While James was setting up the lights, Simon practiced

with the cigar. He opened it and slid the paper ring off, and then he sat with his elbow resting on the chair arm and his face in a furious frown every time he took a suck from the unlit cigar. "I'm getting the hang of it," he said, and looked around for an ashtray to practice tapping ashes into. "When do you reckon they'll let me smoke these for real?"

"Never, probably," said James. "Always someone around that objects to the smell."

"Ah, I wouldn't care. I'm going to start as soon as I'm out on my own, boy. Soon as I turn sixteen or so."

James smiled and tilted a lamp closer to Simon. He had been listening to Simon for some years now, and he had a mental list of what he was planning to do at age sixteen. Smoke cigars, take tap-dance lessons, buy his own Woolworth's, and grow sideburns. Janie Rose hadn't even been going to wait *that* long. She asked her mother weekly, "Do you think it's time I should be thinking of getting married?" And then she would smile hopefully, showing two front teeth so new that they still had scalloped edges, and everyone would laugh at her. James could see their point, though—Janie's and Simon's. He couldn't remember that being a child was so much fun. So he nodded at Simon and said, "When you turn sixteen, I'll *buy* you a box," and Simon smiled and settled back in the chair.

"Might not wait till then even," he said. "You never can tell."

"Well, I would," said James. "Tobacco stunts your growth."

"No, I mean to go out on my own. I might go earlier." He stuck out his tongue and flicked an imaginary piece of tobacco off the tip of it. "I been thinking where I could go."

"It's kind of early for that," James said.

"I don't know. You know Caraway, N.C.?"

James stopped fiddling with his camera and looked up. "What about it?" he asked.

"I just thought you could tell me about it. If that's where you are from."

"Nothing to tell," said James.

"Well, there's hats with feathers on them, and them gold earrings the boys all wear. Do you think I might like that town?"

In the view-finder his face was small and pointed, with a worried line between his eyes. He was leaning toward James with the cigar poised forgotten between his thumb and forefinger, and in the second of stillness that followed his question James snapped the picture. "That'll be a good one," he said.

"Will I like Caraway?"

"I don't see how. Do you ever see *me* going to Caraway?"

"Well, the boys wear gold earrings," Simon said again, and he sighed and rubbed the top of his head and James snapped that picture too.

"Sure, the *boys*," he told Simon. "They're the worst in the state, Caraway boys. Got tight little Church of God parents. All they want to do when they grow up is come somewhere like Larksville. What you want to do in Caraway?"

"I could board with your family," Simon said.

James looked up from his camera with his mouth open and then threw back his head and laughed. *"Hoo!"* he said, and Ansel stirred in his sleep at the noise. "I'd like to see that," he went on more quietly. "Would you turn sideways in your chair now, please?"

Simon turned, but he kept his eyes on James. *"Ansel* says—" he began.

"Ansel don't know."

"Ain't he *from* there?"

"He don't know."

"Well, anyway," said Simon, "I could go and look it over."

"Your mother would love that. Now, quit watching out of the corner of your eye, Simon. Look at the fireplace."

"Do you think she'd miss me?" Simon asked.

James clicked the picture and stood up, squinting at him sideways to see which way to turn him next.

"I think my mother'd say, *'Who* you say's gone? Oh, *Simon!'* she'd say. 'Him. My goodness. Did you remember to bring the eggs?' " He sat forward again then and frowned at James, twining the cigar over and under the fingers of his left hand. "You see how it'd be," he said.

"You know that ain't so," said James.

He stepped a little to one side and got Simon focused in the camera again, all the while waiting for the argument to continue. But it didn't. In the square of the view-finder Simon suddenly sighed and slumped down like a little old man, staring abstractedly at the wet end of his cigar. "Ah, hell," he said. "It don't matter."

That made James look up, but he didn't say anything. Instead he snapped the picture and frowned over at the lamps, measuring how much light there was. "Outdoors would've been better," he said finally.

"I also hear," said Simon, "that they sing all night in the dark. And them plumed hats, why, even the mules wear them. With holes cut for ears."

"Look over toward your left," James said.

"There's six buses going there a day, Ansel told me."

James folded his arms across the top of the camera and watched Simon a minute, thinking. Simon stared straight back at him. In the light from the lamps his eyes seemed black, and it was hard to see beyond the flat surface of them. His chin was tilted outward a little, and his lashes with their sunbleached tips gleaming were like curtains over his expression. Who knew what was in his mind? James uncrossed his arms then and said, "Put your cigar away, now. This last one's for your mother."

"Aw, my mother won't even—"

"She wants a picture she can show to the relatives. What would they think, you with a big fat cigar in your hand?"

"She won't—" Simon began again.

But James said, "You're growing so much, this summer. She wants to get you in a picture before you're too big to *fit* in one."

"She tell you that?" asked Simon.

"Why, sure."

"She ask you out and out for a picture of me?"

"Sure she did," James said. "She said, 'James, if you got time, I wish you'd snap a picture of Simon. We don't have a picture that looks like him no more.' I said I'd try."

"Well, then," said Simon after a minute. He rose and crossed over to the mantelpiece, where he laid down the cigar. When he returned to his chair he settled himself very carefully, tugging his jeans down tight into his boots, running both hands hard through his hair to smooth it back. He looked more posed now; the relaxed expression that he had worn in the other pictures was gone. With both hands placed symmetrically on the arms of the chair, his back very straight and his face drawn tight in the beginnings of a smile, he stared unblinkingly into the lens of the camera. James waited a minute, and then he pressed the button and straightened up. "Thank you," he said formally.

"Oh, that's all right."

"I'll have them for you this afternoon, maybe. Or tomorrow, early. Perle Simpson is coming by for a passport photo and I want to take that before I start developing."

"Okay," said Simon. He stood up, frowningly tucking in his shirt, and then suddenly he looked over at James and gave him a wide, slow smile, so big that the two dents he was always trying to hide showed up in the center of his cheeks. "Well, I'll be seeing you," he said, and sauntered on out, slamming the screen door behind him. When James went to the window to look after him he saw him in the front yard, picking up the bicycle he hadn't ridden for days and twirling the pedal into a position where he could step on it. The buttercup still hung in the spokes, its little yellow head dangling drunkenly from the front wheel and its withered leaves fluttering out like banners when Simon rode slowly off. He rode in the direction of the Terrys' farm; he would be going to see the tobacco pickers, the way he used to do.

When Simon was out of sight, and when James had turned and seen that Ansel was sleeping still, he himself went out the screen door and down the long front porch. The Pikes' window shades were up now. He peered in through the dark screen door and saw Mrs. Pike at her sewing machine, not running it at the minute but sewing by hand on something that was in her lap. "Mrs. Pike," he called gently. She lowered the sewing and looked up at him, her mouth screwed up and lopsided because of the pins in one corner of it. "Mrs. Pike, can I come in a minute?"

"Joan's handing tobacco," she said. Speaking around the pins made her seem like a different woman, like that waitress at the Royal Crown who always had a cigarette in her mouth when she talked. "Did you want to see Joan?"

"Well, no, I just wanted to tell you—" said James. He pulled open the screen door and stepped just inside it, even though he hadn't been asked. "I took a picture of Simon," he said.

"Oh."

"Sitting in an easy chair."

"Well, that's real nice," said Mrs. Pike, and bowed her head to nip a thread off the dress she was sewing.

"Well, I took it for *you*, Mrs. Pike."

"That's real nice of you," she said again. She held the dress up at arm's length and frowned at it. James shifted his weight to his other foot.

"What I actually told him," he said, "was that you *asked* for it. Asked me to take it for you."

She lowered the dress to her lap again and looked over at him, and James thought that surely she would say *some*thing now. But when she did speak, all she said was, "It must be right hard, taking pictures of children"—politely, as if he were a stranger she was trying to make conversation with.

James waited a minute, but she didn't say more. She had lowered her head to her sewing again, fumbling at it with quick, blunt fingers and absentmindedly working the pins from one side of her mouth to the other. So he said, "Well, ma'am, not really," and then turned and quietly let himself out the door again. All the way down to his end of the porch he kept thinking of going back

and trying once more, but he knew already it wasn't
any use. So he entered his own part of the house and
then just stood there a minute, thinking it over, watching Ansel as he slept.

12

The things Joan Pike owned in this world could be packed in two suitcases, with room to spare. She was putting them there now, one by one, folding the skirts in two and laying them gently on the bottom of the big leather suitcase her father's parents had given him to take to a debating contest fifty years ago. Her own suitcase, newer and shinier, stood waiting on the floor already filled and locked. She had saved out her big straw pocketbook, which was hard to pack and could hold all the things she might need on the bus. It stood on the floor, with one corner of a Greyhound ticket envelope sticking out of it. The ticket she had bought this morning, after spending all of Wednesday night lying in bed rolling up the hem of her top sheet while she thought what to do. She had ridden into town for it on Simon's bicycle, and come back with it hidden inside her white shirt. Nobody knew she was going.

When her closet was empty she cleaned it out carefully, picking up every stray bobby pin and button from the floor and bunching the hangers neatly at one end of the rod with the hooks all pointing the same way. Mainly she wanted to save her aunt the trouble, but also she wanted to go away feeling that she had left a clean sweep behind her—not a thread, not a scrap of hers remaining that she could want to return for. She would like to have it seem as if she had never been here, if that was possible. So she closed the closet door firmly and turned the key in its lock. Then she began on the rest of the room.

She rolled her silver-backed dresser set in sweaters, so that none of the pieces would get scratched. Seeing the set, which her parents had given her on her eighteenth birthday, made her remember that she should be bringing back presents for them, and she frowned into the mirror when she thought about it. Always before, after two weeks at Scout camp even, she had brought back gifts for each of them and formally presented them, and her parents had done the same. But this time she hadn't thought far enough in advance; she would have to come home empty-handed. The idea bothered her, as if this were some basic point of guest etiquette that she, always a guest, had somehow forgotten. She shook her head, and laid the wrapped silver pieces carefully on top of her skirts.

Out in the back yard Simon was running an imaginary machine gun, shouting "ta-ta-ta-ta-tat" in a high voice that cracked and aiming at unknowing wrens who sat in the bushes behind the house. She could see him from her window—his foreshortened, blue denim body, the swirl of hair radiating out from a tiny white point on the back of his head. With luck, he wouldn't see her go. He would stay there in the back yard, and his mother would stay in bed for her afternoon nap, and she could sneak out of the house and across the fields without anyone's seeing her. It might even be supper before they noticed. Mr. Pike would fuss a little, feeling responsible for his brother's child. Mrs. Pike was still too sad to care, but Simon would care. He would ask why she had left without telling them, and how would they answer him? How would *she* even answer him? "Because I don't want to think I'm really going," she would say. It was the first time she had thought that out, in words. She stopped folding a slip and looked down at where Simon sat, with his legs bent under him and the toes of his boots pointing out, sighting along a long straight stick and pulling the trigger. As soon as she got home, she decided, she would telephone to make it all right with him.

Then after supper James would come. "Joan ready?" he'd say. "She's gone," they'd tell him. Then what would he do? She couldn't imagine that, no matter how hard she tried. Maybe he would say, "Well, I'm sorry to hear that," and remain where he was, his face dark and stubborn. Or maybe he would say, "I'll go bring her back." But that was something she didn't expect would ever happen now. A week ago, she might have expected it. She'd thought anything could happen, anyone would change. But now all she felt sure of was that ten years from now, and twenty, James would still be enduring, on and on, in that stuffy little parlor with Ansel in it; and she couldn't endure a minute longer.

She turned away from the window and went back to her suitcase. Everything was in it now. The bureau was left as blank as the bureau in a hotel room; its drawers were empty and smelled of wood again. On the back of the door hung her towel and washcloth, the only things left of her. She plucked them off the rack and carried them out to the laundry hamper in the hall, and then she was finished. No one would ever know she had lived here. When she had locked the second suitcase, and stepped into the high heels that she had taken off so as not to make a noise, she stood in the doorway a minute making sure of the blankness in the room. Then she picked up the two suitcases and the pocketbook and went downstairs.

Carrying it all was harder than she remembered. She kept having to switch the pocketbook strap from one arm to the other, and although the suitcases weren't heavy they were big and bulky and banged against her legs when she walked. Before she was even off the front porch she was breathing hard. Then in the yard, the spikes of her high heels kept sinking into the earth and making things more difficult. If she'd had any sense, she thought, she would have called Mr. Carleton and his taxi service. Except then everybody and his brother would have known she was leaving. She waited until she had crossed the road and was into the field and then she took her first breather, chafing the red palms of her hands and looking anxiously back at the house. No one had seen her yet.

All the evening walks through this field with James or the children had taught her the shortest way to town— the straight line through burrs and bushes, leading apparently to nowhere but more field, emerging suddenly upon Emmett Smith's backyard and from there to Main Street. She walked carefully, to avoid getting runs in her stockings, and kept her eyes strained ahead for the first sight of the Smith house. Around her ears the breeze made a hot, lulling sound, drying the dampness on her forehead to a cold thin sheet. Then another sound rose, like wailing, and she turned and saw Simon running to catch up, his brown hands fluttering to part the weeds in front of his chest and his face desperate. "*Jo*-oan!" he was calling. He made two syllables out of it. Joan set down the suitcases and waited, with her hands crossed over her pocketbook. "Joan, *wait!*" he said,

and floundered on. "Oh, Simon," she said, but she
kept waiting.

When he came up even with her he was out of breath,
and covered with burrs. For a while he just stood there
panting, but then his breath came more slowly and he
straightened up. "Can I come?" he asked.

"Oh, Simon—"

"I came in to see what you was doing. I couldn't *find*
you; I thought—" He stopped, and switched his eyes
from her face to the field behind her. "I wouldn't be a
bit of trouble," he said softly. She leaned forward, trying to catch his words, and he said it louder: "I wouldn't
be a *bit* of—"

"Well, I know that."

"Old James came over with that picture he took yesterday," he said. "You were gone off on my bicycle.
He brought it in a special brown envelope like he does
to customers. I said, 'Mama, here is that picture you
was asking for.' She says, 'What?' I pulled it out to
show her. She said, 'Oh,' and then went back to her
sewing and didn't look any more. I put it back on
James's doorstep."

"Well, now, don't you worry—" said Joan, but she
had to stop there, because she wasn't sure what he was
talking about. She stood frowning at him, with the wind
whipping the hair around her face and her hands
clenched white on the pocketbook.

"I won't be a *bit* of trouble," he said again.

She said, "No," and stooped nearer to him. "I can't
take you," she said. "I have to go off, Simon. And you
have to stay with your family. When they are back to
normal, though, you can come and visit."

Simon just stood there, very straight. She didn't know
what to do, because he had his head drawn back in that

way he had and if she'd hugged him he would have
hated her. So she waited a minute, and then she said,
"Well, goodbye." He didn't answer. "Goodbye," she
said again. She kept on facing him, though, because
she couldn't turn first and just leave him there. Then
when she was beginning to think they would stand that
way forever he swung around and left, and she watched
him go. He stumbled through the field in a zig-zagging
line, not parting the grass ahead of him but pressing on
with his hands at his sides. "Simon?" she called once.
But Simon never answered.

When she turned away herself, and bent to pick up
her bags again, she was thinking that out of all the bad
things she had ever done this might be the one sin. It
made her feel suddenly heavy and old; the weight of
her sadness dragged behind her through the fields like
another suitcase, and she couldn't look up or let herself
think about anything but walking, putting one foot
ahead of the other.

The Smith house loomed up suddenly, just beyond a
little rise in the ground. Inside a wire fence the hens
scratched irritably at the dirt, and from the house came
the sound of someone's singing. Joan set her suitcases
down and looked back, thinking to see some sign of
what she had left, but there was only the gentle slope
of wild grass stretching as far as she could see. Behind
that was James, dark and slow and calm, rocking easily
in his chair, and never knowing. And that long front
porch where she and Simon used to shell peas on summer evenings, while Janie Rose sang "The Murder of
James A. Garfield" through the open window. She
picked up her suitcases and walked on, with that sudden
light, lost feeling that came from walking in a straight
line away from people she loved.

The clock in the drugstore where the buses stopped said there were ten minutes to go. Tommy Jones behind the soda fountain checked her bags and handed her the tags, and she said, "Thank you," and smiled at him dazedly without thinking about him.

"Coke while you wait?" he asked.

"No, thank you."

"On the house."

"Oh, no."

Her voice sounded thin and sad. She felt like a stick, very straight and alone, standing upright with nothing to lean against. Surely people should have noticed it, but they didn't; Tommy smiled at her as if this were any normal day, and the two other people in the store went on leafing through their magazines. Dan Thompson's wife came in, wearing one of Dan's baggy printing aprons the way she usually did and carrying a fresh stack of this week's newspapers. The insides of her forearms were smeared with ink from them. When she saw Joan she smiled and came over toward her. "Hi," she said. "You want a paper?"

"I guess so," said Joan. She fished in her purse for the money and handed it over, and Carol gave her a paper off the top of the stack.

"Nothing but the most startling news," she said. "We took it all from the Rockland paper this week. Usually we get it from Clancyville."

"Well, that's all right," Joan said. "I haven't read the Rockland paper either."

"Good. You know what I think sometimes?" She heaved the papers onto a soda fountain stool and began rubbing the muscles of her arm. "Sometimes I think, what if *every* paper gets its news from the other papers?

What if this is twenty-year-old news we're reading, just circulating around and around among newspapers?''

"I don't suppose it'd make much difference," Joan said absently.

"Well, maybe not." She picked up the papers again. "You bring James over for supper some night, you hear? We haven't had the two of you together in a long time."

"All right," said Joan. She didn't see much point in telling Carol she was leaving, not if Carol hadn't noticed for herself. And she hadn't. She went off jauntily, with a wave of her hand, and threw the papers on the floor in front of the magazine rack and left the store. Yet there was Joan, all dressed up in her high-heeled shoes. She looked around at the other customers again, but they went on reading their magazines.

When the bus drew up, she was the only person to board it. The driver didn't smile or even look at her; already she was outside the little circle of Larksville, and only another stranger to the people on this bus. She sat in a seat by herself, toward the rear, and smoothed her skirt down and then looked at the other passengers. None of them looked back except a sailor, who stopped chewing his gum and winked, and she quickly looked away again and sat up straighter. The bus started with a jerk and wheezed up to full speed along Main Street, making a sad, going-away noise. Through the green-tinted windows Larksville looked like an old dull photograph, and that made her sad too, but once they had passed the town limits she began to feel better. Some of that light feeling came back. It crossed her mind, as she was pulling on her gloves, that all she was going to was another bedroom, to years spent reading alone in a little house kept by old people, remembering to greet her mother's friends on the street, smiling indulgently at other people's children. But then she shook that thought away, and folded her gloved hands in her lap and began looking out the window again.

It was almost an hour before the bus made its next stop, in a town called Howrell that Joan had always hated. Gangling men stood lined along the street, spitting tobacco juice and commenting on the passengers whose faces appeared in the bus windows. Underneath Joan was the slamming and banging of bags being shoved into the luggage compartment, and then the driver helped a little old lady up the steps and into the bus. She wore a hat made entirely of flowers. From the way she advanced, clutching her pocketbook in both hands, examining the face of each passenger and sniffing a little as she passed them, Joan knew she would sit beside her. Old ladies always did. She stopped next to Joan and said, "This seat taken?" and then slid in, not waiting for an answer. While she was getting settled she huffed and puffed, making little comments under her breath; she would be the talkative kind. "I thought this bus would *never* come," she said. "I thought it had laid down and died on the way." Joan smiled, and turned her face full to the window.

When the bus had started up again, and was rolling through the last of Howrell, Joan checked her watch. It would be nearly suppertime now. If she were in Larksville she would be sitting at the kitchen table cutting up a salad. She pictured herself there, her bare feet curled around the rungs of the chair. In her mind she seemed to be sitting an inch or so above the seat, not resting on anything but air. She ran through other pictures of herself—sitting in her parents' parlor, sitting on the porch with James, even sitting now beside this old lady on a bus rolling west. In all the pictures, she was resting

on nothing. She turned her mind back to the firmest
seat she knew—James's lap, in the evenings when Ansel
had already gone to bed. But even there, there was a
good two inches of air beneath her and she seemed to
be balanced there precariously, her arms tight around
James. She turned away from the window quickly and
said to the old lady, "It'll be getting dark soon."

"It certainly will," said the lady. "My daughter will
be getting supper on now. The married one. I left them
a cold hen, barbecued the way I like to do it."

Joan went back to looking out the window. She stared
steadily at the clay banks that rose high and red along
the side of the road, and the tall thin tobacco barns from
which little strings of brightly dressed women were
scattering home for supper. Who would take her place
tomorrow at the tobacco table? She stopped watching
the barns. All around her in the bus, people were settled firmly in their seats, with their hands relaxed on
the arm rests and their heads tipped against the white
starched bibs on the backs of the seats. They talked to
one another in murmuring voices that mingled with the
sound of the motor. A little boy was playing a tonette.

"I'm going to my *other* daughter," the old lady told
her. "The one that never married. She has a kidney
ailment."

"I'm sorry to hear that," said Joan.

"She's in terrible pain, and there's no one to take
care of her."

Out of the corner of her eye Joan saw the Larksville
paper she had bought, folded neatly and tucked down
between her seat and the wall of the bus. She picked it
up quickly and unfolded it, and the old lady turned
away again.

There would be nothing interesting in the paper, but

she read it anyway. She began with the first page and read through the whole paper methodically, not even skipping the ladies' meeting announcements or the advertisements. There had been one birth in Larksville this week, she saw, and two deaths. The first death was Jones, Laramie D., whom she had never heard of, but she read all about him anyway—the circumstances of his death, the highlights of his life, the list of relatives who had survived him. The second death was Pike, Janie Rose. The name hit into her stomach, as if she hadn't known of the death until this instant. She started to pass over it, but then she went back to it and read it through:

Pike, Janie Rose. At County Hospital, in her sixth year, of internal injuries caused by an accident. Beloved daughter of Mr. and Mrs. Roy J. Pike, sister of Simon Lockwood Pike. Funeral was held from Collins Memorial Home, July 16, interment in family cemetery.

She read it twice, but it seemed unreal still, something vague and far off. Nothing that bad could happen. When she had finished with it a second time she folded the paper very carefully in half, so that the obituaries were out of sight, and then went on to the rest of the paper. She read very closely now, even moving her lips, so as to shut out all thought of anything she had read before. "Teller-Hokes Wedding Held in First Baptist Church," she read, and although neither name meant anything to her she was careful to find out exactly what the bride wore and who her guests were. Next came the memorial notices, ringed in black like the obituaries. She had never looked at the memorial notices before.

She read about someone named Auntie Peg Myers, who had passed away on July 16, 1937, and was dearly remembered by her two nieces. Then she read about Nathan Martin, who had been taken from his wife in 1941. For him there was a quotation. "Too dearly beloved ever to be forgotten," it said. Further down, for other people, there were little poems, but Joan stopped reading. She had a sudden picture of all the years of this century, stretching far back in a chain of newsprint that grew yellower and yellower as the years grew older. 1937 was almost orange, older than she herself was; 1941 was growing brittle at the edges. How would this year look? The print on January was already blurred. And then she pictured how it would be when today was yellowed too, years from now, and the Pikes themselves were buried and Simon an old man. Then on the third week in every July he would print his notice: "In memory of Janie Rose, who passed away just fifty years ago July 13th. Fondly remembered by her brother Simon." He would be remembering her as someone very small with spectacles, who had lived in the tacked-on bedroom in back of the house. But he himself would be a grandfather then, and nobody Janie would recognize. How would Simon look in fifty years? Joan tried to think, but all she saw was Simon as he was today—hunching his shoulders up, tucking his head down in that uncertain way he had.

She looked quickly out the window and saw the town of Graham rolling up, and the bus station with its line of coin machines. "Is this where you get off?" the woman asked her.

"No."

"Oh. You just sat up so sudden—"

"No," said Joan, "but I think I might buy a Coke."

She stood and wormed her way out past the woman's knees, and as soon as she was out the woman slid quickly over to the window. Joan didn't care. She went down the aisle without looking at anyone, and then descended the bus steps. A team of some kind was waiting to board, a group of boys in white satin wind-breakers with numbers on them, and when Joan stepped down among them they remained stolidly in her path, ignoring her. "Excuse me," she said, "excuse me, please," and then when no one noticed she shouted, "*Excuse me!*" For a minute they stopped talking and stared at her; then they moved aside to let her through. She walked very quickly, holding her head up. Out here she felt thinner and more alone than before, with the team of boys all watching her down the long path to the Coke machine. And when she reached the machine she found she didn't even want a Coke. But she put her dime in anyway, and just as she was reaching for the bottle someone said, "Ma'am?"

It was a young man in sunglasses, standing beside her and looking straight at her. She felt scared suddenly, even with all those people around (had he been able to *see* how alone she felt?) and she decided not to answer. Instead she uncapped the Coke bottle and then turned to go.

"Ma'am?" he said again.

She couldn't just leave him there, still asking. "What is it?" she said.

"Can you show me where the restroom is?"

"Why, it's right inside, I guess. Over there."

"Where?"

"Over there."

"I don't see."

"Over *there.*"

"I don't see. I'm blind."

"Oh," said Joan, and then she just felt silly, and even sadder than before. "Wait a minute," she told him. She turned around and saw two bus drivers walking toward her, looking kind and cheerful. When they came even with her she tapped the older driver on the arm and said, "Um, excuse me."

"Yes."

"Can you show this man the restroom? He doesn't see."

"Why, surely," said the driver. He smiled at her and then took the blind man by the elbow. "You come with me," he said.

"Thank you, sir. Thank you, ma'am."

"You're welcome," Joan said.

The other driver stayed behind, next to Joan. He said, "Can you imagine traveling blind?" and stared after the two men, frowning a little.

"No, I can't," Joan said. She automatically followed the driver's eyes. Now that she looked, she couldn't think why the blind man had frightened her at first. He wore his clothes obediently, as if someone else had put them on him—the neat dark suit with the handkerchief in the pocket, the shoes tied lovingly in double knots. He reminded her of something. For a minute she couldn't think what, and then she remembered and smiled. That slow, trusting way he let himself be guided forward with his hands folded gently in front of him, was like Simon during the first year she'd lived there, when he was six and still had to be awakened at night and taken to the bathroom so he wouldn't wet his bed. He had gone just that obediently, but with his eyes closed and the shadows of some dream still flickering across his face. (You couldn't stop walking with him for a minute, not in a doorway or going around the bend in the hall, or he would think he had reached the bathroom and proceed to go right then and there.) He had held his elbows in close to his body that way, too, against the coolness of the night. Joan stopped smiling and looked down at her feet.

"You all right?" the driver asked.

"I want to go back."

"Ma'am?"

"I want to go back where I came from. Can I take my bags off my bus and wait for the next one going back?"

"Why, surely," the driver said. "You on that bus over there?"

"Yes. I know this is—"

"Women got a *right* to change their minds," the driver called. He was already heading toward her bus, and Joan followed him with her untouched Coke bottle still in her hands.

"I always do this," she said. "But this time it's—"

"You got the right," said the driver.

"This time it's different. I can't help it, this time; I'm not just—"

But the driver didn't hear her. He was walking up ahead of her and laughing over his shoulder, thinking it was all a joke. She stopped trying to tell him it wasn't.

13

Something was wrong at home. James knew it instantly, the moment he stepped out of the pickup carrying his two bags of groceries. There on the porch stood the Potter sisters and Ansel and Mrs. Pike, all huddling together, and Mr. Pike was a little distance away from them. He was facing toward the road, frowning down at an Indian elephant bell that he held in his hand. When he heard the pickup door slam he looked up and said, "James." The light from the setting sun turned his face strange and orange.

"What's wrong?" said James.

"We can't find Simon."

"Well, where is he?" he asked, and then to cover up the stupidity of that question he said quickly, "He was here at lunchtime."

"We thought you might have him with you," Mr. Pike said.

"No."

They all kept looking at him. Even Ansel. James hoisted his groceries up higher and then said again, "No. No, I've been running errands all afternoon. All by myself."

"Well, then," Mr. Pike said. He sighed and turned

back to the others, who still waited. Finally he said, "He's not with James."

"Maybe he's with Joan," James offered.

"No. Joan must have gone off somewhere, but after she left Simon was still around. Lou says so."

James looked over at Mrs. Pike. She was dry-eyed and watchful; her arms were folded firmly across her chest.

"When was the last time you noticed him?" he asked her.

"I don't know."

"Ma'am?"

"I don't *know*," she said, with her voice slightly raised.

"Oh."

"We called the boys he plays with," Mr. Pike said. "And we called the movie-house."

"Did you ask about buses?"

"No. Why?"

"I'd do that," said James. He climbed the steps at his end of the porch and set the groceries on Ansel's chair, and then he straightened up and rubbed the muscles of his arms. "Call the drugstore," he said. "Ask them if he's—"

"Well, I *went* to the drugstore, to see if he'd gone there for a soda. Mary Bennett was on; only been there a half hour or so, but she hadn't seen him."

"Might have gone earlier," said James. "Did you look at the bus schedule?"

"*No* I didn't. What would I want to do that for?"

"Just in case," James said. "Who was there before Mary Bennett?"

"Tommy was, but I can't find him. If it weren't for Lou I'd just sit and *wait* for Simon, but Lou thinks he left with a purpose. Thinks she might have sent him away somehow.''

James looked over at Mrs. Pike again. For a minute she stared back at him; then she said, ''You believe he's on some bus.''

''I didn't say that,'' said James.

''You think it.''

''Now, Lou,'' Mr. Pike told her.

''I can tell.''

''Well, it wouldn't hurt to ask,'' said James. ''I'd track that Tommy down, if I was you.''

''*Oh,* now,'' Mr. Pike said, and accidentally clanged the elephant bell. Everyone jumped. ''Sorry,'' he said. For the first time, Ansel lost his blank tense look; he winced, and leaned back limply against the front of the house. Mr. Pike said, ''Sorry, Ansel. But where would he take a bus *to*?''

''There's lots of places,'' said James.

''Not as many as you'd think,'' Ansel said. ''World's shrinking.''

''Hush,'' James told him. He jingled his keys thoughtfully. ''Roy, can I use your telephone?''

''What for?''

''Let him,'' Mrs. Pike said. The Potter sisters stepped closer to her on either side and patted her shoulders, as if she had suddenly had an outburst of some kind. ''You know where it is,'' she told James.

''Yes, ma'am.''

He walked toward the Pikes' end of the porch, with everyone's eyes following him. At the door he stopped and said, ''Did he have any money?''

''He gets an allowance,'' said Mr. Pike. ''I don't know if he saved it.''

''Did he get some this week?''

He was asking this of Mrs. Pike, but she just shook her head. "I don't know," she said. Finally James turned back again and went on inside.

It was Tommy Jones's mother who answered the telephone. Her voice was breathless, as if she had had to come running from some other part of the house. "Hello?" she said.

"Mrs. Jones, this is James Green. Is Tommy there?"

"No, he's not."

"Do you know where he is?"

"No. Is this about Simon still?"

"Yes, ma'am."

"They haven't found him?"

"No. Do you think Tommy'll be getting back soon?"

"I really don't," she said. "He's off someplace with his girl. Shall I have him call?"

"No, thank you. Sorry to bother you."

"It's no bother."

He hung up and stood thinking a while, and then he went out to the front porch again. In just the short time that the telephone call had taken the color of the evening had shifted, turning from sunset into twilight. The others were standing where he had left them, still looking in his direction as if their eyes had never moved from the spot where he had disappeared. "Tommy's not there," he said.

"Well, *I* could have told you that," Mr. Pike said irritably. He swung his arms down, making the bell clang again, and started toward the front yard. "I'm going to round up a couple others," he called back. "We'll look in all the places where he goes, and ring bells or fire guns if we find him. Want to come, James?"

"I'm not sure that's the way," James said.

"Only thing I can think of. Mind if I use your truck?"

"Well, wait," said James. He came down the steps and crossed over to Mr. Pike. "No, I'd like to take the truck and follow up an idea of my own, I think I—"

"When *I* was a little boy . . ." Ansel announced, and everyone turned around to look at him. He had recovered from that last clang and was standing erect now, placing the tips of his fingers together. "When I was a little boy, I had to tell my mother *every*where I went. It was a rule. And I could never go out of hearing range of this old Army bugle, that my father would stand in the doorway and blow at suppertime—"

"If you could come along," Mr. Pike told James, "and bring a noisemaker of some kind, why, we could start by—"

"I was thinking of Caraway," James said.

"Caraway?"

"I was thinking that was where he might've gone."

"Oh, *Caraway*," Mr. Pike said impatiently. "*I* been there. No, more likely he went off on some hike or other, and forgot to let us know."

"Well, I'd like to try Caraway anyhow," said James.

"But James, that's a waste of—"

"Let him," said Mrs. Pike, and once again the Potter sisters closed in on her and patted her shoulders. "Hush, hush," they whispered. James pulled out his billfold and checked his money; there was plenty for gas. He turned to Mr. Pike.

"I'm sorry," he said. "I just feel I know where he's at."

"Well, that's all right," said Mr. Pike. "Sure wish I could have the loan of your pickup, though."

"I'll make the trip as fast as I can."

"Well, sure." Mr. Pike sighed, and then he set off wearily across the yard. He carried the elephant bell upside down, with his fingers poked through the inward-curling teeth of it to hold the clapper silent. When he reached the gravel road he turned back and said, "Ansel? You feel up to coming along?"

"Not really," said Ansel. "I just feel miserable about all this."

Mr. Pike nodded several times and then continued down the road in the direction of the Terrys'. "Poor man," said Miss Lucy, and then she and Miss Faye began patting Mrs. Pike harder than before.

James said, "Ansel, take in the groceries. And fix yourself something for supper, in case I'm late getting back."

"Well, all right," Ansel said.

"I don't expect you want to come with me."

"No."

James descended the porch steps. In the distance he could see Mr. Pike, far and small already, marching on steadily with his shoulders set. It seemed so clear to James that Simon was in Caraway—where else would he be?—that he felt sorry to see Mr. Pike going to all this trouble. He wanted to call him back, but he knew there was no use. So he just turned around and said, "Ansel—" and bumped squarely into Mrs. Pike, who was standing right behind him. "Oh, excuse me," he said. "I didn't hear you coming." She remained silent, with her arms still folded and her head bowed meekly. "Well," he said. "Ansel, I'm going to call you at the Pikes' number when I get there. To tell you what happens, in case Mrs. Pike is going to be over at the Potters'."

"All right," said Ansel. "Does that mean I can stay at the Pikes' until you call?"

"I don't care, for heaven's sake."

He continued on toward the pickup, and Mrs. Pike kept following after him. When he opened the door on the driver's side she opened the other door, and it was only then that he realized she meant to come along. They stood staring at each other for a minute across the expanse of seat; then Mrs. Pike lowered her eyes and climbed in, and he did the same. He could see that the others on the porch were just as surprised as he was—they came closer together, and turned to look at each other—but Mrs. Pike didn't offer to explain herself. She sat quietly, with her eyes straight ahead and her hands clasped in her lap. Even when he craned his neck around to look out the rear window as he was backing out, she stared ahead. The stoniness of her face gave her a calm, sure look, as sure as James felt inside; she must know where Simon was by instinct.

When they were on the main highway James turned his lights on. Already the opaque white look of early twilight was growing bluer and more transparent, and other cars as they came towards him clicked their own lights on. But he could see around him clearly still: the landmarks of the journey to town slipping by, and then a brief glimpse of Main Street itself before he passed it. It felt funny to keep going straight, instead of turning there. A strange sinking feeling began in his stomach, and he looked into the rear-view mirror and watched the town lights fading away from him. "Don't worry," he said suddenly to Mrs. Pike, but Mrs. Pike wasn't looking worried at all; she only nodded, calmly.

"I'm just waiting," she told him.

"Oh."

"I'll take what I get. Whatever I deserve."

"Yes, ma'am," James said.

He swerved around a little boy riding a bicycle. Where was Simon at this minute? Maybe swaggering down a street alone, trying to look as if he knew where he was going. Searching for some sign—a boy with a ring in his ear or a woman in a red-plumed hat, someone who would expect him the way he had expected them. James frowned. The clomping of Simon's leather boots seemed louder than the sound of the motor; the fuzz down the back of Simon's neck seemed clearer than the road ahead of him.

"It's been a pretty day," he said.

"Yes."

"Where's Joan?"

"I don't know," said Mrs. Pike. She looked out at the road a while, and then she said, "I sewed a dress today."

"Oh, did you?"

"Yes."

"Well, now," James said. He cleared his throat. "I always thought a dress would take *days* to make."

"Anything that happens," said Mrs. Pike, "it's only my fault. My fault."

"Well, now," James said again.

The truck was traveling too fast, he thought. Already the countryside looked like Caraway countryside; not Larksville. In his mind he had added mile upon mile to this trip, stretching the road out long and thin till Caraway might have been in Asia. Yet before they had been on the road half an hour they reached Stevens's Esso Station—the halfway mark—and he braked sharply and turned in. "Need gas," he told Mrs. Pike. She nodded.

The meter said the tank was half full, but stopping this way would slow things down a little.

Mr. Stevens himself washed the windshield and filled the tank, with only a brief smile to James because he didn't recognize him. "Three dollars, ten," he said. "Nice evening." He held his hand out flat, palm up, outside James's window, and James counted out the exact change very slowly. When he had paid he said, "This the road to Caraway?" to stretch the stop out even longer.

"Sure is," the man said.

"How much further?"

"Be there in half an hour."

"Thank you," James said. He started the motor and looked over at Mrs. Pike, but she didn't seem surprised at the questions he had asked. She just looked down at her hands and waited for him to drive on.

Almost no one else was on the road now. He drove at a steady pace, and in silence, looking at the country around him whenever they were on a straight stretch of road. At first it was just the occasional, very noticeable things that he recognized—that humped bridge that looked like something off a willowware plate, the funny barbecue house off in the middle of nowhere with pigs chasing each other rapidly in neon lights across the front porch. But after another ten or fifteen minutes, he began to recognize everything. The objects that flashed by were all worn and familiar-looking, as if perhaps without knowing it he had been dreaming of them nightly. Even the new things—the brick ranch houses rising baldly out of fresh red clay, the drive-ins and Dairy Queens—seemed familiar, and he glanced at them mildly and without surprise. When he reached the town limits it was just beginning to grow really dark, and his headlights glared briefly against the slick white surface of a newly painted sign. "Caraway. Bird Sanctuary," it read. The last time he had been here it had said only "Caraway." And he had looked at it and thought, I'll never see that sign again, not for *any* reason. He hadn't known the Pikes then, nor Joan, nor the Potters; he hadn't foreseen the existence of Simon.

He slowed down as soon as they reached the actual town, and Mrs. Pike straightened up and began looking out the window more intently, perhaps already searching for Simon. James kept his eyes straight ahead until they got to Main Street. Then he pointed to an all-night grill and said, "This is where the buses stop."

"Oh," said Mrs. Pike.

"Do you want to go ask if they've seen him?"

"I guess so," she said, but she was looking at him, obviously expecting that he would be the one to ask. He sighed and swung the truck into a diagonal parking place.

"I'll be right out," he told her.

"All right."

Once on the street, out from behind the shield of the pickup, he felt clumsy and conspicuous. Girls in bare-backed dresses waited with their dates in front of the movie theater next door and when he stepped on the sidewalk they pivoted on their high heels and glanced over at him. He stared back, but there was no one he recognized. And the waitress in the grill was a new one—a fat blond he didn't know. He came up and laid both hands palms down on the counter and said, "Were you here when the last bus from Larksville came?"

"Yes," she said. Her voice was tired, and she seemed hardly able to raise her eyes and look at him.

"Did you see a little boy get off?"

"I wasn't watching," she said.

She began swabbing off the counter with a pink sponge, and James walked out again without thanking her. On the street he looked up and down, hooking his thumbs in his belt and staring over the heads of passersby, but there was no sign of Simon. For the first time he felt uncertain about him, and frightened. He returned to the truck.

"She wasn't watching," he told Mrs. Pike.

"She wasn't," she agreed, and went on looking calmly out the window.

James knew where he was heading, but he was hoping he didn't have to go there. So he drove down Main Street very slowly, looking right and left, peering into the windows of restaurants and soda shops and scanning the faces of people out for evening walks. Several times he saw people he knew. Seen through the truck window, walking in half-dark, six years older and unexpected in new clothes that James had never known, they looked worn and sad to him. He would look after them a minute with a feeling of bewilderment, almost forgetting Simon until Mrs. Pike touched him on the arm. Then he would drive on.

Mrs. Pike didn't ask what he was doing when he turned off Main Street. She seemed to think that this was part of a tour around Caraway that anyone might follow, and she gazed in tourist-like respect at a three-foot-high statue of Major John Caraway. ("This is Major Caraway," James's father always explained to them. "He fought in the Big War." Meaning the Civil War, though there'd been others since. "He certainly was a *small* man," said their mother. Their father never answered that.) Even when they turned down Hampden Street, where there were no statues and only private houses, Mrs. Pike said nothing. She kept on searching the sides of the road, poking her nose toward the window so that the skin between her chin and the base of her throat made one slanted line. James drove more and more slowly. He turned left on Winton Lane and then drew to a stop, letting the truck roll into the grass at the side of the road. They were in front of an old gray house with a great many gables, its yard sprinkled with the feather-white skeletons of dandelions. No one was on the porch. For a while James sat silent, tapping the steering wheel with one finger. Then he looked over at Mrs. Pike. She was still searching out the window, almost as if she thought they were still moving. "I'll be back," he told her.

"All right."

He opened the truck door and climbed out stiffly, careful not to make too much noise. But no dog barked. In his mind, he saw now, he had pictured the dog's barking first. He had imagined that everyone would come to the door to investigate, long before he had reached the front steps; he had seen the long rectangle of yellow light from the doorway and the silhouettes of many people, watching as he walked awkwardly through the dandelions. Yet he came to the door in utter silence, with no one noticing. He opened the screen, which creaked, and knocked several times on the weatherbeaten wooden door and waited. For a while no one came. Then there were footsteps, and he stepped back a pace. He fixed his eyes on a point just a little above his own eye level, where he would see that hard white face as soon as the door opened.

But when the door did open, he had to look lower than that. He had to look down to the level of his shoulders, much lower than he had remembered, into the old

man's small lined face and his eyes in their pockets of
bone. His hair was all white now, gleamingly clean. He
wore suspenders, snapped over a frayed white collarless
shirt which was only folded shut, without buttons. And
his trousers bagged at the knees.

"The dog didn't bark," said James.

"She died," his father said, and stepped back a step
to let him into the house.

14

The first thing Simon said was, "If I'd known *you* were coming, I'd of hitched a ride with you." He was sitting in old Mr. Green's platform rocker, with his elbows resting lightly on the arms of it and his fingers laced in front of him. "Did you just leave home and not tell anyone?" he asked.

"I told *every*one," said James, and looked straight across at the others. They stood in a line behind Simon, the three of them—his father, Claude, and Clara, the one brother and sister still at home. They were standing very still, all three of them in almost exactly the same position, with their eyes on James. When James looked at them Simon turned around and looked too, and just in that one turn of his head, with his chin pointed upwards and the shock of hair falling back off his forehead, he seemed to be *claiming* them somehow, marking them as his own. James's father looked down at him soberly, and Clara smiled, but by then Simon had turned to James again and couldn't see her. "I came on a bus," he said.

"I guessed you had."

"I found them in a telephone book."

Clara said, "James, will you sit down?"

225

"Oh, I guess not," said James. "Did you call the police?"

"I don't hold with police," his father said.

"I forgot."

"We figured you'd come after him. We didn't call no one."

"I see," James said. He folded his arms and stared down at one shoe. "His mother was wondering where he was."

"Well, now she'll know," said his father. "*Your* mother used to wonder."

"Sir?"

"What did she say?" Simon asked. "Did she see I was gone? What did she say about it?"

Instead of answering, James turned around and looked out the open door. There was Mrs. Pike, picking her way through the dandelions and toward that rectangle of light across the porch. She had come unasked, having waited long enough in the pickup, and because she didn't know whose house this was or what she was doing here her face had a puckered, uncertain look. She stumbled a little on the porch and then came forward, her eyes squinting against the light. "James—" she began, and then saw Simon and stopped. "Is that Simon?" she asked. Her finger began plucking at her skirt, and she stayed poised there on the porch.

Simon stood up and looked at James, but he didn't say anything.

"Simon, is that you?" his mother asked.

"Yes."

"Where did you go?" She called this into the room from her place on the porch; she didn't seem able to step inside. "Why did you leave?"

"Oh, well," Simon said uncertainly. He looked over

at James's family, as if they might tell him what was going on here, but they were all staring at Mrs. Pike. "I just came to see these people," he said.

"Oh," said his mother. She looked down at her skirt. The longer she stood there the more distant she seemed to become, so that now James couldn't imagine her *ever* walking in of her own accord. He said, "Mrs. Pike, will you come in?" and then Clara, who had been gazing open-mouthed, came to life and said, "Oh. Yes, *please* come in."

Mrs. Pike took a few steps, just enough to get her safely into the room, without moving her eyes from Simon. "What happened to your hair?" she asked him.

"What hair?"

"I wish you'd have a seat," Clara said.

"Simon, were you not going to come back?"

"Well, I don't know," said Simon. "I just came away, I guess."

"Oh," Mrs. Pike said. She wet her lips and said, "Will you come back *now*?"—not looking at Simon any more but at James, as if he were the one she was asking.

"What for?" Simon asked.

"Why—just to be back."

Whatever Simon was thinking, he didn't show it. He began walking in those small circles of his, with his eyes on his boots. And James suddenly thought, what if he *won't* come back? The same idea must have hit Mrs. Pike. She said, "Don't you *want* to come?"

"Well," Simon said.

"You can't stay *here*."

"How did you happen to come by?" he asked.

"James thought of it."

"I mean, what for? Did you just go off driving?"

Mrs. Pike frowned at him, not understanding. *"James* thought of it," she said. "He thought you'd be in Caraway."

"You mean you came specially?"

"Well, *yes,"* said Mrs. Pike. "What did you think?"

"Oh," Simon said, and the sudden clear look that came across his face made James feel light inside and relieved. It was that simple, he thought; Simon didn't know they had come just for him. "You mean you're here on *account* of my going off," he said.

"Of course we are. Will you let us take you home?"

"Sure, I guess so."

Everyone seemed to loosen up then. James's father said, *"Well,* now," and Mrs. Pike crossed over to Simon and hugged him tightly. He stood straight while she hugged him, looking very stiff and grown up, but there was a little shy, pleased smile pulling at the corners of his mouth. "I came on a bus," he said.

"Wasn't anyone *with* you?"

"No."

"I'm glad I didn't know about it, then. I'm glad I— oh, goodness. Miss, um—"

"Green," James said. "Clara Green, and Claude, and my father. This is Mrs. Pike."

"Your *family?"* said Mrs. Pike. She looked at them more closely. "Well, of *all* things," she said. "I never thought I'd—well. Miss Green, do you have a telephone?"

"In the dining room," said Clara. "I'll show you."

"I want to reach my husband somehow. I hope someone's at the house."

She followed after Clara, with one arm still around Simon, and James watched after them because he didn't know where else to look. Simon walked very straight, holding up the weight of his mother's arm but keeping himself tall and separate from her, and Mrs. Pike moved almost briskly. "They'll be half insane," James heard her say. "Oh, good. Thank you." They were out of sight now. Clara reappeared in the doorway, and James turned away and put his hands in his pockets.

He was standing squarely in front of the fireplace, a small one with a marble mantelpiece. Everything in the room was exactly the way it had been before—the linoleum rug with the roses painted on it, the bead curtains, the turquoise walls made up of tongue-and-groove slats. On the mantelpiece was a Seth Thomas clock that his mother had brought when she came, and a picture of Jesus knocking at the door and a glass plate that looked like lace. At first, not knowing what else to do with himself, James absentmindedly stooped nearer to the fireplace and held out his hands to be warmed. It was only after a minute that he remembered it was summer and the fire unlit. So he had to straighten up again, his hands in his back pockets and his face toward the others. They were all looking at him. Clara had sat down on the footstool, thinner and sharper and with the look of an old maid beginning to set in around her mouth. And Claude was on the couch, twisting a leather lanyard in his hands. He was grown now. The last time James had seen him, Claude was in his early teens and had turned red from the neck up every time he was directly addressed. There had been more of them then. His mother, small and dark, scared of everything, humming hymns under her breath in a tinny monotone as she sewed. His sister Madge, whose one romance they had broken up and who was now in China doing missionary work. And Ansel.

If he had ever imagined coming back here—and it

seemed to him now he had, without knowing it—he had not imagined standing like this, wordless. He had thought that of all the mixed-up, many-sided things in the world, his dislike of his father was one complete and pure emotion and that that alone could send words enough swarming to his mouth. Yet his father stood before him like a small, battered bird, the buttonless shirt folded gently over his thin chest and the worn leather slippers searching out the floorboards hesitantly when he walked. He was making his way to the rocker. All the time that Simon had sat there, the old man must have been watching shyly and eagerly, waiting for his chance to reclaim it. (It had always been his property alone, forbidden to the children. On Bible Class nights, when both parents were gone, James would sit in that chair and rock fiercely, and the other children stood around him with wide scared eyes.) Now James's father sat down almost gratefully, feeling behind him first to make sure it was there and then slowly lowering himself into it. When he rocked, the chair complained; it had grown old and sullen with time.

"Yes, the dog died," he said. He surveyed his three children out of eyes the same startling blue as Ansel's, and he smiled a little, "She died."

"I'm sorry to hear that," said James.

"It happens."

"She had cancer," Claude said.

"Can dogs get cancer?"

"Get everything people get," said his father, rocking steadily. "The vet told us so, at the time."

"I never heard that."

There was a silence. Clara sat forward suddenly, throwing her arms around her knees in that swooping way she had and craning her neck up, and everyone looked at her as if they expected her to say something but she didn't. She just smiled at them, with her lips tightly closed.

"You've got your hair a different way," James told her. Clara went on smiling at him and nodded.

"Yes, I do," she said.

"Every thought of every curl is another stroke for the devil," said her father. "Have you ever thought of that? But *Clara* here don't care; she *likes* short hair."

"Yes, I do," Clara said again. The tone of her voice was indifferent, and she included her father in her smile. No one seemed to be as James remembered.

Out in the dining room, Mrs. Pike said, "Yes? Miss Lucy, I'm glad you're there. I was hoping you would hear the phone and—"

"You're back," James's father said.

The others looked at him.

"You're back in this house."

"Yes," James said. "Just for—" He stopped.

"Just for a while," his father said. "Just for the boy."

"Yes."

"Ah, well."

Mrs. Pike was talking loudly, apparently trying to break in on something Miss Lucy was saying. "Yes, I know," she said. "I know—Miss Lucy, will you try and find Roy? First go and shout for him. Yes, I'm feeling fine, thank you. Then if he's too far away I'll leave a message. But I'd like to have Simon tell him—"

"The phone is a precarious instrument," said James's father.

"Hush, now," Clara told him. "There's not a machine in this world you don't say that about."

"A *wavery* thing," said the old man, overriding her. "On a thin line between what's real and what isn't. Is that person *really* sitting next to you, the way he sounds? When I called you at your neighbors, three Christmases ago—"

"Sir?" said James.

"When Clara called three Christmases ago, and Ansel wouldn't talk to her but stayed in the other room, I happened to be passing near enough to hear what was going on at the other end. Heard Ansel shouting how he wouldn't come. And it seemed to me his voice was trembly-like, unsteady. Is his sickness worse?"

"No," James said. "He's just a little weak sometimes."

"It's the forces from inside that weaken."

"He's all right," James told him.

Simon was on the telephone now. He was talking to Miss Lucy. "Yes, ma'am," he said. "Then I got on the bus. I figured out the schedule in the drugstore." James's father rocked sharply forward and slapped both slippers on the floor.

"That boy is too *young* to travel alone," he said.

"He ran away," said James.

"I realize that. He came to our door and asked to be a lodger. Did you tell him this family ran a boarding house?"

"No."

"He seemed to think you had."

He rocked on in silence for a minute; the only sound was Simon's voice. Then Clara looked up and, finding her father's eyes on her, gathered her skirts beneath her and spoke. "He likes mayonnaise," she said.

"Who does?" asked James.

"The little boy. He wanted a mayonnaise sandwich."

"Oh." He frowned at her a minute, and then looked over at his father. "What were you going to do with him?" he asked.

"The boy? I figured someone'd come after him."

"What if they hadn't?"

"You *did*," said his father. "Someone *did*. I don't hold with police."

"You could have called the parents."

"I don't speak on telephones."

"His sister just died," said James. "His mother had enough to worry about."

"Most do."

"*More* than enough. Clara could have called."

"I never turn a stranger from my door," his father said. He let his head fall back against the rocker. "Can *you* say that? Did *you* never let a man down?" He looked at James from under white, papery eyelids, waiting for an answer. No one said anything. It seemed to James that his father had raised a banner in the room—the same one as in old days, long and dark and heavy. His lowered eyes were asking, "What can you do about it? Can you take my flag down?" and smiling faintly. Yet the lines around those eyes were deep and tired; his children sat limp, not bothering to answer. "Ah me," said the old man, and rolled his head to the other side and then back again and closed his eyes.

"This has nothing to do with me," James said. "It was his *mother* you made worry; it wasn't me."

"Stop it," Clara told him.

"Clara, are *you* against telephones?"

"You could have telephoned here," his father said suddenly. He opened his eyes and looked over at James.

"I was hoping he hadn't got this far," said James.

"I see. Have you got a telephone yet? I didn't think to ask."

"No."

"And money. Have you made a lot of money in your life?"

"No. But I get along."

"Get along, do you." He nodded to himself, several times. "Changed your ways?"

"No."

"No," his father agreed, and relaxed against the back of the rocker again.

Mrs. Pike and Simon came out of the dining room, Mrs. Pike's hand still on Simon's shoulder. She said, "We called collect. I'm sure you're relieved to hear that," and then laughed a little and looked down at Simon. "They're going to relay the message to Simon's daddy," she said.

"Well, I'm glad you got through to them," said Clara. "Will you have a seat?"

"Oh, we couldn't. I'm sorry, I know I haven't said two words to you. Mr. Green, it's nice to see you." She advanced, smiling, heading straight for James's father and holding out one plump hand. He had to rise from his rocker to take it. She said, "You're smaller-boned than James or Ansel. But you've got Ansel's fair skin." The way she spoke of him made him seem like a child being compared to his parents, but he smiled graciously back.

"James gets his skin from his mother," he told her.

"I guessed that."

"He's back in this house now."

Clara said, "Mrs. Pike, I wish you'd sit down and have some lemonade."

"No, we really can't. I have to get Simon home—

and I do thank you for taking care of him." She said that directly to Clara, and Clara smiled at her with her narrow, gaunt smile. "He don't *usually* run away, I don't want you thinking—"

"He's too young to be on his own," said Mr. Green.

"He's *not* on his own."

"James used to run away." He sat down in his rocker and looked up at her, staring out from under white arched eyebrows. Mrs. Pike waited, and then when she saw that he wasn't going to continue she turned to the others.

"I thank my Lord we found him," she said. "I feel it's some kind of sign; I've been let off with a warning." She squeezed Simon tight against her, and he smiled at the middle button of her dress and then broke away.

James stood up, preparing to leave, and Mrs. Pike said, "James, I thought we could go back by bus. You probably want to stay on a bit, now you're here."

"No, I'll drive you back," said James. He crossed over to his father and said, "I guess I'll be going."

"We still have your old bed," said his father, but he seemed to know beforehand that James would say no. He rose again from the rocker, very slowly, and shook James's hand while he looked at the floor. It was a small, clean hand, that offered no resistance when James pressed it. To Mrs. Pike, James's father said, "It began when he was four. He ran everywhere."

"What?" asked Mrs. Pike.

"James."

"Oh," she said. "Well, I'm glad to've met you, Mr. Green—" and she shook his hand once more, holding her wrist slightly curved and offering just the tips of her fingers. "I can't thank you enough for all you've done; any time you're in Larksville you just stop in on us."

"We locked doors and tied knots," said Mr. Green, "but he was like Houdini."

Mrs. Pike shook hands with Claude and Clara and made Simon do the same, and James followed behind them. He shook Claude's hand but Clara he kissed, feeling that she would prefer that. Her cheek was bonier than he had expected, and the skin dry. She would probably never get married, he thought. None of them would.

When they went out the door his father followed them, and stood on the porch in his slippers. "Well, goodbye, James," he said. "You'll be back someday, I expect." But his smile when he looked up at James was timid and uncertain, and James smiled back.

"Tell Madge hello for me," he said.

"All right."

They climbed into the pickup at the edge of the yard— Mrs. Pike at the window, and Simon in the middle next to James. Simon said, "Hey, James, can I steer?" but James was starting the engine up and didn't answer. He looked in the rear-view mirror and saw his father still standing on the porch, his arms hugging his chest, his knees bagging, his small white head strained toward the truck. As long as James took getting started, his father remained there, and when he drove away Mr. Green lifted one arm for a goodbye and stayed that way until the truck was out of sight. James drove staring straight ahead for a while, holding that picture of his father in his mind.

When they had turned into the center of Caraway again, Mrs. Pike said, "It's a nice town, isn't it?"

"Some ways," James said.

"Yes." And she settled back, one hand patting the back of Simon's neck. Simon was restless and fidgety after all his adventures. He sat on the edge of the seat, kicking one foot nervously and gritting his jaw in that way he had when he'd had too much excitement. The passing streetlights gleamed briefly on his face and then left it dark again, and his eyes were strained wide against the night.

"Sit back in your seat," James told him.

"I am."

"No, you're not. You'll go through the windshield."

"Yes, Simon," said his mother, and pulled him back. Simon leaned against her side, still kicking that one foot.

"James," he said, "will we ever go back visiting there?"

"I don't know."

"I better tell Ansel."

"Tell him what?"

"I bet New York is better any day."

"Well, maybe so," James said.

"Those earrings were just teeny gold wires, you know? And there *weren't* no feather hats."

"Well, that was just one summer they had those," James said. "Some kind of free sample."

"Why didn't he tell me that?"

"I don't know."

"Why did he say it was all year every year?"

"Go to sleep," said James. "I don't know."

15

Joan arrived at the Pikes' house in Mr. Carleton's taxi, rattling over the gravel road in pitch dark with the taxi's one headlight making a swerving yellow shaft in front of them. Her suitcases were on the back seat, where they bounced around at every bump in the road, and she sat up front with Mr. Carleton but she didn't talk to him. Twice he tried to begin a conversation. He started off the first time with, "Well, now. Well, now. I didn't know you were even *gone*, Miss Joan." And when she didn't answer that, except for a single motion of her head that might have been a nod, he rode on in silence for a while and then tried again. "Wher*ever* you were," he said, "I sure hope the weather was good." But Joan's face was turned away from him, and she went on looking out the window without even changing expression.

When they turned into the Pikes' yard Joan sat up and opened her straw handbag. She didn't look toward the house. Mr. Carleton said, "Some kind of party?" and then she heard the noises that were floating from Ansel's window. Music, and voices, and someone laughing. The light from that window flooded the yard, fading out the pale yellow of the taxi's headlight. The rest of the house was dark. "I don't know," she said, and reached forward to hand him his money. "Don't worry about my bags; I'll take them in."

"They look pretty heavy for you."

"I can take them."

He climbed out his side of the taxi to drag the bags from the back seat. Somehow the bag that had been her father's had had a strap broken; the strap dangled, looking ridiculous and defeated. When Mr. Carleton handed the bag to her she swayed for a minute, surprised by the weight of it, and then she said, "Okay. I've got it."

"You sure now."

"Sure. Thank you, Mr. Carleton."

"Oh, it's nothing," he said. "Good night." He climbed back into the taxi, slamming the door behind him, and backed out into the road. Joan started for the porch.

The suitcases were hard to get up the steps. She swung them onto the porch one at a time, and then she climbed the steps herself and picked them up again. This all felt so familiar; how many times had she lugged these suitcases into this house? She thought of the first time, coming here in a dust storm, met on the steps by Janie Rose who wore nothing but her underpants and carried one half of a brown rubber sheet that they hadn't been able to get away from her in those days. Now there was no one at all to meet her. When she opened the front door the house was so empty it seemed to echo. She turned on a lamp, and it threw long, black, lonely shadows across the parlor walls.

The first thing she did was put her suitcases back in her bedroom. Whether they had noticed she was gone or not, she didn't want them to come back and find those suitcases. Then she closed her bedroom door and went directly to Simon's room. He wasn't there. The room was black and the door was open, and everything had a strange blank look.

Downstairs, she poured herself a glass of milk from the refrigerator and then wandered through the rooms drinking the milk and switching on every light she came across. Soon all in the house were on, but it didn't seem to change things. When the motor in the refrigerator started up she jumped a little, half frightened for a second. Then she set down the glass of milk and walked very slowly and deliberately out of the house, with that feeling of loneliness prickling the back of her neck as she walked.

The way the music was pouring out, she couldn't identify the voices from Ansel's window. All she heard was words and phrases, and occasional laughter. She stopped at the Potters' window and peered in, but not a single light glimmered there, not even from the very back of the house. They couldn't be far, then. If they planned to be gone for any length of time they turned all the lamps on and sat up a cardboard silhouette of a man reading that was guaranteed to fool burglars. And they couldn't be in bed; it was no later than ten o'clock. She turned away from the window and looked out at the yard, hoping they might come walking up, but they didn't. The only thing left to do was to go on to Ansel's.

No one answered when she knocked. It was too noisy for them to hear her. She opened the screen and knocked once more on the inner door, hard, and then she heard Ansel say, "Wait! Did someone knock?"

"I didn't hear anyone," said Miss Lucy.

Joan knocked again, and Ansel said, "See!" She felt the doorknob twist beneath her hands; then Ansel was standing there, swaying slightly and smiling at her, leaning his cheek against the edge of the door. "Came back, did you," he said.

"What?"

"*I* saw you go."

"I don't—"

"But I didn't tell," he said, and then swung the door all the way open and threw back one arm to welcome her. "Look what *we* got!" he called to the others. "*Who* we got. See?"

Joan stepped inside and looked around her. The room was full; it looked as if someone had tipped the house endwise so that everyone had slid down to James's parlor. Now they sat in one smiling, rumpled cluster—the Potter sisters, the Pikes, Ansel, and James. When Ansel shouted at them they all turned toward Joan and waved, with their faces calm and friendly. The only one who seemed surprised was Simon. He stood up and said, "Joan!" but she frowned at him. "Hush," she said. The voices rose again, returning to whatever they'd been talking about before. Simon shouted, "What?"

"I said, '*Hush'!*" called Joan.

"Oh, *I* didn't tell. It was like I promised you, I didn't—"

The rest of his words were drowned out, but Joan understood his meaning. Nobody had told. Maybe they thought she'd just been to a movie, or off visiting. Maybe they knew that wherever she'd gone, she'd be back. And now they sat here, cheerful and in a party mood—but what was the party about? Just by looking, she couldn't tell. Miss Lucy and Miss Faye were making a silhouette of James—Miss Lucy holding a lamp up so that James winced in the light of it, and Miss Faye tracing the shadow of his wincing profile on a sheet of paper held against the wall. But that was something they always did; some instinct seemed to push them into making silhouettes at parties, and now everyone in the house had at least one silhouette of everyone else. Nor could she tell anything from Mr. Pike, who seemed to be a little tiddly from some wine he was drinking out of a measuring cup. He sat smiling placidly at something beyond Joan's range of vision, tapping one finger against the cup in time to a jazz version of "Stardust" that the radio was sawing out. And the person who confused her *most* was Mrs. Pike, sitting in a chair in the corner with her hands folded but her eyes alert to everything that was going on. "Fourteen!" she called out; she seemed to be counting the swallows Simon took from his own glass of wine. But her voice was lost among all the other voices, and Joan had to read her lips. She turned to Ansel, to see if he could explain all this. He had lain back on his couch now, like an emperor at a Roman festival, and when he saw her look his way he smiled and waved.

"Have a seat!" he shouted. He pointed vaguely to several chairs that were already occupied. "We're celebrating."

"Oh," Joan said. "Celebrating."

"Simon ran away."

"What?"

Simon smiled at her and nodded. "I went to Caraway on a bus," he said.

"Oh, Simon."

"I saw those gold earrings."

"But how did—"

"James and Mama came and got me. They made a special trip," he said. "We're drinking Miss Faye's cooking wine."

Joan felt behind her for a footstool and sat down on it. "Are you all *right*?" she asked.

"Sure I am."

"Oh, I wish I hadn't gone off and—"

"No, really, I'm all right," said Simon. "Look, they're letting me have wine. They put ice cubes in it to make it watery but I drink it fast before the ice can melt."

"That's nice," Joan said vaguely. She kept looking around at the others. Ansel leaned toward Joan with his own jelly glass of wine and said, "*Drink* up," and thrust it at her, and then lay down again. "Ansel had to find his own supper tonight," Simon told her. "He had one slice of garlic bologna, all dried out. James is going to cook him a steak tomorrow to make up for it."

Joan took a long swallow of cooking wine and looked over at James. He was swiveling his eyes toward the silhouette while he kept his profile straight ahead, so that he seemed cross-eyed. When he felt Joan looking at him he smiled and called something to her that she couldn't hear, and then Miss Faye said, "When you talk your nose moves up and down," and erased the line she had drawn for his nose and left a smudge there. Mr. Pike laughed. He clanged when he laughed; it puzzled Joan for a minute, and then she examined him more closely and found in his lap the elephant bell from Mrs. Pike's mantelpiece. "Why has he got that bell?" she asked Simon.

Simon shrugged, and Ansel answered for him. "He used it while hunting for Simon," he called. "Weird thing, ain't it? Such a funny shape it has. Everything Indians do is backwards, seems to me—"

"Fifteen!" Mrs. Pike said.

"*India* Indians, of course," said Ansel. "Not American. Hey, James."

Miss Faye's pencil had just hit the bottom of James's neck. She finished off with that same little bump at the base of it that sculptors put on marble busts, and then James stretched and turned toward Ansel.

"What," he said.

"Funny feeling in my feet, James."

James sighed and rose to go over to the couch. "Well, thank you, Miss Faye," he called over his shoulder.

"No trouble at all. Joan, dear, it's your turn."

"How about Simon?" asked Joan.

"They did me first," Simon told her. "I'm the guest of honor."

"Oh." She stood up and went over to the Potters, still carrying her glass of wine. "My hair's not combed," she told them.

"That's all right, we'll just smooth over that part on the paper. Will you have a seat?"

They sat her down firmly, both of them pressing on her shoulders. The lamp glared at her so brightly that it made a circular world that she sat in alone, facing Miss Lucy's steadily breathing bosom while Miss Faye, strange without gloves, skimmed the pencil around a suddenly too-big shadow of Joan. Outside the circle was the noise, and the beating music and the dark, faceless figures of the others. Their conversation seemed to be blurring together now.

"I had a cousin once who did *group* silhouettes," said Miss Faye. "I don't know how. It's a talent I never had—he could make everyone be doing something so like themselves, even in a silhouette of twenty people you could name each person present."

"That was Howard," Miss Lucy said.

"Howard Potter Laskin. I remember him well. If he was only here tonight, why, we could put him right to work. I wish I knew how he did it."

"Where is he now?" Miss Lucy asked.

"I don't know."

Joan looked at her shadow, staring almost sideways the way James had done. "There is a whole *gallery* of silhouettes in this house," she said suddenly.

"Quiet, dear, you've moved."

"Didn't I have this blouse on the last time? There was that same sticking-up frill around my neck."

"Yes," said Miss Faye. She sighed and her pencil moved briefly outside the shadow of the frill. "Simon had the same shirt, too," she said.

"How do you remember?"

"The collar's worn out. Little threads poking up."

Joan looked over at Simon; he nodded and held up the corner of his collar. "This is the shirt I ran away in," he called.

"Didn't you get dressed up to go?"

"You didn't do the laundry yet."

"Oh," said Joan, and she turned back to fit her head into the silhouette. Miss Faye started on the back of her hair, skimming past the shadows of stray wisps the way she had promised.

"The mornings after parties," she said, "Miss Lucy and I cut these out and mount them. Don't we, Lucy? We talk over the parties as we cut."

"I think we should take a picture," said Simon.

"A what?"

"A picture. A photograph. With a camera." He took a swallow of wine.

"Sixteen," said his mother, still counting.

"I *know*. James could take it when you're done with

Joan there. Me in my shirt that I ran away in. Everybody else standing around.''

"Cameras are all very well," Miss Faye said. "But who can't press a button? If Howard Potter Laskin was here—''

"Howard did *every*thing well," said Miss Lucy.

"I could take you and Miss Lucy drawing silhouettes," James called. He looked up from rubbing Ansel's feet. "Could Howard Potter Laskin do that?''

"Well, now—'' Miss Faye said. She lowered her pencil and frowned into space a minute. "A silhouette of a silhouette? I don't know. But Howard could—''

"I'll get my camera, then," said James. He left Ansel's couch and crossed toward the darkroom, stepping carefully through the other people. But the minute he was gone, Miss Faye finished Joan's silhouette with two quick strokes, ending in a point on top of her head that wasn't really there.

"You weren't *supposed* to finish," Joan said. "How will he have you doing a silhouette if there's no more left to do?''

"Oh, now," said Miss Lucy. "People don't *get* photographed making silhouettes. We'll just sit down, I think—maybe on Ansel's couch, if he doesn't object.''

They began gathering up their pencils and paper. All over the room, people were getting ready for that camera. Simon had buttoned the top button of his shirt, so that he looked as if he would choke, and Ansel was sitting ramrod-straight with his numb feet on the coffee table in front of him. By the time James returned the whole room seemed tense and silent. Even the radio had been turned off. James said, "I don't hardly recognize you all," and everyone laughed a little and then got quiet again. "You're going to have to bunch up now," he said.

They moved closer in, heading toward Ansel who for once allowed someone else to sit on the couch. "Simon can sit on the floor," said James. "That would help. Miss Faye, can you move your silhouettes in?"

"Oh, I don't think—" said Miss Faye, but James cut her off as if he already knew what she would say.

"Sure you can," he said. "*Every*one gets photographed making silhouettes these days." And though Miss Faye smiled, to show she didn't believe him, she brought one of her silhouettes over and set it on the back of the couch against the wall. "That's better," he said. He was carrying his little box camera, and he held it in front of his stomach now and squinted into the view-finder. "Almost," he said. "Joan, where are you? All I get is your foot."

Joan moved over, squeezing in against Simon on the floor. "Ouch," said Simon. "James, are you going to get in the picture?"

"Not while I'm taking it I'm not," said James.

"You should," Miss Lucy said. "You're the one that went and got him."

"No. I hate being photographed."

"Then what's the use?" Simon said. He looked around at the others. "*James* made that special trip—"

"I'll take it," said Joan. She stood up. "You show me how to aim it, James."

"How to—"

"No, Joan should be in it too," Simon said.

But Mr. Pike came to life suddenly and reached down to touch Simon's shoulder. "Can't have everything, boy," he said. "Come on and get in the picture, James. *Joan* didn't go nowhere; she don't mind."

"No, I don't," Joan told James. "Give it here."

"Well, all right."

He put it in her hands and then showed her the button. "This is what you press," he told her. "It's not all that hard."

He went over to sit on the arm of the sofa, next to Ansel, and now even James looked self-conscious. When Joan peered at them through the view-finder she saw all of their faces made clear and tiny, with their smiles stretched tight and each person's hand clamped white around a glass of wine. Ansel's feet were bigger than anyone. He still had them propped up, and when Joan raised her head to glare at them he ducked a glance at her and said, "They hurt."

"They're in the way," Joan told him.

"They hurt."

"If you'd get the right size *shoes*—" said James.

Mr. Pike bent forward to stare at Ansel's feet; his elephant bell clanged again and Ansel said suddenly, breaking in on what James was saying, "I had a *cousin* engaged to a India Indian. I ever mention that?"

"No," said Joan. "Your feet, please, Ansel." She lowered her head and stared into the finder again, but Ansel showed no sign of moving his feet.

"I'd nearly forgotten about it," he said. "This particular Indian used to sing a lot. All the time long songs, India Indian songs, without no tune. He'd finish and we'd clap and say, 'Well, wasn't that—' when oops, there he'd go, on to the next line. Got so we were *afraid* to clap. On and on he'd go, on and on."

"Are you *sure* we shouldn't just sit in a chair?" asked Miss Lucy.

"Wednesday came and went," James said. "When will you remember your shots?"

In the finder of the camera Joan could see them moving, each person making his own set of motions. But the glass of the finder seemed to hold them there, like figures in a snowflurry paperweight who would still be in their set positions when the snow settled down again. She thought whole years could pass, they could be born and die, they could leave and return, they could marry or live out their separate lives alone, and nothing in this finder would change. They were going to stay this way, she and all the rest of them, not because of anyone else but because it was what they had chosen, what they would keep a strong tight hold of. James bent over Ansel; Mrs. Pike touched the top of Simon's head, and Mr. Pike sat smiling awkwardly into space. "It starts near the arches," said Ansel, "right about here . . ."

"Be still," said Joan.

She kept her head down and stared at the camera, smiling as if it were she herself being photographed. The others smiled back, each person motionless, each clutching separately his glass of wine.

THE TIN CAN TREE

A Reader's Guide

ANNE TYLER

A CONVERSATION WITH
ANNE TYLER

Q: *The Tin Can Tree* is one of your earliest novels, written almost forty years ago. Has your opinion of the novel and the characters within it changed at all since you wrote it? In what ways?

Anne Tyler: When I wrote that novel, I was doing the best job I could do at the time. I must have sent it out feeling that it was worth sending. But now I think it's very young and very inept.

Q: How would you define your own writing style? How has it changed since you wrote *The Tin Can Tree*? How does this novel compare to some of your others stylistically?

AT: I have been aiming all these years for a style that is transparent—that lets readers lead the lives I'm describing without thinking about who's describing them. But I was a long way from that goal in *The Tin Can Tree*. Also, it seems to me that I didn't properly trust my readers' intelligence in those days. I overexplained.

Q: When you sit down to write a novel, do you always go through the same process? Has this process changed significantly in the last forty years? How?

AT: That part is very much the same. I fall in love, you might say. I become riveted on a character, a situation, or a what-if and I long to know every detail of it.

Q: How long do you typically spend between novels? How do you know when you are ready to begin writing again? Do you need some time to say good-bye to the characters of your last book before you can begin creating new ones for the next?

AT: When I finish a novel, I generally spend the next year or so closet-cleaning and drawer-sorting and, oh, just ordinary living, as opposed to writing. Then gradually I start feeling that closets are perhaps not the be-all and end-all that I had imagined. But *The Tin Can Tree* was a different proposition. I had just had my first novel, *If Morning Ever Comes,* accepted for publication when my agent advised me to begin my next one, because he felt that writers often develop a sort of mental block with their second novels. So I started *The Tin Can Tree* immediately. I think I should have given myself more time to "refill."

Q: What planted the seeds of *The Tin Can Tree?* Are the characters based on any real-world counterparts, or are they entirely products of your imagination?

AT: The seeds of the story were sown fifty-odd years ago, when I was a child so young that my mother and her friends talking over their coffee didn't worry that I was hearing what they said. A woman told my mother that her friend had just lost a daughter, and that the daughter had been the less favored of two. My mother said, "Oh, yes, it's always so much harder when it's the one you love less." Even as a child—well, especially as a child!—I was fascinated by that. Why wouldn't it have been harder to lose the one you loved more? I thought about it for years, and *The Tin Can Tree* is what came out of it.

Q: The book begins with a funeral for a six-year-old child, which sets the mood for the entire novel. Is this reflective of your mood at the time? Was this an emotionally difficult book for you to write?

AT: At the time, I was a young wife with no children. I could never have written this book if I had had a child of my own, particularly a child Janie Rose's age. (Years later, when I wrote about the death of a child in *The Accidental Tourist*, I made very certain that the child was younger than either of my own two were at the time.) I was able to write about Janie Rose's death only because it was a sort of abstract problem—why is it harder if the child is less favored?—and not in the least reflective of anything going on in my life.

Q: The characters in the three-person row home of *The Tin Can Tree* are a somewhat motley crew, thrown together by chance and circumstance. Despite their various disappointments in their previous family lives, they have all managed to come together and form a sort of makeshift family. How important do you think it is for people to feel included, to have a particular group to which they really belong?

AT: I do believe we all need to belong to some kind of nesting unit to feel happy, and I love to see the odd forms that some of those units can take—the "artificial families" that compensate for situations where the biological families are less than ideal.

Q: The book shows several instances of people testing others' love for them. Simon tests his mother by running away from home; Joan tries to test James by running away as well; and Ansel tests James on an almost daily basis by making extraordinary demands of him, such as foot rubs and meals served on trays. Do you think this is often the case in the real world? Do people do hurtful things to test one another, to find out how much others are willing to do for them?

AT: I'm not sure I agree that these people are testing one another. Simon and Joan are acting out of pure pain, and Ansel is so self-involved that he probably doesn't realize how he strains James's good will.

Q: *The Tin Can Tree* takes place in a very short time span and deals with a very specific situation—namely, the aftermath of a child's death. It provides a snapshot of its characters at one of the hardest times of all of their lives, revealing some at their worst and others at their best. How differently would the characters have behaved had the book spanned a longer period or shown them in more ordinary conditions?

AT: Well, for starters, I don't think they'd have been very interesting. These are the most commonplace people, really, leading nearly motionless lives. Probably that was my unconscious motivation in confining the book to such a small window of time.

Q: Who is your favorite character in *The Tin Can Tree?* Is there one character with whom you particularly identify? Who is your least favorite?

AT: My favorite was Janie Rose. She began as merely a puppet—I just needed a lesser-loved child who had died, period—but then it seemed she asserted that spiky personality of hers, announced all her quirks and her funny habits and small distresses, and I was won over. My least favorite—no surprise—was Ansel, although I suspect I may have liked him better back when I was writing about him.

Q: It seems to me that Joan and James are responsible to a fault. Their sense of obligation to others—though a very honorable trait—prevents them from ever being truly happy themselves. Do you think familial/interpersonal responsibilities often get in the way of people's romantic happiness or ability to live their own lives? Are such obligations too burdensome to be realistic? Where do you draw the line between positive and negative self-sacrifice?

AT: I think that's a line that can be very blurry. James, in my opinion, has been crippled by an unwarranted sense of responsibility, but I'm not sure we could say the same about Joan.

Q: Some characters—Missouri and the Potter sisters in particular—can be quite quirky and funny at times. Did you have fun writing their scenes?

AT: I did. I enjoyed the tobacco-stringing scene particularly—I always love situations in which women get together and talk without thinking about it while they're involved in some occupation. And I found the Potter sisters a relief from the mournfulness of the other characters.

Q: Several characters in the book attempt to escape their problems (often by running away) but ultimately fail. Even James, whose resolve is the strongest, cannot break entirely free from his unsatisfying family life in Caraway; he remains burdened with an overly demanding and needy brother. Do you think that people are basically stuck with whatever problems life deals them? Is there ever any point in trying to escape our problems, or will they follow us wherever we go?

AT: Probably they wouldn't *have* to follow us, but I think people often have a sort of signature problem that defines their lives, and I'm always fascinated by the ways in which they cling to their particular problem when it might conceivably be possible to dump it.

Q: The characters' speech patterns seem to say a great deal about their mental and emotional health. Mrs. Pike— a former chatterbox—falls completely silent after her daughter's death, while hypochondriac Ansel and the spinster Potter sisters talk almost incessantly to whoever will listen. What do you think a person's verboseness or lack thereof says about his or her overall emotional well-being?

AT: Obviously Mrs. Pike's uncharacteristic silence reflects her grief, but the other characters' talkativeness has more to do with my interest in run-on speech. I always think, when I come upon such people in real life, How can they talk so much and say so little? But then I begin to notice the little plums that drop from their speech without their realizing it—the secrets they give away unintentionally. I love reproducing that sort of speech on paper.

Q: At one point, Joan feels homesick, "but not for any home she'd ever had" (page 130). The whole novel, in fact, has a feeling of nostalgia and longing for experiences not yet had. Do you think this is a common feeling in the real world? Can people be nostalgic or homesick for people, places, and things they've never experienced? Was this an issue that particularly interested you at the time?

AT: As near as I can remember, that reference to Joan's homesickness has to do with the fact that she didn't have a real family when she was a child—or not the Dick-and-Jane kind of family we imagine all families to be. So when she longs for "home," it's not a home she's had any personal experience of. Anyone who feels the same lack will probably experience that same sense of homesickness, but I don't mean to imply that it's a common emotion.

Q: The party in the final chapter seems to be a sort of return to normalcy for the Pikes, Potters, and Greens. There is an overwhelming sense that, despite Janie Rose's death, the entire cast of characters will ultimately be all right—at least as all right as they have ever been. Did you choose to end on this note in order to reassure your readers that recovery is possible or even inevitable?

AT: I suspect that what I wanted to say was, human beings have a way of going on, even after experiences that seem unbearable. I don't think that the Pikes will ever be the same, but I do think they'll start getting up in the morning again and gathering with their neighbors again, and they'll even manage to laugh sometimes.

Q: What was the most frustrating aspect of writing *The Tin Can Tree*? What was the most rewarding?

AT: I don't remember any frustrating aspects—perhaps if I'd been more frustrated, the book would have been much better! I do remember my pleasure in creating what amounted to a portrait in negative space—defining Janie Rose by all the qualities that were missing now that she was gone.

READING GROUP QUESTIONS AND
TOPICS FOR DISCUSSION

1. The story begins after the death of six-year-old Janie Rose. How do the different characters mourn her? Are their individual mourning styles reflective of their respective personalities? In what ways does the child's death propel some of the characters' lives into action? In what ways does it stop other characters' lives in their tracks?

2. Joan has lived her entire life feeling like a guest in other people's homes—even the home of her own parents. Is this something she brings upon herself? Or is she a victim of circumstance? What does this say about her character?

3. How would you characterize James and Ansel's relationship? Is it symbiotic or parasitic in nature? Would Ansel be able to survive without James? Would James without Ansel? Is James's caretaking more helpful or harmful to his "sick" brother? After running away and abandoning the rest of his family, why is James unable to cut that final cord and leave Ansel?

4. James and Ansel have both run away from their home in Caraway, and both Joan and Simon attempt to run away from Larksville. What are they trying to achieve by running away? Are they running toward something positive in their lives, or merely running away from some-

thing negative? Does running away ultimately solve these characters' problems? Whose experience with running away is the most successful and whose is the least so? Why?

5. What do you think James's love of photography reveals about him? Does his need to preserve and protect his memories stem from his rocky family history and his parents' abandonment? He claims that he can photograph people exactly as he remembers them; does this mean that he sees the people in his life as two-dimensional? In what ways is he himself two-dimensional?

6. After Janie Rose's untimely death, Ansel becomes obsessed by the concept of his own mortality. He seems to be more concerned with how he will be remembered in death than with how well he is treated and loved in life. In what ways does his fixation on and fear of death prevent him from being able to fully live his life? Why, for instance, does he cut short his attention to Maisie Hammond? Do you think he has written off the possibility of a romantic relationship in his life? If so, why?

7. Missouri and Joan scheme to restore Mrs. Pike to emotional health by putting her back to work. Why does this plan ultimately fail? Was Missouri right in claiming that the only person who can pull Mrs. Pike out of her silence is Simon?

8. Joan is constantly attending to other people's needs and wants, often at the expense of her own. Is this a positive character trait? Do you see her return to Larksville after her attempt to run away as a continuation of putting others' needs before her own, or do you think she is finally doing what she really wants to do? Is her decision to return a demonstration of strength or of weakness?

9. Simon learns to deal with loss at a very early age. How do you think this will affect his emotional development throughout his life? At the end of the book, he seems happy to have won back his mother's attention; is his recovery that simple? Does his grieving period end with the close of the last chapter of the book, or will it continue?

10. Why did Anne Tyler name the novel after Janie Rose's tin can tree? What significance does the tree have for Janie's mourners?

11. The picture Anne Tyler paints of Janie Rose is a colorful juxtaposition of great optimism (drawing pictures of apple trees where only barren bushes exist in reality) with great self-doubt (wearing layer upon layer of underwear for comfort and security). Can you imagine Janie as an adult? Do you think her optimistic side would have overcome her insecurities, or vice versa?

12. The world of *The Tin Can Tree* is divided into responsible caretakers and those they care for. Which characters fit into the first category and which fit into the second? Is there any overlap between the two?

13. Anne Tyler creates some very humorous characters, such as Missouri and the Potter sisters. What do you think of these characters? Are there aspects of their behavior that you find particularly amusing? Are we laughing at them or with them?

14. What significance does clothing hold for the characters in *The Tin Can Tree*? Janie Rose used to take comfort in wearing multiple layers of underwear and would often cry while putting on her dresses; Mrs. Pike's state of emotional health can be gauged by how much she cares about her clothing and appearance; James uses Joan's clothing

to determine what season it is and "resents" any new clothes she buys until he has gotten used to them. Why do these characters put so much stock in what they—or other people—are wearing? What do their various attitudes toward clothing say about them?

15. Missouri claims that the "bravest thing about people . . . is how they go on loving mortal beings after finding out there's such a thing as dying" (page 96). Do you agree? Would you characterize this human propensity to love as bravery? Which characters do you think exhibit this quality, and which do not?

16. How would you describe the ending of *The Tin Can Tree*? On the most basic level, is it a happy ending or not? Do you think James's prospects look hopeful? What about Joan's? Where do you see the characters five years after the book ends? Ten years? Fifteen?

ANNE TYLER was born in Minneapolis in 1941 but grew up in Raleigh, North Carolina. She graduated at nineteen from Duke University and went on to do graduate work in Russian studies at Columbia University. This is Anne Tyler's second novel; her eleventh, *Breathing Lessons*, was awarded the Pulitzer Prize in 1988. She is a member of the American Academy and Institute of Arts and Letters. She lives in Baltimore.